"Jane Kirkpatri[...] that touches th[...] with her histori[...] Lord. If you haven't tried Jane's books, I highly encourage you to do so. She's one of the best."

Tracie Peterson, bestselling author of
The Heart of Cheyenne series

"Jane Kirkpatrick's writing evokes a powerful sense of the challenges and strengths of women who settled the West. In *Across the Crying Sands*, she affectionately tells of a remarkable woman who longed for adventure and did not allow the restrictions of her time to keep her from finding it. Kirkpatrick's sense of time and place and her understanding of the trials of women of another century have made her one of the West's most beloved writers."

Sandra Dallas, *New York Times* bestselling
author of *Where Coyotes Howl*

"Jane Kirkpatrick has an incredible talent for discovering courageous women from our past and sharing history that might otherwise be forgotten. Exploring the rugged coastline of Oregon in *Across the Crying Sands* was a delight I won't soon forget. As Mary Edwards Gerritse and her new husband help build a road through the wilderness, they learn what it takes for a relationship to succeed in the face of adversity—a lesson we can all use!"

Karen Barnett, award-winning author of *Where Trees
Touch the Sky* and the Vintage
National Parks Novel series

ACROSS
the
CRYING
SANDS

Also by Jane Kirkpatrick

Beneath the Bending Skies

The Healing of Natalie Curtis

Something Worth Doing

One More River to Cross

Everything She Didn't Say

All She Left Behind

This Road We Traveled

The Memory Weaver

A Light in the Wilderness

One Glorious Ambition

The Daughter's Walk

Where Lilacs Still Bloom

A Mending at the Edge

A Tendering in the Storm

A Clearing in the Wild

Barcelona Calling

An Absence So Great

A Flickering Light

A Land of Sheltered Promise

Hold Tight the Thread

Every Fixed Star

A Name of Her Own

What Once We Loved

No Eye Can See

All Together in One Place

Mystic Sweet Communion

A Gathering of Finches

Love to Water My Soul

A Sweetness to the Soul

Novellas

Sincerely Yours

A Log Cabin
Christmas Collection

The American Dream
Romance Collection

Romancing America:
The Midwife's Legacy

Nonfiction

Promises of Hope
for Difficult Times

Aurora:
An American Experience in
Quilt, Community, and Craft

A Simple Gift of Comfort

A Burden Shared

Homestead

Eminent Oregonians:
Three Who Matter (coauthor)

THE WOMEN *of* CANNON BEACH · 1

ACROSS

the

CRYING

SANDS

JANE KIRKPATRICK

Revell

a division of Baker Publishing Group
Grand Rapids, Michigan

Published by Revell
a division of Baker Publishing Group
Grand Rapids, Michigan
RevellBooks.com

Printed in the United States of America

Library of Congress Cataloging-in-Publication Data
Names: Kirkpatrick, Jane, 1946– author.
Title: Across the crying sands / Jane Kirkpatrick.
Description: Grand Rapids, Michigan : Revell, a division of Baker Publishing Group, 2025. | Series: The Women of Cannon Beach ; 1 | Includes bibliographical references.
Identifiers: LCCN 2024039376 | ISBN 9780800746094 (paperback) | ISBN 9780800747145 (casebound) | ISBN 9781493450657 (ebook)
Subjects: LCSH: Self-realization in women—Fiction. | LCGFT: Christian fiction. | Novels.
Classification: LCC PS3561.I712 A65 2025 | DDC 813/.54—dc23/eng/20240826
LC record available at https://lccn.loc.gov/2024039376

Scripture quotations are from the King James Version of the Bible.

Dana Huneke-Stone, "Walking Papers," in *Amuse-Bouche: A Taste of Melancholy* (Sticks and Stones Press, 2022). Used with permission.

This book is a work of historical fiction based closely on real people and events. Details that cannot be historically verified are purely products of the author's imagination.

Photograph of woman © Magdalena Russocka / Trevillion Images; Cover design by Laura Klynstra

The author is represented by the literary agency of Linda S. Glaz Literary Agency.

Baker Publishing Group publications use paper produced from sustainable forestry practices and postconsumer waste whenever possible.

25 26 27 28 29 30 31   7 6 5 4 3 2 1

To dear Jerry,
one more time.

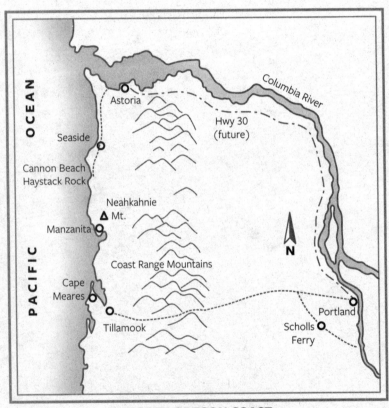

NORTH OREGON COAST

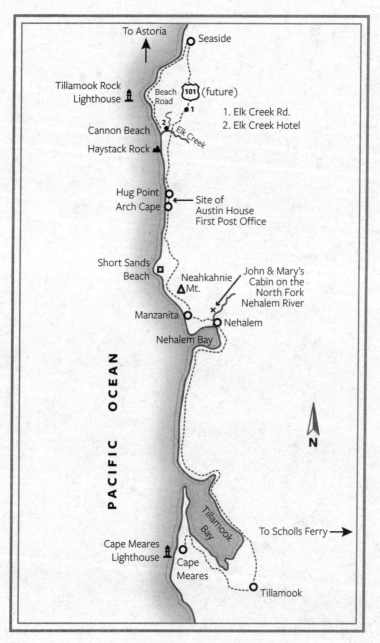

To Astoria

Seaside

Tillamook Rock
Lighthouse

Beach
Road

US 101 (future)

1
1. Elk Creek Rd.
2. Elk Creek Hotel

2
Cannon Beach
Haystack Rock

Elk Creek

Hug Point
Arch Cape

Site of
Austin House
First Post Office

Short Sands
Beach

Neahkahnie
Mt.

John & Mary's
Cabin on the
North Fork
Nehalem River

Manzanita

Nehalem

Nehalem Bay

PACIFIC OCEAN

N

To Scholls Ferry

Tillamook
Bay

Cape Meares
Lighthouse

Cape
Meares

Tillamook

Maps not to scale.

cast of characters

Mary Edwards—sixteen-year-old daughter of William and Amanda

John Gerritse—sailor from the Netherlands

Herbert Frank L. Logan—British remittance man and entrepreneur

Joe Walsh—remittance man

Amanda Edwards—Mary's mother

William Edwards—Mary's father and dairyman

***Jewell**—Nehalem/Clatsop Indigenous friend of Mary's

James and **Lydia Austin**—owners of the Austin House

Will Batterson—teacher, justice of the peace, and father of Merritt, young friend of the Edwards family

* fully imagined character, representative of historical record

Walking Papers

Further, each day.
Anointed with spray.
Holy water.
Wayward Daughter.
For sky. For stones.
For strength in my bones.
Salted air.
Walking is prayer.

—DANA HUNEKE-STONE
IN *AMUSE-BOUCHE:*
A TASTE OF MELANCHOLY

prologue

ave Woman tells the story. Her grandmother told her and that woman's grandfather had told her and so the story wove through many seasons. Wave Woman shared the story as though she had seen with her own eyes. That is the best way to tell a story, bring the listener inside.

A schooner—the ship was called with a second name, *Shark*—tried to come into the mouth of the mighty Nch'i-Wána, the Columbia River, where it met the sea. The ship and the river fought. The river won, pushing the ship onto the spit of sand. The captain tossed large guns over the side, hoping to free the *Shark*. The river broke up more of the ship, and a chunk the size of a whale separated and took three guns with it, dropping them on the sand. The tide pushed and buried one, maybe two. Cannons they were called.

Seasons passed. One cannon was spit up by the sea, miles south on a flat, golden beach. A Crying Sands Beach named for a great sadness. The sea and sand took it back. It left a new name behind, named by the white men who knew of the ship's great loss. Cannon Beach. And so the search for the cannons began.

PART I

chapter

1

Like a clarion call to adventure, Mary Edwards cherished the sound of the swooshing surf on the golden sands beach. She'd kept the window open though it was November, and wind off the Pacific rolled in, brushing the shore as flat as an adze-smoothed table before reaching her primitive room. *November 8th, 1888*, Mary wrote in her journal with the note, *Happiest day ever—so far. Grand adventures lie ahead*. She did like excitement. Adventures reminded her that she was alive. And goodness, she was alive this week, her wedding week.

Mary wrapped the journal in a leather pouch, set it on the duck-down pillow beside her, and lay back, pulling her rust-colored braid over her shoulder, hands over her stomach. She savored the peaceful moment in Herbert Logan's cabin (that would one day be a hotel, he claimed) on Ecola Creek, the Clatsop People's word for *whale*. Some people called the area Cannon Beach—and another dozen names. Mary preferred the cannon reference because it came with a good story.

She heard rustling next door where her fiancé, John Gerritse, and Herbert Logan himself had spent the night. Herbert hailed from England and came to the area as a remittance man, sent as the second son and, like English women, therefore not able to inherit. Instead, he received a monthly remittance from his elder brother. The money gave him income but also served as a reminder of his expulsion and that he'd never be welcomed home. Mary felt sorry for him and other remittance men who had found their way to the coast for being banished by family. What did one have if not family, so vitally important to her.

Still, Herbert had made the best of it and planned to build a hotel on this lovely though remote beach. He'd also been a good friend to John and Mary. Knowing Mary liked to read and write poetry, he'd introduced her to an English poet named Edward Lear. One of Mary's favorite poems now was "The Jumblies," a whimsical verse with a ballad rhythm. Mary memorized several stanzas and recalled one this morning.

> They went to sea in a Sieve they did,
> In a Sieve they went to sea.

Sometimes with John so large in her life and with his willingness to try new ways, Mary wondered if they were going to sea in a sieve. They were certainly sailing to places she'd never been before, marriage being one.

Hearing the men next door stirred her own rustling to rise. So much excitement ahead. The wedding, the party, moving to John's claim—though he'd been secretive about that. A surprise she guessed. Mary liked surprises.

She finished her prayers of confession, gratitude, and requests, then rose in the dark, pinned up her braid, and readied herself to make the last leg of their journey south to her and her parents' home at Nehalem, on the north Oregon coast. They'd take the upper inland trail, she supposed, as that's the way they'd gone north nearly the week before to Astoria. In that bustling town, she'd bought a wedding hatpin and had two teeth pulled, the latter giving her even more information about her John. He'd been both practical and tender.

Her tongue kept finding the holes those teeth had departed from, and pain still darted into her mouth. John had held her after the chloroform wore off, and they'd stayed an extra day so Mary could recover. John washed out the rags lodged in her mouth to stop the bleeding. Even without them, she felt like a gopher with chubby cheeks. He caressed her shoulder as he sat beside her, spoke kind words. He was a gentle man despite his size.

Other than the teeth-pulling, it was almost like a honeymoon in that bustling city where the Columbia River met the sea. John knew his way around Astoria, and they walked along Young's River, climbed to a high point to see just where the Columbia River passed into the ocean. The Bar, it was called, and it put seamen like John into peril crossing it. On certain days, ships broke up or had to wait a day or two until the sea calmed. Mary thought it was a bit like life—surviving suffering times, having to wait.

"Ready?" John asked as he knocked on her door, interrupting her reverie.

"I've been waiting on you lazy boys." She grabbed her knitted cap, stuffed her braid up under it, and opened the door.

"A man needs his beauty sleep." John leaned in and kissed her cheek. "But you sure don't."

"What you see is what you get, cotton cheeks and all." She reached up to gentle his sideburns. Soft.

"You look much the better."

"I've been awake just listening to the waves," Mary said. "They're a lullaby. I'd love to live here one day."

"Anything is possible." He put his arm around her shoulder, and they walked to the porch. Beyond, he'd already saddled the horses. It was nice not to have to do that herself.

In two days, she'd be Mrs. John Gerritse, wedded to this stocky man with arms the size of thighs, light sand-colored hair, and a high forehead he told her meant he had "big brains." He stood nearly six feet tall. Fortunately, her parents had approved of the match though John was eight years older than her. He'd be twenty-four on their wedding day which was also his birthday. "This way I won't forget the special event, ja?"

His booming voice appealed to Mary along with his worldly

ways. He'd sailed around the globe, leaving from the Netherlands as a boy, landing in America to stay.

They'd marry on Saturday but the party would wait until Monday so their revelry wouldn't sweep into Sunday. That had been their compromise. That, and no alcohol served. She could only push her dear parents so far. They did indulge her, her parents. Only-children were often as spoiled as rain-soaked cabbage. That's what her mother said. But they seemed to like John and his dream of great things. Mary dreamed of splendor too: a family and a way to serve those around her, and hopefully a regular dose of adventure.

John pulled a woolen hat over his head and ears. "You follow me, Mary." Her future husband rechecked the cinch. Some horses liked to hold their breath during saddling to keep the cinch from being tight. But Jake, John's faithful horse, wasn't like that. Mary appreciated John's sweet gesture and that he knew about horses even though he was a seaman.

Mary stepped into John's palms, and he lifted her to the saddle. Jake might be owned by John, but the gelding was fast becoming Mary's. She patted the sorrel's neck. His ears twitched in happy response. She eyed the dark ocean. "Shouldn't we wait until dawn?"

"Horses see the ocean well by moonlight."

They were taking the beachfront trail. The ocean could be tricky in the dark. A large rock called Haystack was ahead of them, and in this light they wouldn't see it until they were almost upon it, standing like a sentinel of the Pacific and Cannon Beach. They'd barely make out the tide line.

"Aren't we taking the upper trail?"

"Nee. The beach beckons. You say that in English, ja? Beckons?"

"Yes, that's the proper word." It was a shorter path, but only if the tide receded.

The upper trail through the manzanita and spruce wouldn't be good in the dark either, she supposed. "And the tide? Are you sure it's going out?"

"Will you question my every decision, woman?" He grinned, but she heard the edge in his voice.

"No. It's just that—"

"You two are arguing like a married couple and you've yet to say 'I do.'" Herbert laughed. He popped on his derby hat as he stepped up onto his sorrel. He didn't have to ride south with them, but he planned to attend their wedding after taking care of business in Tillamook, the county seat. He'd spend tonight in Nehalem rather than alone at his cabin.

"Alright. I defer to the man of the house," Mary said. "This time." She grinned.

"That's my girl. I know the ocean. I delivered mail for a time from here to Hoquarton."

Mary corrected him. "They call it Tillamook now, in honor of the Indians. Hoquarton is its old name."

John grunted. "Let's go."

Mary made a mental note: John didn't like being corrected, at least not with another man to hear it. Maybe no one liked to be corrected with an audience.

At least he didn't deny that she knew something too.

She pressed her knees into Jake, and the horse's hooves spit up sand as he sped Mary forward.

Mary's russet tendrils escaped from her cap, matted against her face in the morning mist. Like most coastal women, she'd long ago succumbed to the sea air's sense of style. She lived with caps and hats. Her split skirt let her ride astride with ease. A fawn-colored wool sweater kept her warm and protected her white blouse while riding boots kept her feet dry. She sighed. A beach ride on a good horse was a bit of heaven, even in the half dark.

They passed the imposing Haystack Rock on their right.

They spoke little as the ocean swiped their words and tossed them into the breeze. Mary liked the wind, the feel of it on her face. Gulls stayed quiet, waiting for dawn. The sleepyheads. A white froth highlighted by the gibbous moon etched the waves. The ocean filled the world to their right as Mary reached down to pat Jake's neck and to check her leather pack.

She didn't have it! She'd left it on the bed. She had a mind like a sieve sometimes. Hopefully John would share his lunch that Herbert had provided them. And he'd be silent about her forgetting her pack. She'd have to go back one day for the journal, though. Maybe on their real honeymoon they could stay at Herbert's cabin again and sleep in until the sun was high overhead—if the sun chose to shine that day.

They were long past Haystack, and now, on their left, another large rock outcropping appeared at the end of a wooded promontory. Dawn peeked over the ridge, sending pink shafts of light over the sea. This chunk of granite was called Hug Point. At the base the sand glistened in moonbeam and Mary caught her breath at the stellar scene. She blinked back tears: the vast ocean, in the company of a loved one and a friend, all announced that her life was on the lip of something grand.

John shouted for them to pull up. "Sand looks smooth as silk but . . . Gallop full force till we pass it, ja? You follow me, Mare. Herbert, bring up the rear." He gave a whooping shout and kneed his horse.

Mary chirped at Jake, who galloped forward just as Herbert passed her like a shot, one hand holding his derby hat tight against his head.

"Whee!" Herbert shouted.

Anything else he'd planned to say was lost when Herbert's horse jerked as a sleeper wave nearly as high as Hug Point hurtled toward them. The horse reared, his front feet piercing the air, tumbling Herbert into the explosion of surf. Agape, Mary heard John shout as his horse sank into a deep, deep pool, submerging man and mount.

The numbing cold thrashed thoughts from her mind as the wave hit her, knocking her from Jake, plunging them both into surf.

chapter
2

Swim!

Mary surfaced. Thrashing, she reached for Jake, the stirrups, anything to grasp.

His tail! Thank God!

Her cold fingers grasped the coarse wet hair as the animal
lunged toward Hug Point, and she let herself be taken, sputtering
at the water over her face. John's blue shirt flashed before her, then
was gone, pushed under again, carried around the rock.

Jake scrambled onto that rock, Mary behind him, her heart
beating as she scraped her legs like stumps of wood on the barnacles. Bent over, she coughed the seawater, gasped in air, squeezed
water out of her skirt.

Alive!

And alone. Her father had told her that in time of peril she
was never really alone, but it felt that way. Prayers rose from her,
prayers for John and Herbert, prayers going every which way. She
swatted her arms for warmth. Her teeth chattered. There was nothing to build a fire from even if she did have a dry match. Which
she didn't. She removed her sodden boots, heavy as tombstones,
pulled her knees up, and wrapped her feet in the wet wool of her

skirt. She'd lost her hat. Salt dried on her cold cheeks. From the ocean or the tears that fell, she didn't know nor care.

A noose of panic wrapped around her throat as she struggled for air; a knot of fear twisted in her stomach. Deep sobs of despair racked her.

Alone.

The wool sweater, heavy with seawater and kelp, weighted her exhausted body against the sharp rocks. Should she take it off? Keep it on? She'd survived, but what did it matter? John was gone, all the hopes, the dreams they'd shared submerged in the surf, the sleeper wave carrying him across the Crying Sands Beach. The Indians had named it that and now she understood why.

Move!

She couldn't. Her body, laden with exhaustion, trembled.

Move!

John would want her to make the best of things.

Move!

She made her way to Jake, felt the warmth of his flesh. She ran her hands across his withers, down his legs. No serious damage or cuts. She leaned into him.

Shivering, Mary watched the tide. They were marooned but above the tide line. People did try to reach the inland trail from this rock, hugging the granite as they pressed against natural footholds, but she'd never tried the hazardous route. But the tide would go out. She and Jake could leave together then. She had to keep moving or that cold-wet on her body could make her think strange. She'd heard of such things in blizzards and near drownings.

This would never have happened if they'd taken the inland trail. Why hadn't she stood her ground with John? It was her fault for not standing firm, for wanting to please John. It was always important not to argue, not to challenge, to please, wasn't it? Or one could be left alone.

Her mind looped to something from long ago, an encounter, being left, but the memory shivered away. She recalled Scriptures, one about fearing nothing; another about days being numbered, that we may get a heart of wisdom. They'd gone to sea in a sieve and this was the result. She fist-rubbed her crying-strained eyes. She was a widow now—or did one have to be married to be one? What would she tell John's family? Or Herbie's family in England, if she could find them?

There was nothing to do but wait out the sea. She moved as she could on the rocks, always returning to Jake, taking in his warmth, his scent, rocking herself like a child. Time and peace sifted through her, closing every hole in that once fateful sieve.

Seagulls squawked overhead. The sun was well up in a cloudless sky when Jake nickered, looked toward the upper trail, pulled back on his tether.

"Easy now." *What worries him?* She stood, patted his neck, and scanned the upper trail area, her hand a shade over her eyes. The rustling continued, followed by a snort.

Then the bear appeared.

She flapped her arms. "Shoo! Shoo!" She picked up loose rocks and pitched them uphill toward her intruder. Would there be no end to this traumatic day?

The bear looked at her as though to consider her a worthy adversary or not—then waddled away. The bear must have been on the trail, the one they should have taken. Maybe it was a sign for her to start climbing up. She took a deep breath, struggled to put her boots back on.

Scrambling sounds again; loose rocks falling. Jake whinnied. Was the bear coming back?

Then like an apparition, a moment so glorious she wondered if she dreamed it, she saw him.

"John!"

"Mary! Oh, thank God!" John stumbled from where the bear had disappeared. Clambering down, lumbering like that bear, he reached her, pulled her close, his arms like a warm blanket even though he was damp and his linen shirt now smelled of the sea. They cried together. She'd never felt a man's sobs on her cheeks, relief kisses on the top of her head. She washed her own tears with his, her cold fingers warmed in the curls of his hair, the firmness of his neck.

"How . . . ?"

"It washed me around, pushed me up against the shore." He had made his way up from the beach, through timber and onto the old mail trail, then back north, taking the morning to do it. "I didn't know if you . . ."

John was safe. And so was she. Mary started crying again, this time, tears of relief.

"Herbie?" John asked.

"I saw him sink, never surfaced. The sleeper wave was so forceful."

"Ja. We need to look for him," John said.

They stood in silence watching the sea breathe, survival and loss like two oars moving the ship of life forward whether they were ready or not. They would have to grieve later. "At least try to find his body so we can let his family know." Would they understand the risks of the sea?

As though action would settle him, John ambled over the rocks to Jake, ran his hands down the horse's legs, and stroked his neck. He opened the saddlebag. "I hoped we'd have matches secured in the beeswax."

"I left that bag at Herbie's. I'm so sorry."

As the gulls called out, John lifted her chin, looked into her eyes. "I apologize, Mary. You were right to question me about the tide. I'm grateful that the Lord has granted me another hour or day or week to let a woman guide my way. Now and then, ja." His lips grazed her cheek, each one. Warmth on her skin.

"I'll put that apology in my satchel to pull out on a future occasion. If I remember my satchel."

John pulled her to him. "Ja, we are quite a pair. Think it's alright to leave now?"

Mary surveyed the sandy beach, the rhythm of the ocean. "I do. Let's see if we can find Herbert and the horses."

Like a cautious child, John led Jake off the rock, across the sand, and around the Point as Mary followed. As they neared caves at the

26

south side of Hug Point, Jake nickered about the same time they saw both Herbert's and John's mounts, heads down among driftwood.

"The horses made it!" Mary clapped her hands.

"Maybe Herbert's in one of those caves." John handed the lead rope to Mary, then scrambled over the midsize boulders dribbled like giant toys near the caverns.

"You look. I . . . don't want to see a . . . body. I'll catch up the other horses."

"Ja, I don't want that for you." John took a deep breath and bent to enter the largest cave while Mary led Jake toward the animals, easily caught up their reins. She checked them for injuries, praying all the time that Herbert might have made it too. She led the mounts, saddles still attached, back toward the caves, her head down hoping to avoid the tide pools, each footstep a prayer in the sand.

"Verily, my hat will need to be replaced." Herbie's British accent! "And lo, I wished for my horse and there he is!"

"If wishes were horses, beggars would ride," Mary said as she approached the caves, a grin wide on her face.

"Ah, I am beholden." He shaded his eyes with his hand. "The sun has passed its prime. I've been out awhile." He rubbed his neck.

John gave his friend a bear hug then as Mary had done. He looked over all the horses, found scratches, but nothing broken nor sprained. "It's amazing." He shook his head. "A miracle."

The trio stood in the silence broken only by the sea. What had happened here this day stunned Mary, her heart a pool of gratitude. Tears welled in her eyes. The silent men appeared humbled too.

"Let's head out. We've a wedding to prepare for. Ja."

They all three mounted up, Herbert without shoes or stockings.

What a story she'd have to tell. Mary would write about it in her journal when they picked it up on their way to Astoria for their honeymoon. At least she hoped that's where they'd be going. And then she realized a honeymoon didn't matter much. Being alive was what was precious; being alive, with loved ones and friends, despite having taken to the sea in a sieve.

chapter
3

John wanted to tell her, but maybe tonight was not the time. Actually, he hadn't found any good time. He pitched grass hay into the manger of his future in-laws, working beside his future wife. He had meant to tell her of the situation about the claim on their way back from Astoria, but then they'd had their own "situation," their survival still a miracle to consider.

She'd been excited to tell her parents about their catastrophe with the accompanying joyous responses. And then she went right into chattering about their "cabin," the one he was supposed to have built. And how excited she was to see it. She'd asked a dozen times, but he'd put her off, not wanting to see her disappointment.

Earlier, she hadn't seemed to notice his silence while they ate hot chowder Mary's mother had made. He guessed he'd find out how she dealt with disappointment. He just hated that he was the bearer of it.

Jake nickered as John thrust the hay into his trough. He turned toward his future wife. Here she was, helping, even though they were all exhausted, reaching her parents' home on the Nehalem River well past dark. Still, after eating, she'd joined him, her auburn hair wrapped into a bun at the top of her head. She stood barely to his shoulder with eyes a deep-pool blue. He could sink into them.

Instead, he said, "Aren't you tired?"

She'd brought out feather pillows and quilts for him and Herbie. He and the remittance man had the barn for their evening slumber. Herbie conversed with Mary's parents, giving the lovebirds, as her father called them, time alone after this perilous day.

"I want to help." Her resilience after their near-death encounter was just one of the reasons he'd been drawn to her. He hoped for a stalwart mate, one who could partner with him as he built a life as a farmer and more. He had ideas. Mary had not hesitated when he'd shown up to invite her to a dance last summer. Instead of waiting to see if she'd appear with her friends, the sight of her making his hands sweat and tying his tongue into tangles, he'd asked her out, met her parents. He loved her laugh and her wit and especially her care for the sea.

Growing up in the Netherlands with its dikes and windmills, he could be wary and inspired over his relationship with the ocean. He supposed it was one of the reasons he'd signed on to work on ships, to have a new sense of the sea—and stoke different dreams. After he and Mary started courting, he found another view. Magnificent. He began to see Mary that way too, though as humble as she was, she'd be embarrassed to think of herself as magnificent. But she was.

"Jake's scratches look good." Mary bent at the horse's legs. "And your Baldy seems no worse for wear either. We're so fortunate."

"That we are." John put grain in the horses' nose bags. He added more hay.

He heard Mary inhale. "Don't you love how the smell of summer is let loose in that grass?"

She saw the world in inventive ways.

Mary didn't appear to mind that he'd jumped ship in Astoria a few years before. A great many sailors had done so, he'd learned. And when she complimented him about his English instead of teasing as some did, she'd seemed impressed that he'd taken English classes at night after working for a farmer near Astoria. He did pretty well, though he bumbled the grammar when he was nervous. He had higher hopes than just farming. And his dream would need a woman of fortitude.

He was so grateful to see her alive after the episode near that hugging rock. She'd been right about the tide. He should have listened to her. Still, she never said "I told you so."

She saw so much that happened as God's plan. That wasn't his take on things—at least it hadn't been. But he liked her hopefulness and adaptability. He counted on it.

"We'll build a barn once we're on the claim and bring your horses there. I can hardly wait." She rubbed Jake's legs with liniment, the smell filling the stall. "Can't we slip away and see it before the wedding? Is it two rooms or one?"

John winced. *Tell her now?* "Ja, every homestead a barn, needs. Ach. My bad English." She smiled at him, reached up to kiss his cheek, carried the scent of liniment with her. "No. No time to visit. You have your marriage attire to fit, ja? And I have a surprise to arrange."

"I can hardly wait."

He pulled her to him, loved how she molded into him, so trusting. Then he pushed away. He was such a rat! He didn't mean to be, it was just how it happened.

"What's wrong? Is it something I've done?"

"Nee. Just tired. Ready to bunk in. You must be too." He kissed her nose.

Mary squinted at him. She could already tell when he wasn't upright in his words.

Tell her. Get it over with.

He couldn't take away the joy of this day.

"I am tired," Mary said. "And excited that you are here beside me, for as long as God allows."

"Aye. Ja. We are good together. I look forward to calling you my wife."

"Sleep well, my soon-to-be husband. I'll send Herbie out."

She spun around and darted through the barn door, then turned to wave, her grin brighter than the lantern she carried. He'd harbor his disappointing news. It was the price guilt forced him to pay.

chapter
4

"Green is lovely with that rusty hair of yours." Mrs. Pye, the dressmaker, watched Mary swirl around. The velvet felt extravagant, and Mary knew her parents had sacrificed to buy the cloth and have it shipped all the way from San Francisco. Loving parents did that, put themselves out for their family. Two rows of silver buttons marched down the tight-fitting bodice of moss green. They accented her trim figure, made her feel taller than her five foot two inches. Made her stand straighter. "And here's something special I made for you." Mrs. Pye pulled the turban hat onto Mary's head. "It's the perfect topping to your dress."

And so it was. Mary's auburn hair showed just enough to frame her eyes. Since John had told her on the ride back from Astoria that they wouldn't be taking a wedding trip, she didn't need a "going-away coat." That made her sad for a moment or two, but as she looked in the mirror, she decided the wedding hat made up for the loss. And it meant that she and John would be starting their married life sooner—on their own little claim.

"What do you think, Amanda?" Mrs. Pye addressed Mary's mother.

"It's lovely." Her mother looked wistful. "Those buttons came from Minnesota."

"Something you brought with us?" Mary always sought information about her past. Sometimes she'd walk in on her parents' conversations and hear "New York" and "Minnesota" and they'd stop talking when they saw her. She remembered Minnesota, a land of lakes and snow.

"Can we trim the hat with silver thread?" Her mother acted like she hadn't heard Mary, spoke instead to Mrs. Pye. It was just like when she interrupted her parents, only this time her mother had Mrs. Pye to cover for her.

"Absolutely. Maybe a flower or—"

"A butterfly," Mary said. "I have a hatpin I bought in Astoria. Butterflies are my favorite, especially those orange-and-black ones we see in the fall and spring coloring up the milkweed."

"You're quite the little botanist." Mrs. Pye removed the hat, stroked it. "I'll get right on that. A silver outline of a Monarch will make it special. And I don't have much time. Tomorrow's your big day. Did your father get all the licenses and certificates signed? That's always a journey going all the way to Tillamook." Mrs. Pye packed up her sewing kits.

"Oh yes. He had to give his consent because I'm not seventeen yet."

"Then the clerk wrote it right onto the license," her mother added. "'Minnie Edwards to marry John Gerritse.'"

Startled, Mary said, "Minnie? That's not my name."

Her mother slapped her hand to her mouth like she'd said a foul word.

"Mother?"

"Of course it isn't. Silly me. I'm sure *Mary* is what your father wrote. Where is my mind these days? You'll come to the party on Monday, won't you, Mrs. Pye? Mary wants everyone there, the entire north Oregon coast if she had her way." Her mother's cheeks were pink, and she spoke rapidly. "Isn't that so, Mary?"

"Yes. The more the merrier." She looked at her mother, who refused to look at her.

"I wouldn't miss it." Mrs. Pye moved aside her sewing to get a better look at Mary. "It's special that you get to wear your dress twice, too, before it gets taken apart and made into winter toddler clothes."

"That's down the road a way." Mary turned from the mirror. "I wish I had a sister I could hand it down to." She stroked the silver buttons. "So, you were able to bring these with you. It seemed like we left in such a hurry from Minnesota. The middle of the night almost. What else did you pack away?"

"No time to talk about that now."

"Oh, a mystery," Mrs. Pye chortled. "Everyone loves a mystery."

"Time for you to change, Mary." Her mother used her hands to shoo Mary toward the bedroom. "Let Mrs. Pye get on with that embroidery."

"But you never—"

"And I'm not going to now, either. Go on. There's work to be done before your big day."

Mary sighed, put a little stomp into her sway. She removed the velvet, then donned her wool dress, attaching the white collar, pondering: What was that about "Minnie"? On her wedding license? And why did her mother keep changing the subject? She'd never do that to her children, she was sure of that.

chapter
5

For the Clatsop-Nehalem girl, it was a special day at her grandfather's hut in a place the Clatsop people once called *NeCus'*, before the big flood that made the sands cry. A small fire outside the opening brought the scent of cedar into the dwelling. Jewell planned to attend the wedding of her friend Mary Edwards. She dressed in her regalia to be certain she had all the accoutrements, including the basket hat her grandmother had woven for her from cedar root. It would cover her hair, black as a raven's wing. She'd don the cedar bark skirt with a cloth blouse made from calico. Her shoes were cedar bark slippers worn rarely, but they were desirable for Jewell's small feet, to keep them dry. She would carry an eagle's feather fan from the bird that could fly between the People's world and that of the Beyond. And she would hold a purse made of spruce roots with a dog design woven into it, a gift of her mother no longer on this earth.

Jewell had many family members who were in the Beyond. Here, she had her grandfather who had raised her after the sickness took her family. Together with other Nehalem, they wintered in their cedar houses near Tillamook Bay or north near the big river. Summers they moved closer to the mountain and formed huts of reed mattings layered to keep summer squalls out. Jewell and her grandfather chose to nestle their summer home in the spruce trees not far from Ecola Creek, which flowed across the Crying Sands Beach into the ocean. That is where she had met her friend Mary years before.

Jewell looked at her image in the piece of mirror her grandfather had found after a summer intruder left it behind. The summer tent communities appeared each spring like temporary skin eruptions, and the inhabitants dug for razor clams, searched for sand dollars, or walked the beach. When they left, they sometimes gave up treasures like the section of mirror that caught sunlight and her image. Now, Jewell checked her hat, her cheeks, and called them "good."

He'd given permission for her to look at her reflection. "You are old enough not to search for your image. You know it is you." The first time she'd looked at herself, she'd studied the sandy color of her skin, lighter than her grandfather's. She was pleased to see that her brown eyes were large and round, just like his. Her mother was a Nehalem, but her father was Finnish, giving her the sand-colored skin.

She would walk the seventeen miles to where the wedding was being held, starting out one day, camping on the beach near the mountain, then arriving the next day. The walk would give her much time to think about her friend and to pray for the happiness that such a day promised.

She undressed and began to pack the regalia into her cedar bag she'd carry on her back, remembering that early meeting. She and Mary had found beeswax together in the sand. Mary's father sold the lumps—some as big as a Clatsop baby—to Tohl's store and split the money with Jewell. This was important. Mary treated her as though she was a sister, an equal. Jewell had no real sisters. Neither did Mary. Nor brothers either. They had this in common.

Mary thought it curious that in days past, the Spanish ships carried the beeswax as ballast, but also to help the Black Robes inland meet the requirement that they make all their religious candles out of beeswax. Not deer or elk tallow, the latter more readily available. This was the story handed down to her. Jewell didn't care how the beeswax had come to their shores, only that it offered a way for her to help support her and her grandfather. The ship that held them had sunk many moons ago and still it gave up wax after a king tide. She liked being among these Edwards people and other Anglos. One day she imagined being more among them. A wedding gave her new wisdom for how to be with those who were not of her people.

Jewell added the gifts she planned to give.

"The tea is prepared," her grandfather called to her. His hands shook when he gave her the cup. "Are you ready to make your journey?"

"It is so." Jewell sipped. "The strawberries taste good. We dried them when they were at their ripest."

"Aha. I will have enough for while you are gone. You have left me all I will need. I should go with you, but I will wait. When you return, we will head north."

"You can stay warm here. I am able. Is that not what you say to me?"

Her grandfather drank, then said, "It is a long and dangerous trip but yes, you are able."

Jewell smiled at him. "Not so dangerous. You have told me how to use the beach and to be careful if I have to use the mountain trail."

"Maybe you will meet the boy of your dreams at this wedding place."

Jewell sputtered, strawberry tea spit onto the dirt floor. "You think this is why I make the trip for Mary Edwards's wedding? No! It is for her. To show my happiness for her."

"You are of an age when babies should be your companions, not Anglo friends."

"That is not my dream, Grandfather."

"Maybe it should be."

He was a wise elder, one to be taken seriously, but he had no one but her to share this wisdom with. Soon, when she returned, they would move north, closer to the Columbia as the Anglos called the Nch'i-Wána. They would winter with others of their kind near a place where the Anglos Lewis and Clark had wintered. And the Shoshone woman, Sacagawea, who her grandfather said kept the Anglos from making mistakes. "Strong women do such things." But Ecola Creek was where he had spent his days. He told her the memories were as good as friends. She would remember that image when she left this ocean and take memories of friends like Mary and her wedding with her.

Jewell left that afternoon. A fog settled like a sitting hen over Ecola Creek, the route she followed to the beach. Once through the seagrass and driftwood onto the sand, she headed south, sensing rather than seeing the Haystack Rock, wishing she could see the puffins with their gray beaks this time of year. The rock stood between her footsteps and the sea.

She heard the seals barking and kept her eyes out for beeswax that might appear as a gift on this afternoon. She could smell the sea; inhaled its scent. Another gift: she bent to collect feathers, gray and white, of the flycatcher and the yellow fluff of the hermit warbler. Delicate as a hummingbird nest, she gentled them into her shapta'kai. These she would give to her grandfather for his duck carvings and the feathered hats he made.

The fog lifted, giving way to a drizzle. Fitting for the moon month her people called "moving inside for Winter." No beeswax, just strings of flotsam, kelp, driftwood that she stepped over, meandered through, forcing her in places to walk closer to the waves. She chose a place to stop at the base of the mountain, up from the tide line, and put up her tarp. She would eat dried fish and berries, listen to the rain, and finish her trip in the morning. She built a small fire. One day, the sale of beeswax would help her pursue a dream she had. A dream she had not shared with her grandfather, for it would mean leaving him in order to save him. Sometimes one person's dreams could seem another's nightmare until one saw the wisdom that comes only with time.

chapter
6

Herbert Logan's remittance was lower than expected. After spending the night in the Edwardses' barn, he'd ridden to Tillamook, the county seat, as Americans called it. With the remittance so low, he was glad he could meet with potential investors and then had time to return to Nehalem Hotel where he'd taken his second hot bath. He wasn't sure he'd ever get warm after Thursday's plunge into the sea. Resting on the bed, he took his packet out. It had been sealed in beeswax well attached to the saddle, so had survived the surf. Now he had to survive his brother's venom. The scarcity of his payment might suggest troubles in England, but he doubted it. Just his older brother being miserly. The letter had claimed the difference wouldn't be forthcoming and to spend these pounds wisely. Even thousands of miles and an ocean away, he could hear his brother's controlling voice.

He shivered. Still cold. In that cave, when he'd come to, he warmed himself by thinking of his beloved Devonshire and its elegant beaches and cream tea. And other warm sands of the United Kingdom like Brighton's shore, pebblier than the one where he'd built his cabin—that would one day be a hotel if all went well. Devonshire had similar miles of attractive beach a mere fifty miles or so from London. This Oregon sand was nearly eighty miles from Portland, the biggest population center in the region, but unlike Brighton, it attracted only hardy people wishing to escape the inland summer heat or to hunt and fish in the fall. He wanted to make it easier for everyone to find what beaches offered: a place of refuge, contemplation, spirit healing, a place for walking prayers.

At first, he'd imagined ranching near Victoria in the province of British Columbia after he and a pal, Joe Walsh, had arrived in Astoria in 1885. They'd traveled north but turned south after Joe decreed the Canadian province too much like the old country, with no place for the wit and wisdom of the Irish. "Except for you, Herbie," he'd said, "the Brits are stuffy as a head cold." While Herbert didn't agree, he did share Joe's love of the Oregon coast, especially where he'd settled, Cannon Beach or Arch Cape or Golden Sands. The natives called it Crying Sands Beach. He'd promote it as Cannon Beach. That's how he thought of it. You couldn't swim far out in either Brighton or Cannon Beach with the tides too strong—or at least you ought not to. A toe dip on a hot summer's day might suffice. But one could walk the sands, hand in hand if you had a lover, or fish the rivers that poured onto the beach, blending salt water with fresh. He had explored up and down the coastline between Astoria and Tillamook and kept coming back to "his" beach. It was where he'd built his small cottage out of driftwood. It didn't suit for the winter months. Those he spent in Astoria. Then this past year he'd acquired sufficient funds to build a real cabin. It had two bedrooms, and one day he'd add to it, making it his Elk Creek Hotel, right on the river he referred to as Elk Creek. Easier for people to envision what they might see—big herds of elk splashing in the surf—than figure out what Ecola meant. A local man, James Austin, had a hotel in Seaside, but he'd heard a rumor that Austin wanted to build one where the cannons might reappear. That meant a rival for his own accommodations for tourists.

He got off the bed, pulled on a wool sweater, and reread his brother's letter. It had been years since he'd been back to England. Actually, since he'd been sent away with only memories and the promise of a remittance each year assuming he would stay away so as not to embarrass his dear brother, the great heir. What they expected him to do that would embarrass them he wasn't sure of. Fail? Commit a crime? Who was he deceiving? It was all about Olivia.

Herbert had found a comrade in John Gerritse, a sort of renaissance fellow, willing to try new things, take a risk now and then. John didn't have much money, but he was a friendly opportunist, taking advantage when he could without harming others. He had shared a plan he had with John, which was why he had traveled with them to Astoria their wedding week. He wanted John to see the strengths and barriers to the possibilities—possibilities that almost didn't make it with that plunge in the sea.

He put away his satchel and brushed his mustache. The hotel used a lavender soap. He'd need fragrances—candles, soaps—in his hotel. He crawled beneath the blankets, tucking his nightshirt around his legs. They ached tonight. He hoped he could sleep. Tomorrow he'd visit with the mercantile owner. He might be willing to invest in Herbert's idea: building a seven-mile road to reduce the current seven-and-a-half-hour journey from Seaside to his Cannon Beach. He'd attend the wedding party on Monday but wouldn't attend the wedding. It was a family affair, and besides, weddings didn't sit well with him anyway, the one he'd once planned to be a part of foiled by his brother. But that was another story. He blew out the oil lantern and prayed for sleep.

chapter 7

"Come in, Jewell. You're just in time for the wedding breakfast." Amanda Edwards welcomed her daughter's friend. The girl must have gotten up early to arrive before the sun did. She sniffed. Sometimes these people carried an unpleasant fishy smell, but Jewell didn't. A promised sunrise cast a glow on the Edwardses' Nehalem porch. Shep, their dog, stopped barking and circled the newcomer who patted his yellow head before the dog turned away to flop down on the porch.

"I did not know that I might not be on time."

"No. I only meant . . . Well, please. May I take your bag?" Amanda closed the door gently, keeping Shep outside. Dogs could be so dirty.

"You're here!" Mary skipped from the table and wrapped her friend in her arms after dropping her linen napkin at her plate. "You came such a long way."

"It is my gift for your tying. That is one way we call a marriage. I also bring you this." Rather than hand it to Amanda, Jewell opened her cedar bag she took from her back. "Your people have guests bring gifts, is that not so?"

"Yes, but it isn't necessary. You're being here is enough."

"At our weddings, we give gifts away." She pulled out a blanket.

It was white as an egret with a black-and-red stripe at one end. "It is a trade blanket, from Hudson's Bay Company. My grandfather received it many years ago. It kept him warm, then Mother, then me. Now it will keep you and your John warm."

"It's beautiful," Mary said, handing it to Amanda, who smoothed her hand on the soft wool. She hoped there weren't fleas in it. Or did the Indians have a way to deal with those critters? Amanda would have to ask. Fleas and chiggers were such a bother.

"And it can keep you warm one more evening. Here," Mary added.

"And then your babies." Jewell bumped Mary's hip and the friends laughed.

"Let's sit, girls. Jewell, we're having backstrap, eggs, and johnnycakes. Do you like venison?" The girl nodded. "Of course you do. It's likely a staple."

"We eat more fish than deer or elk," Jewell said. "Easier to catch and clean." She smiled.

Amanda served the newcomer, then her daughter, then herself. William was at the barn with John on this wedding morn. The girls chattered together. They seemed so young to Amanda, so unprepared for what life had to offer them. Amanda certainly hadn't thought she'd only have one child to raise, and Mary came not as a pregnancy but as a gift after Amanda and William had grieved all the babies who came but didn't stay. And now she'd be losing her one and only. It was as it should be but still, Amanda would miss her, did not relish the changes her departure would bring. As all children did, Mary worked for the family. She took the butter to Tillamook for sale, sometimes rowed the canoe alone. It was Mary who herded the sheep up the mountain. Mary who helped milk their seventeen cows. All that help would end with her marriage. She wasn't sure how they'd replace her efforts, let alone her happy spirit. Amanda had neither the energy for farming nor that optimistic state of being.

She checked herself. William encouraged her to think positively. Mary wouldn't be far away. John's claim was upriver and Amanda could visit by boat or, if she had to, walk in the tangled path through the trees and ferns and manzanita bushes.

42

She'd be able to see anyone taking a boat upriver, too, so she could still protect Mary from . . . She ceased her thinking about her fears. It didn't go anywhere helpful. And it made her careless, as she'd been yesterday at Mrs. Pye's fitting. Telling of the license with the name "Minnie," which was Mary's legal name but which they had never shared with her—nor the reasons why.

Amanda checked the stew she would have for the wedding supper later, then heated maple syrup for the girls' next batch of pancakes. She touched the braid wrapped around her head. She'd have to redo it before the ceremony to capture the errant gray strands. Her husband William and John had finished eating and were taking care of the milking so Mary didn't have to on her wedding day. It would be a day of changed routines. Uncertainties. Would the pastor make it? He was traveling clergy. William had asked the justice of the peace to attend just in case. Would the witnesses remember? Did she have enough food prepared? She wished she could enjoy the disruptions. She liked predictability. Certainty. Yet much of her life had been anything but. She'd been born in New York, married William, headed to Minnesota in haste, only to leave quickly again to the Willamette Valley, then to this coastal place. They couldn't move any farther west without stepping onto a boat out on the Pacific. Mary was safe here, that was what mattered.

Amanda prided herself on serving meals, keeping their cabin neat and tidy, and fixing lunches for Mary when she headed off to school. *School.* Mary hadn't attended since seventh grade. But with her vows this day she'd truly go from being a girl to a woman.

The girls whispered. Mary rubbed her silver spoon on her skirt, then placed the bowl of her spoon on her nose, the handle extended out. Jewell laughed and tried it, both girls giggling at each other's spoon handle resembling an elephant's trunk stretched out.

"What keeps the spoon from falling?"

Mary crossed her eyes to more raucous laughter. "Magic," she said.

"Girls!" But Amanda laughed with them, trying to ignore her worries.

Had she and William been too lenient in allowing this marriage to go forward? Had they given Mary the skills she'd need to have a happy married life? Could John protect her?

Amanda feared for her daughter, but she feared for herself too. Once Mary and John left . . . Amanda's heart pinched at the thought. She noticed the time. Mary should consider getting dressed. She wished she had one more day with her daughter as just her daughter, not a married woman. It would be so lonely when John and Mary were gone. In the evening, she'd knit and watch her husband read, miles away into whatever world his books took him, leaving Amanda wondering if she could survive the impending trench of sorrow.

chapter
8

"Could I have a minute, sir?" John halted his future father-in-law at the barn door. They'd milked the Jersey herd, poured milk into pans to separate, and turned the animals out into the paddock, their warm cow scent still permeating the shed.

"We'd best be heading in. Your nuptials await. Don't want to keep your bride waiting." The man smiled, but it didn't reduce John's heart pounding nor his sweaty palms. What would he do if William Edwards said no?

"Ja. A minute it takes." He corrected himself. "It will take but a minute." William Edwards nodded. "You see, there's been a bit of a delay." John cleared his throat. "With my claim. And it would serve us well if we could stay here with you and your missus for a time. Make it easier for Mary to keep making that butter. And do the milking, of course."

He'd put off the request long enough. It was one of his flaws, he supposed, putting things off. But didn't everyone have to have some bad habits? He neither smoked nor drank.

"It was our belief you'd be heading up the North Fork. That you had a claim there."

"Oh, I do, I do, ja. But I've had to take a mail contract to help support us, and that puts me away most of the week with but one night at the claim site. So, I haven't made much progress clearing land."

"Maybe I could get a few neighbors together."

"I don't wish to trouble you, nor them. It's my responsibility to provide. It'd be better for her if she stays here, ja? Only for a short time. Until spring. I could pay you rent."

"Oh, now, we're family. Rent isn't necessary, but I appreciate the offer." William scratched his back on the door jam. "Our house is small as you know. Just the two rooms."

"I was thinking about that. I could haul a load of driftwood and we could add a room on if you're agreeable. Herbert Logan is considering bringing a sawmill to the coast, but until then . . ."

"Mary's alright with this?"

He lowered his eyes. "She will be. I'm not so good yet with the timing of what I tell her."

"Aha. Well, you'll find that sharing information for discussion rather than just a telling will bring you a happier wife. Which is why I'd want to talk with Amanda before I say yes. She has a little harder time with changes, though I think this one might actually please her. She's been a little sad about seeing Mary go."

More delay. He deserved that. It put off seeing Mary's disappointment. That was a price he had to pay, and it was better than running away to the sea.

"But that would be . . . lovely," Amanda said. The men had come in, hung their coats on the wall pegs, and sat at the table. Mary served berry pie to her father and future husband while her mother finished whipping cream for the topping. Jewell had slipped away to sit beside the fireplace, braiding eight strands of straw while Shep (having snuck in with the men) lay beside her, his nose resting on Jewell's moccasins.

"What say you, Mary?" John looked up at his future wife, who wore a confused look on her usually pleasant face. He did love that face, those blue eyes he could sink into like a drowning man reaching a saving ship.

"It comes as a bit of a . . . surprise. Not that I don't like surprises, mind you. I do. But I imagined tending my own hearth with my husband."

"It'll be fun, Mary." Amanda Edwards was an ally John hadn't realized he'd need. "Two married women sharing the house. We can hang a quilt to separate us in the bedroom or you can squeeze into the loft. Well, the two of you."

"Is this how decisions work in marriages?" Mary put on her curious face, eyebrows raised. "Seems to me there's something amiss here. You've put the cart before the horse, John." Mary tapped her upper lip.

John noticed she did that when she was perturbed. He had wanted to avoid that gesture. The truth was, having this discussion with the backing of her dad—and now her mother—worked to his advantage. How could she really protest?

"We'll make up the kitchen for the two of you. Hang a blanket to separate your bed from the table. It'll be your own little space, not so tight as the loft." Amanda clapped her hands. "Why, we'll have such fun together, the four of us."

"I won't be joining you often, what with the mail route. It'll put me here just one night during the week. And weekends. Till we build on the claim."

Mary frowned. His stomach knotted. He didn't want to hurt her. He'd have to find a time when they were alone to reassure her that in the future, he'd involve her in decisions. If he could, though wasn't it a man's task to set the course?

"How long?"

"Oh, just until spring."

"I can help, you know. I helped Dad burn out stumps and clear ground. A lean-to is all we'd need."

"You'd be alone there because of my mail route."

"Oh." Mary paused. Then her face lit up. "It would be an adventure. We'll move into a cabin in the spring?"

"Sometime around then." He wanted to change the subject. "I do have a surprise for you, Mary. One you'll like."

"Can I afford any more?"

John walked to Mary, held her gently at the waist. Did she resist? "Where's that optimism I so adore in you, Mary?"

"It's most hopeful to think of the possibilities, true, but everything doesn't always turn out fine, John. Has our miracle survival gone to your head?"

He laughed. "Nee. I show you Monday, before the party. You'll like this surprise." He turned to his future in-laws. "Thank you, Edwards family. We have a boat to put into the sea, as they say."

"With hopefully no leaks," Mary chirped.

It was John's turn to feel his face grow hot. There was so much yet to tell her, but that could wait. This was their wedding day and he'd brought her enough uncertainty.

chapter
9

"Y̲ou'll always have a home if you need it, wherever we live, Mary, you know that." Her father had entered her parents' bedroom, where Mary had dressed for the ceremony. Mary's heart was a drumbeat and her arms felt tingly beneath the long sleeves of her fitted velvet dress. "We're family."

"Thank you, Papa. John and I will have a house of our own before long, but I am so grateful for this home and how you set the pattern for me to follow. Generosity and kindness." She slipped her arm through his elbow. "You'll always be my first family."

He kissed her forehead and she sensed he wanted to say something more, clearing his throat, and when he did, tears came unbidden. "I love you, Mary. As does your mother, more than you can know." He coughed then. "Let's expand this family and get you married off."

It was the first time her father had ever said he loved her.

The ceremony went forward on Saturday at 11:00 a.m., held at the Edwardses' home, with the scent of chowder wafting through the room. The officiant was the Justice of the Peace, Will Batterson, who was also Mary's former teacher. It was a small affair with a few friends and her parents. Mary wished she'd had a sister or brother to share the day with and was especially glad to have Jewell attend. John's family lived in the Netherlands, so he had no one to represent his side when they said their "I dos." His eyes held hers through the vows as her heart filled to the brim, their love a porcelain cup of joy and hope, especially as it was a miracle they were there at all.

After the ceremony, Jewell brought her blanket up and asked Mary and John to stand side by side facing out, while she wrapped the blanket around them. "We do this at our weddings," she said. "Bind you together facing friends and family who witness your day."

Mary snuggled into John's side as he held her tight. Binding. Yes, they were attached forever now.

"Come, come," her mother said, pressing them toward the table. The traveling pastor finally arrived in time for pandowdy composed of dried apples refreshed with rare sugar and spice.

"Justice Batterson made it legal. I'll make it permanent," he said, and Mary and John repeated their vows "before God."

When they told him of their near death, he raised his eyes to heaven. "Praise God from whom all blessings flow." He blessed the nuptials, and Mary and John finally sent the guests into the night to do chores, most being farmers, while she and John took a walk along the bay's shore, their journey lulled by the tempo of the soft-slapping waves. Mary slipped her arm through her new husband's and decided she was brave enough then to tell him of her thinking. Shep trotted along behind them, sniffing at driftwood and sand creatures capturing the night. Mary looked up. An overcast sky would keep the stars out of sight. She would have liked the witness of their light.

She dipped her toe into the stream of marital conflict. "Now that we're married, I'd like you to include me before you make big decisions. Talk with me first, before my father. Or anyone else." She wouldn't talk about feeling betrayed.

"It's my job to look after you, ja? A man can't be waiting for his wife to decide important things."

She felt her heart pound in her ears. "No waiting required if you chat a bit with me beforehand. I'm an easy decider." Mary kept her voice light though her stomach clenched. "You won't have the misery of my being annoyed if you follow that sequence."

John stopped. Still. He released her arm, then bent to pick up a pebble and toss it into the water. Mary heard it plop.

She took a deep breath. "See, if you had told me you hadn't made progress on the claim, I could have been working on it for us."

"I didn't want you alone out there, Mary."

She swallowed. "But I will be eventually, what with you taking on the mail contract. And maybe, in the years ahead, one or the other of us will be forced to fill the purse away from the farm. Leaving the other behind."

"The mail route is temporary. I'll make a go of farming, you'll see. And you've never been alone like that."

"Not overnight, no. But up on the mountain I've been by myself all day with sheep and cows. I rather like the solitude of birds and insects, quiet plants and grazing elk. I don't feel lonely. Besides, there's no time like the present to figure out how I'll manage our separations. I've prayed to be brave, John. It was my prayer the day at Hug Point when I thought I'd be alone forever." As the only survivor, the aloneness had weighed like a stone on her heart. "But I realized that to answer that prayer I have to face something fearful. I want you and me to anticipate those dangers together."

John threw another rock. "I'm used to making my own decisions, not having to defend them."

"But I might have something worthy to offer and it'll work better if I offer it before the fact instead of after. It's worth a try, don't you think?"

John grunted. She had her work cut out for her in figuring out how to make this part of marriage work—and it was but a few hours old.

When they returned to her family, no Contrary Woman quilt hung on a clothesline strung across the main room. Instead her parents' bed was freshly made up. Her mother beamed. "We're spending the night with friends in Nehalem, to give you private time." Her mother looked away. "Come along, William. Let's leave the newlyweds to their . . . escapades. Where did I put my night bag? We're leaving Shep with you."

Jewell walked outside with them and would sleep under her tarp before visiting relatives the next day in Tillamook.

Mary's heart started that drumming again as she undressed in the kitchen while John did the same in her parents' bedroom. Months before, Mary had probed her mother about the intimate side of marriage. Her mother's face had turned pink, and she'd scrubbed the cast-iron kettle like it had been full of soot. "It'll come to you natural," her mother told her. "You'll learn as you go."

Natural? Mary had vowed to talk further with Mrs. Pye the dressmaker before the wedding night. Which she had.

Neither had told her how tender a husband could be, how easily John comforted her, sighing, as she came through the door carrying the beeswax candle. "Beautiful, you are." He stroked her cheek, her chin, and kissed her as deep as ever she'd been kissed. Pulling back, he'd gazed at her, the candlelight flickering. "I love you, Mary Gerritse. I always will."

Tingles like fireflies flittered down her spine. Twice in one day she'd heard those words from the two men she most loved. "And I love you," she whispered back.

They believed in each other and had the blessing of God and family. What greater hope could there be than that?

chapter
10

After bidding Jewell goodbye outside in the early dawn, Mary woke John. "Hey, sailor. Grab your socks. Time for coffee with your first mate. We don't want to be late for church."

John groaned but turned to her and accepted the steaming mug she handed him. "A man could get used to this."

"My very plan. I'll fix flapjacks and bacon and then we're off. Folks will expect us."

"Looking innocent of our evening antics, ja."

Mary's face grew warm.

Church was in Uppertown on the Nehalem Bay. During the week, the building served as the school. Slates and maps of the world and charts of letters offered a bit of whimsy to the traveling pastor's harrowing descriptions of what will happen to sinners if they don't repent. Mary settled next to John, skirts swishing as she considered this, her first church service as a wife. Today, the preacher's emphasis was on the role of parents in the nurturing of their children's souls. She and John had never shared how their faith might reflect on the raising of children, only the numbers: Mary wanted a dozen; John said half would do. "Though the trying wouldn't bring me sorrow." He'd followed that comment with a grin and a kiss.

Today, standing in front of the church, Mary called out to attendees. "Don't forget our wedding party tomorrow night. Seven o'clock, after chores."

"Been waitin' all year for a good dance," one of the men said.

"You're really waiting for Amanda and Mary's cookin'," his wife said, poking her husband's paunchy ribs.

"We've a child tender so feel free to bring your little ones too. We'll squirrel them away in the coatroom so they don't interrupt our revelry." Mary waved to one of her schoolmates and shouted, "Don't forget!" The girl waved back as she mounted her horse.

"Mary, a lady's voice, please," her mother cautioned.

Mary would be pleased someday soon to not have to fit into her mother's ideas of proper behavior. What was a good shout among friends? Besides, she was a married woman now and could establish her own rules, couldn't she?

Mary curtsied to her mother, then turned her back when Mr. Effenberger asked, "Still want me to bring my accordion?"

"Absolutely," John said. "It wouldn't be a party without it."

"Count the Battersons in," her old teacher said.

Mary was glad they were coming. Maybe the festivities would cut into some of the sadness of that family.

"We'll have egg coffee for you Finlanders." Mary spoke to another couple who had immigrated from that cold northern clime to work in the woods felling timber. "And plenty of stewed chickens from Mama's old hens that stopped laying."

"So glad children can come." Mrs. Effenberger slipped beside her husband. "You know our little crab cakes love music."

Mary'd never heard of children being called crab cakes before, but grinned. It seemed fitting for coastal babies.

A few others offered congratulations and confirmed their attendance, letting her mother know that they'd bring bread and cheese and Arbuckle's coffee and promised to keep any liquor outside. It felt festive as Christmas that was still a month away.

The four of them returned to a quiet afternoon at Mary's parents'. The same old schedule, with Mary lamenting the lack of a view from their own cabin.

"I've some unfinished business to attend to," John said after the cold meal of smoked fish, dried huckleberries, and her mother's wonderful biscuits. The jam Mary and her mother had made that summer sank into the soft pastry, and Mary sighed with delight. Thank the Lord for her mother's way with flour.

"It's the Sabbath," her mother protested. "Time for quiet and reflection."

"I'm honoring the day by finishing what I started." He wasn't afraid to challenge her mother, Mary noted.

"I'm sure the Lord loves a good worker, Amanda," her father said.

It had always been her mother who kept the Sabbath, expressing concern over not upsetting God by working even though there were chores that had to be tended to. Her father always replied that the Lord would be distressed if they didn't care for their stock. "Not to mention how distressed the cows would be not getting milked."

"I can go with you," Mary said. "Wherever you're off to." She rose to put on her slicker. It had started to rain.

"You can go as far as the barn with me. Then Baldy and I are off to the neighbors, and you'll just have to be patient, Mrs. Gerritse." He helped her with the hood on her slicker. "I won't be long."

At the barn, Mary watched John mount up on Baldy, a slow-walking horse who reminded her of a recalcitrant child dragged to chores.

"Is this another of your decisions that it might be well to have involved me first?"

"A man can't surprise his wife without getting into trouble?" He had an edge to his voice that was almost a warning.

Jake gave a low whinny, turned to look at Mary. Maybe that horse felt her tension? Mary exhaled. "Not challenging you, dear sailor, just not wanting any more big adjustments coming my way."

"Ja. This I understand. I think you will like this. But if not, it is reversible."

"Ah, something to wear."

John laughed, then prodded Baldy as he rode out the lane beneath a dripping sky.

"What do you think that man has in mind?" Mary brushed Jake's winter coat. The horse was becoming the closest thing she had to a sibling, one who had rescued her from the sea.

She must have been in the barn longer than she'd thought for she heard John's deep voice, and he appeared in the doorway. "It's time for your surprise." Her father would be out soon to milk his eight cows while she'd milk the other nine.

"Is it?"

John invited Mary closer.

"What could it be, Jake?"

He handed her a new halter and lead rope. Mary put the leather to her nose, inhaled the smokey smell.

"This is wonderful work. Did you do the braiding?"

He nodded. "It comes with something else." John motioned her to the door. Mist filtered the late afternoon light. "Wait here."

Mary admired the workmanship of the halter until John appeared from around the side of the barn leading a tall gray horse. "His name is Prince," he said. "I've worked him since he was a colt. He's three years old. Gelded him earlier this summer. He has a huge heart and he'll be perfect for you. Jake's getting older. It was lucky he had the stamina to carry you through the wave at Hug Point. Prince will be with us for years to come."

Her own horse!

Mary approached Prince and pressed her hand along his wide gray cheek. "Sixteen hands?"

"About. He's stable, sturdy, and smart."

She stood off to the horse's side so he had a good look at her, then she stepped in front of him. She stroked the velvet of his nose. The horse nickered, lowered his head to her, then put his chin on her shoulder.

"He likes you already," John said. "I knew he would."

"He's a wonderful wedding present, John. I've never had my own mount. Thank you."

Mary put her arms around John's neck and kissed her husband.

56

It was her gift but would help him too. With Prince, John would have a backup horse for his mail delivery if Baldy or Jake came up lame or needed a rest. Baldy was so slow-moving, John would be delivering Christmas cards at Easter if he had to rely on him every day.

"Can you wait until tomorrow for my present to you?"

"I'm an impatient man." He leaned his back against Prince, pulled Mary to him. "About some things." His breath on her neck made Mary shiver. "I'm asking you to wait on a home of our own, so I guess I can wait a day for your gift. Meanwhile"—he kissed her—"I could be distracted by other things."

Those tingly feelings crept up her spine. Surely it wouldn't be proper to have antics in the barn. On the Sabbath. What would her mother say? Did she care?

"Hmm . . ."

"You'll have to get to know when I'm teasing or not, Mare. I do tease a lot."

She poked his chest. "I'll work on detecting that impish side of you, my sailor."

John held her finger and winked.

chapter

11

I think we have enough for an army." Mary's mother wiped her forehead of the sweat as she leaned over the fireplace. Mary loved a party and she wanted this one to be memorable, as it almost didn't happen. Nothing gave her greater joy than serving food to family, friends, and neighbors as a celebration.

Jewell helped John load the baskets and milk buckets onto the boat, then John took Mary's hand to settle her onboard and they paddled toward the schoolhouse. The outgoing tide would whisk them along the Nehalem River toward the bay. A second craft brought Jewell and Mary's father and mother, and more food. At the schoolhouse, Mary helped her mother from the boat. Her mother's eyes darted about. "You'll be fine, Mama. Just think as if we're going to church."

"Just more people than I know here." Her mother's hands wrung, washing with air, and Mary knew she was sacrificing to be here. Her mother was a wary person and, except for church, didn't venture out much.

"You'll keep busy at the food table. It'll be fine."

Settlers and homesteaders gathered at seven, and in an array of aromas, Mary and her mother put out the roast beef, chicken pie, potatoes, onions, carrot dishes, pitchers of milk, butter and bread and Arbuckle's coffee, deviled eggs by the dozen. And the wedding cake.

Joe Effenberger started playing his accordion while guests from up and down the coast began swinging to the music. Everyone knew John, it seemed.

"You two go dance," Mary's father told her and John. "Your mother and I'll manage the food."

Mary kissed her father's cheek, and wearing her green velvet wedding dress, she and John swirled to the music. Mary had earlier removed her turban hat as the room warmed with active bodies, even with the doors open to the night air. John was a good dancer and playfully allowed others to cut in. Mary noticed—as farmer after logger danced the two-step or the waltz with her—that John never danced with another. He just smiled, standing in his white blouse and blue pants. When he took her in his arms again, he said, "I've captured the most vibrant woman in the world. Vibrant is a good word, ja?"

"It is indeed. So that's what that grin was about?"

"Ja. I'm a most lucky fellow."

It was midnight when the violinist broke two strings and laughter halted the dancing.

"A good time to feed our bellies," John announced. He held Mary's hand, and they stood behind the plank table to serve their friends. Mary watched her mother scan the crowd.

"Are you looking for someone, Mama?"

"Oh! No. Just counting heads, wondering if we have enough food."

"Not to worry. You've done us proud."

The chatter of happy celebrating people sounded like music to Mary, louder than the rain pelting the shake roof. And when the Batterson boy said loudly, "When ya gonna open presents?" John clanked his spoon against a glass and the crowd made a semicircle around the gift table.

Little Benjamin Effenberger was one of several "crab cakes" who attended, but it was the Batterson boy, Merritt, who set himself right next to Mary and John as they perched on high stools, ribbon-wrapped presents before them. Merritt's older brother had died of typhoid and his mother, it was said, had returned to California with his only sister. Lucy Batterson couldn't handle the change from a nice home in Sacramento to the wilds of the coastal homestead where she had to carry water up a steep hill instead of it running from a pump in her kitchen. Her son's dying had been the last stone on the grave of Lucy and Will Batterson's marriage. At least that's what Mary had heard. She shook her head and vowed not to think of unhappy marriages, at least not this day.

"Merritt," his father called out to him. "Come away now."

"It's alright," John said. "Let the lad be."

Will Batterson, Mary's former teacher, faded back into the crowd.

"I wonder what's in that one," Merritt said with enthusiasm. He pointed to a bucket with a red cloth spread over it.

John lifted the cloth and inside were razor clams piled high.

"Oh, wow! Clams," Merritt announced to the crowd. "I wonder how many there are in there. We'd better eat 'em or they'll spoil."

Everyone laughed. From the back a neighbor shouted, "He's right. Part of the gift is the promise that we'll fill that bucket once a week for you for the first month of your marriage, so you won't have to take time away from cuddling and—"

"Stop right there," a woman called out.

People chuckled. Boxes abounded. One contained an almanac cased in beeswax to keep it safe from sudden rains or even bugs. Jewell's blanket graced the table and Jewell had also put one of her woven baskets beside the cake. Into it, she'd enmeshed a design made of cattails, spruce roots, and maidenhair ferns. Mary held it up for all to see.

"Wow! It's so beautiful," the boy said.

"Mary can pick blackberries into it," Jewell told him.

"Or just look at it," Merritt said. "I like pretty things. They make me feel better."

"Do you want to give me your present now?" John whispered in Mary's ear.

"I can," she said. "But it won't be announced by little Merritt. It's not wrapped in any package." The rain had paused as though it knew Mary's voice would otherwise not be heard. "It's a poem I wrote for you." She felt her face grow warm. "Maybe I should save it for just your ears."

"Do as you please, but I'd like to hear it." He angled his head and grinned. "Besides, how many men have a poet for a wife? I'd be proud to have you recite for me, ja?"

"Alright."

"Wow!" Merritt the eavesdropper announced, "Mrs. Gerritse's gonna recite a poem. Maybe it'll be all mushy." He shouted the words to the chortles of the guests.

"Shush, Merritt," his father said. "I'm so sorry."

"I wonder the same thing." John smiled and squeezed Merritt's shoulder while looking directly at Mary. "Let's hear it."

Mary took a deep breath. She'd worked on the poem for a few days, and it felt festive for the public reading. A wedding ought to have a little whimsy along with love. Inspired by the ballad rhythm of the Lear poem Mary cherished about the Jumblies who went to sea in a sieve, she began:

> "The Puffins mate for life, you know
> For life, the puffins mate.
> Their lives are promises of note,
> As they honor that sweet fate.
> Like them I vow to you, my love,
> My love, this is my vow:
> Like puffins on that Haystack Rock,
> I'll stay—no matter how.
> I'll stay; no matter, calm or strain.
> Like the puffins, I will stay.
> And pledge to you my love and life.
> My love grows strong each day.
> And so I vow to you, my love
> My love, this is my vow:
> Like puffins on that Haystack Rock,
> I'll stay—no matter how."

Applause rose up. Mary lowered her eyes. John kissed her, just a sweet one. "I wrote 'Love, Mary Edwards' on your copy," she whispered to him.

"Wow! That there is pretty!" Merritt's words met another shushing by his father.

Jewell stood then. She'd been silent off to the side after her basket had been presented. Most of the evening she'd chosen to be the child tender. "If you read it again, Mary, I will drum to it."

"Oh, wow!" Merritt shouted.

Mary nodded and recited the poem again as Jewell tapped her hand on the table. Soon Merritt picked up the rhythm and pounded beside her. The banjo player plinked a tune, and by the time she'd finished reading—having repeated the lines about vows—everyone sang together. "'And so I vow to you, my love, my love, to you I vow. Like Puffins on the Haystack Rock, I'll stay no matter how.'" Raucous applause followed this time, and Mary beamed with the community of it, the joined voices and perhaps the vows that went beyond those of her and John to each of those in the crowd, vowing to be there "no matter how." It could be a coastal settler's mantra.

John leaned down and kissed Mary. "You've made me proud to have a poem writ for me." He turned to the crowd. "Thank you for all of you coming. Let's wind up the music, then dance until dawn." To Mary he whispered, "You signed it Mary Edwards?"

"I wrote it before we were married."

"Alright then."

"But I think any poem I write I'll sign as Mary Edwards. It'll be my pen name—that's what author's call a special name attached to their work."

"But why wouldn't you carry my name?"

"On everything else I'll be Mrs. John Gerritse. Keeping 'Edwards' means I was something before I married. It's my birth name." Her mind flashed on "Minnie," the name her mother said her father wrote on her marriage certificate. Was her name really Minnie Edwards?

John was about to protest more, she could see, so she was glad Herbert Logan approached.

"That's the ballad beat, like the Jumblies poem of going to sea in a sieve, isn't it, Mary?" Herbert had been dancing but, like the rest of the crowd, had quieted for Mary's reading. He rubbed his lower back.

"It is. It's easier to remember with those special beats. Are you hurting?"

"It's nothing." To John he said, "Truly that is quite a pledge of love and loyalty to you, old boy. We should all be so fortunate. And tonight we all received a present."

He said the words with a wistful sigh, and Mary made a vow that evening to be there not only for family but for friends—no matter how.

chapter
12

For Amanda, John's delay in building on his claim kept her daughter close at hand. It turned out to be surprisingly comforting for Amanda, having her daughter still at home. Mary continued to work at something she seemed to like doing—tending animals, milking. And once a week when John stopped midway on his mail route, and on weekends, Amanda cooked for an extra person. No problem there.

Amanda clucked at her chickens as she pulled warm eggs from beneath them. Egg collection prompted the rare times when she went outside. She wasn't good at clearing brush or milking cows. She had to be vigilant, stay close to the house, keep Mary safe.

Back inside, Amanda beat an egg into the soup, sloshing chowder onto the stovetop. The hiss of heat caused her to step back. She counted to ten. Or was it twenty she should count to when there was a spill to prevent it from happening again? She made up rules for herself, but didn't everyone?

William and Mary should be coming inside soon. She looked out the window. She liked the way their home sat on their homestead. She could see what came down the road. It would seem strange to some that such building placements would matter. But when they'd lived in Minnesota, there'd been a very close call that made Amanda have strong feelings about where they lived and how they set buildings on the claim.

She caught her breath at the memory, her heart pounding as though it just happened, her breathing shallow.

William had taken shakes to market that day, so she was alone. Mary had gone with her father, her ten-year-old legs swinging as she sat on the wagon seat, waving to her mother, bundled up against the Minnesota winter.

The man had simply appeared out of nowhere. He said he was looking for the Edwards family, on behalf of a friend back in New York. "Have I found the right people?"

"I'm sure I have no idea." Why had she answered the door? "There are many Edwards and certainly not all are related to us." *Keep your voice calm, calm.*

She didn't invite him in, a sin of prairie hospitality for sure, especially in the cold November.

At first, Amanda thought him a salesman of spiders and other cookware. Or thread maybe, but he didn't have a pack animal or wagon. In fact, he'd walked down their lane. She saw his footsteps in the snow.

"New York?" Amanda acted like she was contemplating. "We don't have any friends in New York." She didn't say anything about family nor that both she and William had been born there.

"I'll keep looking, then," he said. "Thanks for your time."

It was after that when she made the first request of her husband, that they go farther west, to somewhere more remote. And when William had filed the claim near the mouth of the Nehalem River, she'd been grateful, suggesting the placement of the house and barn. If someone else came looking, she didn't want Mary to finish milking the cows, walk out and see a visitor, and start asking questions. She was a gregarious child, chatting up strangers and friends alike. Amanda had to protect her. Which was why she could permit the marriage, knowing John had filed a claim upriver which was even more remote. No one could find her there and tell her about her beginnings. Mary would hopefully forget about Amanda's slip of "Minnie" on the marriage license. Amanda had to keep Mary from knowing—and keep William from some of the details she'd never shared with him either.

She scrubbed at the burnt chowder, counting her strokes.

Families came in many shapes depending on how a mother blended them. She must keep things from spilling onto a hot surface. She counted to twenty.

chapter
13

"You got us here, Logan. What is it you were thinking aside from spending a tad of your remittance on our drinks?" James Austin fingered his handlebar mustache, smiling.

Austin wasn't bad. It was the Portland banker with his cigar and sly look that got Herbert Logan's gut twisted like a nautical knot. He reminded Herbert of his brother, that was it. The smug visage of a man in charge. He knew he wouldn't inherit, but his father had promised he wouldn't be banished. But here he was, having to prove himself once again.

These property owners in Astoria, Seaside, Portland, and places more developed than the golden sands of Cannon Beach smoked their cigars in the saloon of the Austin's hotel in Seaside. At least they'd shown up.

"I want this as much as you," Austin said.

Of course he did! Austin planned to build a rival hotel south of Herbert's and he had a personable wife too. That always fared well for an inn's operation. Herbie had no one but himself to greet guests at his hotel, no family to rely on.

"I say, we surely can come up with a plan that each of us can agree to, can't we, gentlemen? Austin here knows my idea has merit."

The banker—who sounded like Herbert's arrogant brother—said, "Doing business with a foreigner? Are the economic interests of Oregon ready for that?"

"I say," Herbie said. "This whole country was once peopled by foreigners. Except for the Indigenous of course. And a pound spends as good as a dollar."

Couldn't these money men understand that getting tourists and travelers *to* that beach was the key? More than just fishermen or clam diggers, Herbert imagined families with children, building sandcastles, flying kites. An equestrian stable where people could rent horses to speed along the beach. Churches. Schools. Artists showing their wares. A sawmill, fish hatchery. Maybe even a place of retreat. He had to convince them, not only for his own investment's sake, but to prove to *his* family that he was something.

"I'm putting in the lion's share," Herbie said. "You can be in on the beginning of something grand or sit back and watch your favorite foreigner race ahead of you. What's it going to be?"

"He's right," Austin said. "Except for when the tide goes out, there isn't a road anyone can count on to get them safely to Cannon Beach without undue strain. We all agree on that much?"

Herbert eyed the banker as did the others.

"That fellow from Portland who traveled with Gerritse's mail run must have had a megaphone to the entire city. So many complaints I've heard since then." This from a Seasider. "Every time someone hits the town from the city, they tell me about that 'poor fellow who nearly died.'"

He couldn't let them rehash old stories.

"We have to reclaim the idea of adventure rather than danger in getting to the coast." Austin set his pipe aside, crossed his hands over his stomach.

"By Jove, you've hit on it exactly." Herbert stood now. "It's all about making the way to get to that glorious beach something memorable rather than horrifying as a Frankenstein novel. We need to 'illiterate the competition,' as my friend Joe would say. Present company excluded." He nodded to Austin. "Let's make Cannon Beach a rival to Portland for its beauty, its hope, its banquet for families, its unique commerce that only a beach can offer." His words could be an advertisement. "Are you in, gentlemen?"

He'd lose them if they focused on the impossibility of things ever being different than they currently were or saw danger instead of success. That was the trouble with history: it suggested not only the way something was but often cemented in the brain that it was the *only* way it could ever be. He tapped his ivory walking stick against the table leg to get their attention. "Gentlemen. I have formed the Elk Creek Road Company and today is the day for you to climb into the best investment you've ever known."

Would his capacity to communicate ideas and dreams be enough for them to part with their cash? He was about to find out.

His eyes held those of the banker, who blew cigar smoke toward the ceiling. *He isn't my brother.* But would he act against him as his brother had?

chapter
14

Even though Prince was Mary's wedding gift, she rarely got to ride him. The winter months with heavy squalls, high winds, and occasional snow meant John needed the most sure-footed of mounts for his mail route. But John had left Prince for her today as he rode off on Jake. Her marriage turned out to be a constant hello and goodbye instead of the highs and lows of learning about each other, making their lives fit like an intricate puzzle. Her stomach curdled as it did whenever she felt sorry for herself.

She burped. She'd been doing that a lot lately, which had inspired this trip to Tohl's store in Nehalem on the wharf. She dismounted, grabbed at her stomach. She shouldn't have waited to pick up Hostetter's Celebrated Stomach Bitters, nor the other supplies her mother had asked for.

"What can I do you for?" The Tohl's clerk leaned over the counter with a smile at Mary. His apron was sea-sand beige.

"Good morning, Mr. Anders. You can hand me a can of Arbuckle's."

"Newlyweds drinking lots of coffee these days?" He turned and reached for the tin. "Figured you have other things to keep you awake." He winked.

She sniffed like he'd offered her snuff instead of his opinion. Why did people think newlyweds were fair game for mirth?

"It's for my parents. We're staying with them. Well, it seems like I am. John's only around a couple of days a week." Holy Jumblies, she was expounding when she should be keeping herself to herself.

The bell above the door jingled and Merritt Batterson came in, head down. He perked up at the sight of the adults.

"Hi, Mr. Anders. Hi, Mary. I mean Mrs. Gerritse. My pa says I'm to call you that now that we aren't in school together anymore. I'd sure like to get out of going to school once in a while. I guess I'd need to get married to do that."

Mary laughed. "You're welcome to come over to our house *after* school if you'd like." She missed attending, but returning would be truly admitting nothing had changed with her marriage vows.

"Wow! That would be grand. I like to throw that there ball for old Shep."

"Don't you have a dog?"

"We did." He sighed. His freckled nose ran and he wiped it with his jacket sleeve. "But he died. Right after my brother did, and Pa hasn't had the heart to get another one. He says taking on a dog is like preparing your heart for loss."

Mary nodded. "Same with a horse. We fall in love with them, don't we? But they give us such joy. Maybe that's worth the heartache at the end. And we do have memories to help us."

"I miss my brother."

"I'm sure you do. You and I are both without siblings."

"What's a sibling?"

"A brother or sister." Mary felt a little guilty feeling sorry for herself when here was little Merritt dealing with significant losses. And she'd told herself she'd check up on him and hadn't. Here it was already March.

"Oh," Merritt sighed. "I got a sister but she's in California. Somewhere. Pa says when I'm older I can go visit. It's too far to walk, though."

"Did you walk here?" Mary asked. Merritt was a wiry child, and though it wasn't much more than a mile between the town on the bay and the Batterson claim, he was listless and pale and looked tired. Maybe he had what she'd had at Christmas and then her birthday in January, her stomach roiling and tossing itself up in the outhouse. It had gotten better, but she still felt odd at times.

"I did." Merritt turned to Anders. "I'm to pick up some slates my dad ordered for the school. I hope they aren't too heavy or I might have to make a couple of trips."

"That's a lot of walking," Mary said.

He shrugged, then cheerfully added, "I get to see boats on the bay, and ducks."

"Does it tire you out?"

"A little. But Pa's been hovering over me since Orson died."

"I have a little time. Would you like to ride Prince? We can put the slates in the saddlebags."

"Oh, wow!"

"You were such a good announcer at our wedding party letting everyone in the back know what the presents were when they couldn't see them. I never properly thanked you. So thank you."

"It weren't nothin'."

Should she correct his grammar? No, he carried enough weight with the separation from his kin without another adult picking at him.

The clerk returned with a box. "We'll unload the slates into the packs," Mary said. "Or would your pa like the box? It could make up into a good chair." The two stepped outside to where Prince stood, the clerk behind them.

"We got chairs we brought from California. Ma didn't take anything with her when she left 'cept my sister and some of their clothes." Merritt's voice dropped, and Mary could see a cloud of sadness cover his face. "I can still smell her on the pillow she stitched."

Mary blinked back tears. Her own separation now and then from John each week paled. "Let's get these loaded. Ol' Prince will like the change of paths."

Merritt patted the animal's nose, then bent to help Mary open the box and transfer the slates into the packs.

"Go ahead and step up," Mary told Merritt. "I'm going to walk instead of ride. Prince will follow me right along. I haven't been feeling so good, and walking and breathing in the ocean air, well, that makes me feel better."

They waved to the clerk and as they walked along, Merritt reprised his wedding excitement, introducing what he saw with his exuberance. "Wow! A blue heron! Wow, there's a dory. I think they got a fish on! Oh, wow! The neighbors got new pigs. We got new pigs, too, Mary. Mrs. Gerritse. Wish they'd follow me around like your horse does."

The boy needed a dog, Mary thought.

Another burp. "Excuse me," she said. Her face grew warm.

"I do that all the time. Wanna see?"

"Not really."

"Yeah, Pa would say that's a child thing and I'm being a man now. I hope you ain't getting sick. That typhoid is the devil come afoot."

Mary'd had no fever, but her stomach didn't seem to like food. Her mother thought it was nerves. She said she got like that too sometimes when she was troubled.

But Mary wasn't troubled, not really. Confused, more like it. She wished she had a better sense of what she was supposed to be doing in her life besides being a daughter during the week and a sometimes wife. And being treated like a seventeen-year-old girl instead of her mother seeing her as a married woman.

"Oh, wow, Mary. Did you see that? I think it was a whale blowing way out to sea. I've never seen a whale close up, have you?"

"I have," Mary said. "When I was at Cannon Beach with my father. I was about your age, and we looked for the beeswax. Have you done that? Look for beeswax."

Merritt shook his head. "What would I do with it?"

"You could bring it to Tohl's. They'd buy it. You could melt it down, keep a little, and make candles that don't have that tallow smell. John coats his packet with it, to keep the rain out. My Nehalem friend, Jewell, puts some onto her grandfather's wooden ducks, and they use it to put feathers on the ducks to lure mallards into the lakes."

"That would be fun."

"Yes, it would," Mary said, "though a little cold and wet. Maybe one day we'll do that, if your father approves."

"Swim in the lakes?"

"No, no. We'll go looking for beeswax. Maybe you can come up with something else to do with it."

"I'll think on that, Mrs. G."

She smiled, glad he'd settled on what to call her.

They arrived at the Batterson claim, and Merritt jumped off Prince, calling to his father. Will came from around the back of the cabin with a shovel in his hand.

"Mucking the pigsty," he said. His boots were thick with the evidence of his efforts. He farmed, taught, and was also the justice of the peace.

"Mrs. G let me ride Prince and we got the slates in the saddlebag."

Will Batterson leaned his shovel against the cedar planks of his house. Mary saw the remains of what had been a garden. Lucy was probably the keeper of the carrots and peas, and the garden had been neglected once Lucy left. It took so many people to make it on these coastal homesteads. Almost impossible with just a man alone. Or a woman alone.

Her stomach started to roil again. She swallowed quickly as saliva filled her mouth. Catching her breath, she asked for the privy and Will pointed. Mary fast-walked past him. Whatever this was, it came on quickly, leaving Mary breathless. She deposited her breakfast, then sat for a moment, her head throbbing. Could the Battersons' farm have exposed her to typhoid?

She had no fever, though. Maybe something she ate. Dried mushrooms. The little red umbrella ones, dotted with white. Some of those mushrooms Jewell had told her were poisonous. She'd be better off looking for beeswax than mushrooms.

"Are you alright, Mrs. G?" Merritt knocked on the outhouse door.

"I'm fine. Maybe bad eggs." She opened the door, the air cooling her face. "I'd best be going on home."

Merritt's father had a worried look when Mary returned.

"It's nothing," Mary said. "Something I keep eating, usually for breakfast. That's when I get sick."

"Ah," Will said. "Thank you for helping with the order."

Sickness in the morning.

Holy Jumblies! It came to her like a small berry pressing through a hole in a sieve. John would be so happy! Wouldn't he? She'd been longing for a new adventure. She was about to begin the biggest of her life.

chapter
15

I say, John, I do intend to finish my hotel, because when guests have an easier way to get here, they'll come in hordes."

Herbert Logan and John sat on Herbert's porch drinking hot tea with a bit of whiskey added "for warmth," as Herbert said. John had declined the additive. He would spend the night here at Cannon Beach, then move along north to Seaside, bringing the mail and accompanying supplies. Herbie appreciated that John didn't seem to mind stretching the federal postal system by dropping off anything Herbert ordered. It saved him from having to go to Seaside to pick it up. This time, it was a new felling saw, long and thin, to tackle the largest Sitka spruce trees that marched right down to the sea. That horse of John's hadn't batted an eye at the odd cargo.

A flight of pelicans pierced the slate sky as the waves hushed a lullaby. Herbert sighed as he watched the graceful pod. It wasn't his beloved England, but this was a special place. He wanted others to know it.

"An easier way to get here, ja. There's the challenge. Just me and the packhorse have trouble in places," John said. "Not sure how you'd get a stage, say, coming south from Seaside through the trees and swamps."

"I've been talking to investors, John. I've discovered that Austin wants to build a hotel here, too, similar to the one he has in Seaside. He's sure those cannons will reappear, and he wants to be on the beach to get them. I think other people will want to come looking for them too."

"What good are they?"

"Oh, just the novelty of being the one to find them, I'd say. And it would firm up the name of these nine miles of beach as *the* Cannon Beach though it stretches to Arch Cape."

"I suppose one could make the case for people to come not just for fishing or clamming and crabbing or elk hunting but to be the discoverer of the cannons."

"People always find things to do on the beach," Herbert mused. "You know the rumors about the buried treasure somewhere on the mountain, brought by pirates?"

John nodded. "Last year, Mary's parents hosted four men who came to hunt for it. They paid the Edwardses for room and board and went up the mountain every day, looking. Guess their money ran out. They left empty-handed."

"Exactly what I mean, old boy. Exactly what I mean. Just the possibility of a treasure intrigues people. We could offer a place to stay—my hotel—and a guide." Here he paused. He wanted John on board for something else, but he might be more likely to be involved with the treasure hunt. "What would you say about being such a guide?"

"Me? I'm not very . . . personable. That's the English word?"

Herbert joined in John's laughter. "You are, my boy. Look at all the people you've had to deal with working on the ships and farming at Clatsop and now here, carrying the mail. I think you could put up with dandies. You put up with me."

Herbert expected John to say something like, "Oh, you're not so bad." He would have liked to hear such words from his father before his death. He never expected any praise from his older brother, but it was hard to keep enthusiasm for implementing good ideas without a little encouragement, especially from family. At least John wasn't being critical. They shared a survival experience that brought them together in a way he didn't have with anyone else on the coast. It almost made him family.

"I think me being a guide puts the cart before the horse, as Mary would say. The road is what'll make a difference. We could offer any number of activities to lure the Portland folks south then, but the road has to be passable from Seaside to Ecola Creek."

"Yes! I'm going to rename it Elk Creek once I've secured investors—and I have them close to committing. I've formed the Elk Creek Road Company. The route will start in Seaside and end right here where we're sitting." He tapped the railing with his cane. "I hope to buy the mill in Seaside once we start actual road building. And of course money has to come first. But I see this as the beginning of something big for our little section of the coast." He hoped he wasn't overstating his case, but he needed this, needed to prove to his brother—and others—that he wasn't a lackey.

"Resources to invest in such a thing, I don't have," John said. "I guess you know."

"But what about being a contractor, use your horses to help clear logs, grade the road. It'll have a zillion turns in it to avoid taking out the bigger trees. I was an engineer back in England, and I've mapped out most of it with the help of a local. But I'll need someone who's strong and who could direct a crew."

John sat silently for a time, then finished his tea. "Keep me in mind," he said. "One thing I've learned about this north coast is that people have to be jacks-of-all-trades to make a living. You can build a house out of driftwood and such, but it's not enough just to have shelter."

"Right. Streams give up fish, the beach gives up clams. The lake nestled in the trees has ducks for the taking so you can feed your family. Contracting does that."

"But you must have trade or cash for the other things like bedsheets or flour."

Herbert laughed. "That's quite a combination. But you're right. You'd be paid in cash." He'd work on that. "It could set you and Mary up. And once finished, at least a portion of your mail route would be easier to traverse."

"Ja. But while building I'd need to give up the mail."

"Only for a short time. The future always has risks. And you noted, people have to be inventive. I'd like you to be a part of my vision, that this'll be a community people want to come visit. Maybe even stay."

"Mary says such as that. She'd like to live on Elk Creek. But where we are is closer to her parents. She likes that too."

"Marriage does enter into decision-making. Or so I'm told."

"We'll talk, Mary and me. You keep me on your list of folk willing to be some part of your grand dream. Maybe Mary is too, but she probably wants a home of her own first." John yawned. "I'm ready to hit the sheets. We talk again, ja."

As Herbert stood, his knees buckled and John caught his elbow and kept him from falling, frowning. He didn't want John to think he wasn't up to the task they'd just been exploring. "Been sitting too long, old boy. Nothing to fear. I'm good for another ten years." Why did this have to happen now, just when John expressed interest? He steadied himself as John let him loose. "Thank you. I'll see you in the morning." At least he hadn't had this collapse in front of the investors.

chapter
16

The wind whipped around Neahkahnie Mountain, blasting John in the face, keeping him from the view of the distant beach hundreds of feet below. At least it wasn't raining. He secured his black bowler hat. At the rock outcropping, where the trail narrowed to single file, he dismounted and led Jake and the packhorse behind him. Both animals carried saddle packs of letters, lanterns, seeds, and silks and satin, the latter a heavy load that John was careful to balance. One shift on this treacherous trail and he could lose the animals as well as the cargo. He shouted "Hello!" and waited for anyone coming the other way to let him know they had the trail—or with no response, he could continue. He paused, didn't hear any reply. He hoped the wind hadn't stolen his words. He did not want to meet up with someone on this trail on a windy March day. In the summer, sometimes one could step on the upside while animals passed by each other, but it was treachery.

"Easy, boys," he cooed to his horses.

Mary told him she envied his mail route and all his possible adventures. Little did she know! How would she take Herbie's suggestion that he let the contract go and work on his road? At least they had time to discuss it. He'd committed to that, too, not making those one-way turns, as Mary called his deciding without her suggestions. It hadn't been easy.

Around another bend, the wind rested, and John had a reprieve from the blast to his face. The Indians walked this route, possibly following game. It was why this part of the coast hadn't developed, because who wanted to take a trail such as this to go anywhere? It was as bad as the route to Cannon Beach through the timber and manzanita and the swamps leaking toward the sea. But the mail would go through. He was a man who kept his word. He thought of his nonexistent cabin. "I'll get it built—in time." His horse shook his head, rattling the bridle rings. "I'm glad you agree."

A hawk flew below him out toward the sea as the scent of smoke came up from the shoreline. He frowned. It wasn't a good time for someone to camp at the base. Rains could come at any time. Maybe the Indians were smoking salmon, but usually they had small fires, low flames of alder to dry the fish.

John continued to walk, gingerly stepping, noticing where he placed each of his brogans. Jake didn't need to be led, so John had tied the reins around the saddle horn. He wasn't thinking about anything but putting one foot in front of the other when the packhorse whinnied. John turned to see what was up.

A twist of his ankle. A rock cascading. That smoke again. John's right foot stepped into the air.

chapter
17

Jewell and her grandfather and a dozen other Nehalem gathered at the foot of Neahkahnie Mountain's southern point. It was perfect weather, early in the morning, before the winds would pick up. Her grandfather, being the oldest of the band, spoke in Nehalem, marking the activity every few years that would bring fresh grasses to the meadows to feed the deer and elk. Prayers completed, Jewell helped her grandfather soak the torch in kerosene and light it. Then young men touched their twists of dried grass into the center torch, followed by dribbling fire along the base of the mountain. The community of Nehalem people watched the flames rise up the slope, smoke twirling. The People had done this for years. Not every year. Just when the shrubs threatened to overtake the mountain meadowlands. Jewell loved this tradition of burning the old to make room for the new.

The homesteaders had not liked this practice, but Jewell's grandfather had explained it to them at a gathering, years before, how this tradition would help them as well. Settlers also grazed their sheep and cattle on the mountain. In time they had come to see the wisdom of this effort. They hunted there too, and burning brought elk and deer herds to feed both white families and the People.

This day, the People would watch the flames, and when the blaze reached the top, send praise for the wind that put out the fires.

Finished with the ritual cleansing—that was what the burning did—Jewell helped her grandfather walk toward their hutch north on Ecola Creek. She loved coming to the mountain, hearing the story of Ekani, the Supreme Being of her people, the Being who'd turned to stone on the mountain and was there still. As a child, Jewell had heard the story and wondered why the Being had chosen such a challenging place to live. She preferred their summer lodgings made of rush mats where Jewell dug for clams. She'd find mussels and kelp and, like the young boys, sometimes climbed and stole eggs from the birds' nests, hoping the parents didn't return while her hands reached into the sticks and twigs. The views were worth the danger of snatching hawk and eagle eggs.

"The fire burns out," her grandfather said, his eyes reaching to the mountain's top. "Rocks swallow it." He looked to Jewell, "Like a life if we forget to keep the flame glowing. Do not let your fire burn out, Granddaughter."

"You are my flame," she said. She walked beside him. How many years would she be able to continue this journey with him? The weight of the answer licked like a flame around her heart, squeezing. He was all she had.

"I will not always be here." He coughed. "Not much time to hold your children in my old arms."

"Let us not talk of such things," Jewell told him. Rain started, slanting against them.

"Ah," he shouted above the deluge. "The rain works with you today. But maybe not tomorrow." His toothless grin made Jewell smile, duck her basket hat into the wet wind, her arm through his.

For now, they headed north again with Jewell worried over her grandfather's slowing gait. What would she do if she lost him? She had to find a way to work with the woman doctor serving on the Clatsop Plains. But to do so, she would have to leave her grandfather. There were always choices and sometimes none of them were good.

chapter
18

Y ou think so?" Mary's mother said. "Seems awfully soon."
Her mother put a bowl of oatmeal before Mary. Steam
rose up. She inhaled.

"When you were pregnant with me, did you have morning sickness?"

Her mother frowned, turned away, busying herself at something Mary couldn't see. "Some women don't, you know."

"Lucky them. Here I go again." Mary raced to the outhouse, making it in time, though she wasn't sure if the scent of the privy might not have added to the discomfort. She'd need to bring coffee grounds to neutralize the smells next time. How long did such things go on? It didn't matter. What mattered was that they were starting their family. Birds chirped their support. The river gurgled its delight. She rubbed her tummy. "It'll be fine," she whispered. She could hardly wait to tell John, to talk about what she needed to be a good mother, what John needed to be ready to be a father. He'd want to do all he could to make this baby arrive happy and healthy. So did she.

Back inside with a sunbreak in the morning rain, Mary drank tea and put her mother through the inquisition. "Could you feel me moving? Did you talk to me? How long does the sickness last?"

She's more interested in scraping dried egg off the stove than listening to me. "Was the delivery hard? Is that why you don't like to talk about it?"

Her mother turned, sat, sighed. "Nothing like that. I just don't remember much. You'd think I would, wouldn't you." Her eyes looked over Mary's shoulder. "Hand me that whetstone, would you please? This knife is so dull it couldn't cut butter if it tried." She laughed, then took the stone Mary handed her.

"Will I have to take one of the older mothers aside and pepper her with questions about having a baby?" Mary heard the edge in her voice, irritated that her mother was dulling this happy occasion, didn't share the joy. Maybe the Cape Meares Lighthouse library had books about babies. She'd have to ask John to look when he dropped off the mail there. She'd make notes in her journal, so she'd remember for when her daughter asked questions about her birth. It was as though her mother had amnesia. But she remembered other details.

Maybe she and John stuck in her parents' home was good right now. Especially if she had complications. Or maybe—her heart lifted like an arrow sped into the sky—maybe this would be the impetus John needed for them to get the cabin ready. She had to get John to let her and maybe others help on his claim—their claim—so that they could be there when the baby came. She'd tell John when he stopped on his loop as he delivered the mail. She looked at the old clockface. He should be here in another hour if he didn't get tied up at the Tillamook post office. Postmasters were good gossips and everyone like that needed an audience. She didn't need her mother's experience. This would be her own—their own, hers and John's together, like a real grown-up family.

That decided, she helped her mother prepare supper, sauerkraut scents not bothering her much. Then Mary put the pie in the oven.

"I'll keep time," her mother said.

"And I'll put the saleratus back, if you're finished with it."

"Yes, do."

Mary pushed the package onto the top shelf in the small closet used as a pantry. She pushed. The package stuck, bumping up against something. She found the short stool, and at eye level saw a fat book. The size of the family Bible, its cover had a painting of a stork flying with a baby toward a rainbow-lit sky. Her baby book? Her story.

She pulled the book down, stepped off the stool. When she opened it, a photograph drifted out. It was of a woman with a small girl standing off to the side. The woman had her arm around a boy. A dog lay at his feet. They stood next to a house Mary didn't recognize. She blinked back tears, confusion threatening her breathing that came short and hard.

Alone.

The girl in a dirty pinafore stood alone.

Mary turned the picture over. Nothing. She looked at the next page in the book. The words were in mother's handwriting.

1882. Redwing, Minnesota. He said his name was Fisk. I gave him no sense that the name meant anything to us. When William came in from the barn, I told him of the visitor. We prayed together then made the decision. I packed little. Silver buttons from my wedding dress, Mary's clothes. Thank goodness Mary was at school. She will miss her Minnesota classmates but it isn't safe here any longer. We must protect her.

Another entry: *Arrived in Scholls Ferry in the State of Oregon. Tomorrow we go with William's cousin to the coast. Mary and her new dog, Shep, are excited. We pray that we have left the Fisks behind.*

There were more documents behind the notes—

"Mary!" Behind her, her mother hissed her name, grabbed the photograph, the album, stuffed the picture back in the book. "This is private, Mary. You have no right."

"I . . . I didn't realize."

"I've honored your privacy as a married woman. You need to honor mine."

Heat rushed to Mary's cheeks. "I . . . I didn't know. I thought it was my baby book, that you'd written things you don't remember now."

"Every pregnancy is different. Stop asking questions. And this"—she held the book to her breast—"is not your business. Let's finish up supper. Your John should arrive before long." Her mother backed out, the album, notes, and photograph like a shield against her breast.

Stunned, she watched her mother turn her back on her. There were people named Fisk who were somehow entangled in her parents' lives. Maybe in hers, based on her mother's reaction.

She would talk with John, grateful that she didn't have to navigate this unsettling ship alone.

chapter
19

Jake had been prescient and had moved forward just at the moment John turned and his foot swung out into space. Instinctively, John grabbed the stirrup as he was losing his balance. His heart pounded; he hoped he wouldn't throw his horse off-balance. Or the pack animal's. "Steady, steady, boy." He pulled himself up, still shaking.

John could smell his own sweat that had seeped from him at the moment when he thought he was gone. If it had happened a bit farther on, the slope was such that he might have been able to scramble up diagonally back to the trail. But here on this narrow section . . . three hundred feet to the sea.

Smoke whipped up from below, and through it John could see low flames licking toward them. The Nehalem were doing their burn. The yellow flickers were quite distant, and now the rain began its torrent and would win the battle with the fire. At least he wasn't going to have to jump flames with his horses.

John secured his hat. They had only a few more feet and they'd be onto the wider trail and past the loose shale and onto clay. He tried not to rush the animals, but he could feel his own worry about reaching safety. Once past the danger point, John remounted. His mind had been on other things. Investments. Contracts. Mary.

Now he added a prayer of gratitude. He remembered that little ditty from Mary's wedding poem, *"Like puffins on that Haystack Rock, I'll stay no matter how."* He had stayed today, at least, with Jake's help; that was how he remained alive.

The surprise danger cemented in his mind that carrying the mail on this route demanded a man to do it. He'd indulged Mary's hint about her wanting to be a mail carrier. Even with sturdy mounts, all danger couldn't be anticipated, and even if it was, the response required a quick-thinking man, not the best-intentioned woman. He'd do what he could to turn away any more conversations about "Mary the mail carrier."

chapter
20

"A re you feeling alright, John?" Mary delayed sharing her happy news as they stood in the barn. John had barely spoken to her, brushing the horse with more vigor than usual.

"A long day."

Mrs. Pye had told her that a good wife always listens first to her husband's stories of woe or triumph, though usually the former, she'd said with a smile on that day she finished Mary's wedding dress.

"What adventures did you have on the trail?" Mary handed John a brush to finish cooling Jake.

"I delivered a letter to Herbie. Spent the night there. He has some ideas for development. And the Nehalem had their annual burn on Neahkahnie Mountain." At the last Mary thought his voice shook a little.

"Up for a walk at the bay?"

"Maybe later. Tired, I am, ja."

"But it's a beautiful night. There are stars sparkling like fireflies. I miss those little lights. I saw them last in Minnesota. Did you have them in Holland?"

"Ja. Even a festival celebrating fireflies."

"That sounds lovely." She paused. "I have some news, John. Good news. Please can we take a walk?"

"Alright." John took the lantern from the nail.

He's about as enthusiastic as a man pulling a sliver from his backside.

She bubbled with enthusiasm, clinging to his elbow, skipped as they skirted seagrass, crossed over low dunes spurting out onto the sand. Shep trotted into the water, then shook himself of the wet, the droplets lit by sunset. The dog disappeared into dusk, then back into the kerosene lamplight that John carried. The beach seemed clear of jellyfish, no "purple sailors" as the translucent shells were called. Those sea creatures were stinky and she didn't detect their scent as they walked. If she had smelled them, she would have been sick again and that would have told John all he needed to know.

"I'm . . . we're expecting a child. Oh John, can you believe it!"

He turned to her, stopped. "That's, that's, well . . . well, I guess I wanted that, though maybe not so soon."

"I should have asked Mrs. Pye about the, well, you know. They were married two years before a little one showed up."

"No, it's just fine. It is Vunderbar." He grinned, his straight white teeth shown in the dusk. He pulled her close, setting the lantern down. He stroked her belly in a soft circle. "Is a good thing. When would it arrive?"

"August, I think."

"Ja. It's good we stay at your parents' house, then. I'd worry if you were at the claim alone with a baby on the way."

"I can see the advantage. But we could work on the weekends to make progress. I can help. Oh, John, we're becoming a real family!"

"Ja. But I wouldn't want you to do anything to harm the little guy."

"Women have had children forever, John. I like to keep active." Mary slipped her arm through his elbow, pulling him close. "And it might force my father to look for another helper. He has to get used to the idea that I won't be here to milk and make butter forever."

Mary hadn't thought about that as a reason to go upriver to

work on the claim, but getting her father accustomed to the idea of her being gone was good. Her mother had gotten used to them all there, though ever since Mary had found the album, her mother's penchant for counting buttons in the button jar had made her forget to check the huckleberry pie. No one complained about the dark crust.

"How far along is the cabin at the claim? Are there walls? A roof? You've never said."

"Not so much." He'd started walking again so she wasn't sure she heard him. He moved a bit faster than she did. She trotted to catch up, grabbed his hand.

"How much?"

John sighed. His shoulders sank. "I'm still clearing trees for the cabin site. That's why I haven't wanted you to see it. There's nothing there. No lean-to. No shelter of any kind."

Was that shame she heard in his voice? "Oh."

She couldn't fault him. He worked five days delivering mail, then helped with the extension to her parents' home. He worked in the pouring rain, dealt with muddy trails, camped out if he had to. But still. She had hoped they could move into their cabin before the baby came.

"Maybe my father's idea of having others help build is worth considering."

"I'm a man who does things for himself, Mare. Not one to accept charity. Besides, we have a nice place to stay right here. Even more reason to do so now with a baby on its way."

"You are either very proud or just stubborn." She kept her voice light, not wanting it to sound like a critique. When he didn't reply, she added, "I think my mother is getting weary of having another married couple in her house."

"Starting our family. In the grandparents' haus. And a good thing for you to be in a safe place too." He said *good ting*, the *th* sound hard for him to pronounce.

"I thought just the opposite. Our child should be born in his own home. We have different ways of looking at things, that's for certain."

"Ja, you'd be there alone when I was delivering mail."

"Maybe I could have a dog."

"Hmm. You'd be far from a near neighbor. And there are bears."

"I think a woman knows when she's about to deliver." *Do they?*
"I can walk to Mrs. Effenberger's if you're gone. She'd help with the baby."

Maybe she was being naive. After all, it had taken her several weeks to conclude that she carried an infant all tucked away inside of her. Her mother, oddly enough, didn't have a plethora of baby knowledge either. Still, her mother could be the answer.

"I'll ask Mama. Maybe she could plan to stay with me at our home after the baby comes."

"Ja, now you are talking. We wait until there is a house. A baby. Your mother visits. I can hardly wait to tell our friends." He kissed the top of her head, her cheeks, her fingers.

That wasn't her conclusion. Her mother coming to stay was a solution to *his* worry, not an excuse to remain at her parents'. She'd have to be persuasive in a more subtle way.

She had thought the good news would propel them forward. Instead, it seemed to cement John's plan to keep them right where they were.

chapter
21

Amanda felt clammy and panicky when she saw the stranger walk up from the dock. Something about him—perhaps the cap rather than a hat with a brim set her off. A cap meant it was only the visor that mattered, as in a Midwestern town in April, less worry over keeping rain from one's ears. She pulled the curtains, hoping he hadn't seen her do so. Let him think that no one was home. She was alone.

Maybe he was a salesman. He looked too young. Mid-twenties? That was the right age of course. That's what made his presence so frightening.

He walked up to the door and knocked. Shep was with Mary or he'd have barked a warning, maybe sent the man away. But more likely, the dog would just wag his cream-colored tail and greet the stranger; he was that kind of pet, not wary of anyone.

"Anyone home, the Edwards house?"

A Midwestern twang, the long *o* in *home*.

Amanda could hear her heart beating and wondered if he could. She breathed shallow so he wouldn't hear the gasps she wanted to take, holding her breath.

Go away! Go away!

Where had he gone? Out of sight. A knock on the lean-to door in the back. Had she caught the latch? She wanted to yell at him to go away, to leave them be. They'd made an agreement and kept their part, so why were they now being harassed? And she did consider it harassment, these visits by someone seeking Mary, this the third. Three times was supposed to be a charm.

She slid down the side of the wall, her knees noodles of weakness, the anxiety of what might happen if ever this man and Mary were to meet up. William told her she worried too much, but here they were, at the farthest outcrop of the continent and someone from that family had found them.

One. Two. Three. She counted her breaths. It relaxed her.

She prayed that Mary wouldn't return, that she wouldn't meet him on the road as she came home.

Home.

Mary needed her own home. It had been selfish of Amanda to keep her and John with them, to enjoy being the mother with her child—at seventeen she was still a child—to bake together, laugh together. Amanda didn't have friends to speak of, merely acquaintances who sewed wedding dresses or who had a home large enough to hold a quilt frame where women sat around and chatted while they stitched. Amanda could stitch . . . but she kept herself to herself, as her own mother used to say.

He knocked again. "I believe you're in there, Mrs. Edwards. I only want to talk. I mean no harm. I'll leave a note where I'm staying."

Amanda remained as still as a heron standing on one leg in the bay. She waited another half hour, counting and counting her slowing heartbeat. She looked out the window. She was alone. She opened the door and retrieved the note, crushing it like a dirty roach, throwing it into the fireplace where it flamed. She was safe for now, but they needed to make a change. He came too close.

chapter
22

We could take the boat upriver," John told her. "That might be easier than trying to ride the horses along the trail. It's so muddy after the rain. The claim is on higher ground, you'll be happy to know."

"I'm happy we are at last going to see our home, however we get there. Remember that time we took the boat up Elk Creek for that party in the woods?"

"And the tide went out leaving us high and dry." John laughed. Most of the coastal rivers were affected by the tides, salt water turning into clear, well up into the trees. It was what brought the salmon in season. "We partied all night till the tide came in to whisk us home."

"I wouldn't want to have to wait till the tide comes in today," Mary said.

John hadn't disagreed and they finished saddling the horses, Jake and Prince, leaving Baldy where he was, munching on hay. The elk moving down to play in the surf had made this trail beside the Nehalem River. Shep sniffed at elk scat as he trotted in front of John on Jake, Mary and Prince following. They left behind the black oystercatchers and listened for the twitter of songbirds in the trees.

Mary had read dime novels about cowboys in the West riding through sagebrush wearing leather chaps, and she wondered if such attire might not be useful in this coastal forest of dense shrubbery and trees. Keeping those brambles out was why they roached the horses' manes and bobbed their tails. An occasional spring seeped across the tree roots, muddying their route, but it was the perfect day beneath a blue sky broken only by treetops.

The child moved inside Mary and she gasped, this being making itself known in the gentlest of ways. "Our child is expressing his or her opinion about horseback riding."

"And what is that opinion?" John shouted over his shoulder.

"That he'd like a smoother road, I suspect. Oh!"

"Are you alright?" He rode back toward her, concern on his handsome face.

"He just kicked up a storm for a second. Come here, feel that?"

John maneuvered Jake around, put his hand on her belly. "Like a butterfly." John leaned over and kissed her, his blue eyes sending thrills of love through her very being.

This was what she'd imagined her family would be: Joy and hopefulness, her husband, tender as a baby quail, this new life filling them both with wonder and awe.

"I'm not nauseous, which is a fine improvement. Speaking of progress, how far are we from the claim?"

She had visions of a meadow, maybe a split rail fence, something to mark the boundaries at least. They had purchased a stove that was sitting at Tohl's waiting for them. She already planned their first meal. A rich, thick clam chowder with potatoes and herbs Jewell shared with her, and two raw eggs added just before serving. She could almost taste it. John hadn't been too complimentary about her cooking, which surprised her because it was something she did well. If someone cooked for her, she'd praise them no matter what, so they'd want to do it again.

The horses had to work to gain purchase against the muddy incline before arriving at a widened area stubbled with stumps and surrounded by pines. "This is it," John said. "My claim. Our claim."

She wouldn't let her disappointment show.

Several stumps dotted the forest before them, blackened by the attempt to burn them out. But that was the only evidence of taking a patch of timber into a clearing wide enough to harbor a canoe, let alone expansive enough to build a home. She had helped her father do the same on their claim. It was dirty work, but unless the stump was of a size that a horse could pull it out, firing them was the only way to move them. He hadn't been able to move many.

"I know it doesn't look like much, ja? I tried to tell you."

"No, no, I can see that you've toiled." They were a long way from this place being a home. All the more reason for her to do work on her own here while John kept to his mail contract. She'd prove to him she could be a real helpmate. With a little compromise and effort, they'd have a cabin of their own to bring their child to.

"It wouldn't take much to round up a brigade of coastal folk. They'd be happy to help put up a cabin. People helped my parents. They reciprocated. It's the way of things here. Oh, John, I can see where the chicken house would go and the barn." She dismounted, walked an imagined outline of a house. "Look at the view we'd have, of the river, of our garden right over there."

"I bring you here, to show why we are grateful to have a bed and board with your parents, now more than ever. It makes no sense for you to be here even in a tent, alone."

"But I'm not alone now. I have the baby and you once a week and the weekends when we can work together."

"Nee. It is not, how do you say it, feasible. Right. Nee. I am humbled to need your parents, but we do. No more talk of this. We go home now."

"But we are home."

"It takes more than wistful thinking to make such a thing, Mary."

He put his hands out to help her mount, and as she put her arm around his neck, he bumped her hat off. He lifted her into the saddle, then bent to retrieve her straw hat. "Please. Let us not fight this, Mare. Maybe as you say it is God's will we have a place with family."

His words were strained as though his shirt was too tight

against his throat. She wouldn't push him, though her disappointment threatened to.

John's shirt felt scratchy against his neck, embarrassment like a rope tightening at his throat. "You expect the baby when?"

"August."

"Ja, this fall maybe after he arrives we work on this place. Save funds now so I can leave the mail and work the claim. Once started we have to finish the cabin." He mounted up.

"You need to teach me how to shoot, so I'll be able to defend myself when you're not here."

Was she still thinking they could build here before the baby came? She could be obstinate. Was it better to ignore her when she pricked at him like poison nettles? Or be firm, bark his voice as his own father did to John's mother? How did his father-in-law manage his wife? He'd have to pay more attention.

"I hope Shep doesn't get lost." *Change the subject.* That might work.

"I saw him wander off. Well, he's probably back at your parents' home by now. Not a great guard dog." He stroked the gray horse's neck. "Take Prince, here. He's a good guard horse, in addition to being the best postal horse around."

"Oh, there he goes again," Mary said. "Put your hand here."

John reined his horse around, leaned over. He felt the quickening, as they called it. It was as if his son was reaching out from the womb to greet him, trusting that in his presence, all would be well. It was what he wanted for his family, to trust him. He looked up at Mary, and tears came to her eyes. He saw them through his own.

John knew that Mary's plan was to get up a tree-felling-stump-burning-cabin-building cluster of family and friends to raise a structure. But he wanted to do it on his own. That's what a man did. It didn't look like he was up to it right now—from her pinched-mouth expression when they arrived at the plot—but he'd earn her trust. He would.

After chatter about where the garden would go, they started back.

"What's that?" Mary pointed to a structure across the river about a half mile from their claim.

"A homestead, I expect. Nestled in there. Looks abandoned. So many are. It is a hard life, proving up a claim."

"Or a neighbor. I might not be alone much at all—once we're here."

She could be like a dog with a bone, hanging on even when there wasn't any meat on it. Resilient Mary could turn into stubborn Mary. He hoped her parents could help her see the wisdom of staying with them. It was his job to keep his family safe even if it did upset her.

chapter
23

I t's time for them to move onto their own claim," Amanda told her husband. "I know I said I'd enjoy having them here and all, but a baby will make it too crowded."

"I would have thought the baby would make you want to keep them here longer." William tapped his pipe on the porch rail, then cleaned out the bowl with a rounded wooden spoon he'd carved himself. He leaned back in the rocker he'd also made but didn't light his pipe. He always took a few restful moments before donning his hat over his white hair, then starting the evening milking. Amanda didn't mind the smell of pipe tobacco but not in the house. Dusk on the porch was the perfect place for such, but he was only chewing on the pipestem. He did that sometimes when he was worried. She didn't know what might be worrying him. She didn't want to ask. Their marriage had done well by her being a silent one, acting at times and giving limited explanations when pressed. It was how Mary had come into their lives all those years ago.

William continued. "John is a hard worker, but I can see that he'll be away often from their claim. Mary will have to stay there in order to prove it up successfully. It does surprise me, you *now* deciding they should move onto it."

"He's probably further along than he's led Mary to believe."

"Maybe."

A pair of mallards fluttered across a sky the color of tarnished silver.

"But keeping them here until the baby comes will ensure Mary has access to a midwife and one of us to go get her. Unless you're feeling capable."

"I can pickle fruit and cucumbers, but no, I wouldn't be able to do that. Perhaps I could stay there with her during her last month."

"Then why not just wait? Let them be here. The extra room is finished."

"No! She needs to have her own house, her own rhythms to invite her child into." She should tell him about the visitor, but he'd only minimize the consequences. Mary had to be kept in the dark about the Fisk family, she just did. There were things William didn't know.

"Alright, alright. Don't have a conniption fit."

One. Two. Three. Four. She counted breaths. "It's essential that you understand that they need to depart."

"You'll be the one to tell Mary, then, not that I think she'll mind. She's been chomping at the bit to be on her own." William sighed. "I need to hire someone to help anyway, but I'll miss her. Them. And I was looking forward to having a baby around."

"Trust me, William. She'll be safer there, away from . . . I appreciate you indulging me. I know you were happy at Scholls Ferry closer to your cousin. But I didn't feel—"

"Safe," he answered for her.

"Yes. And I do here. It's just Mary I'm worried about."

"Maybe we should just tell her."

Amanda gasped. She didn't ever want Mary to know that her mother had given her away. And Amanda didn't want William to know that that mother had later changed her mind.

chapter

24

"Y ou head to the house, Mare," John said. "I'll tend the horses and help your dad with the milking." Shep stood up to greet her.

"You deserter," Mary said and scratched his head. He panted and let himself be petted.

Her mother made a rare appearance in the barn. "You're back. Good. I was starting to worry," she said. "When the dog came here without you."

"You know Shep. He gets to sniffing and he's off on some adventure." Mary held her belly. "Isn't it amazing, this new life?"

"So how was the claim?" her mother asked. They left the men and walked into the house, where her mother busied herself looking out the window, then wiped down the plank that served as a cutting board. Mary could hear her counting under her breath. "Did you like what he'd done?"

"Not particularly encouraging." Mary didn't want to denigrate John, but truly, there was much, much more work to do than what she had imagined. But she was up to it. The best remedy for boredom is action.

"Oh? You didn't like the cabin?"

"There were no structures, Mama. Just stumps. He's still in the clearing stage. I think we need to round people up for help or we'll be here with you until the babies are ready for school. Though I know you'd love having us all around, I think we should put up a lean-to. I can work on the claim during the week or until I convince John to accept a little help. There's a spring close to the site where a house might go. Will go."

"How fast do you think you can make that happen?" Her mother tasted the stew she had on the cookstove. "It needs salt."

Mary had trouble following her mother, who wasn't looking at her at all while she spoke. "How fast can I make what happen? Move to the claim? I don't know. John is relieved that we have a place here." Mary's hands circled her belly, naturally settling there, a protection to her child. "Of course I am grateful too. Hmmm. That smells so good. Did you add wild onion?"

"Your father and I have been discussing this, and we think it would be wise for you to have your own place and be all settled when the baby arrives." She cleared her throat. "Before the baby comes."

Mary blinked. What odd timing her mother had. Just when John was certain they should remain, her mother pushed them to move.

"Naturally, as time gets closer, I'd come and stay with you. August will be a lovely time to be in the woods. You can plant coneflowers. They'd bloom in August. Your father and I can help you get the bed there and move that cookstove from Tohl's. There's a lean-to for sure, isn't there? John wouldn't have slept out in the rain."

"He had a tent."

Mary felt like she'd been rounding Hug Point in the calm only to be swirled to the other side by a sleeper wave. "I . . . Mother . . . I—"

"We'll work it out, you'll see." Her mother looked at her at last. "I just think it's time you're on your own. Maybe by next week?" Her mother patted Mary on her head. "Best remove your hat. Ready for some stew?"

Whatever would she tell John? They were being evicted. He'd have to accept help now.

chapter
25

Jewell stood on the Crying Sands Beach looking out at Haystack Rock. In the distance rose the lighthouse that had taken years to build and broke the landscape her people had shared for generations. "Terrible Tilly" it was called, and to arrive there, one had to risk one's life and yet it had been built to save lives. She turned back toward the tree line and Ecola Creek, watched the wide ribbon of blue kiss the sand on its way to the sea. For Jewell, this was the best season. Summer. She and her grandfather would fish for salmon when the precious catch made their run up the creek. Their arrival was cause to celebrate as it meant hearty meals and a special camas root celebration with water served first, then salmon as the gift of the Creator. The fish's return was a sign of the faithfulness of the Creator and the survival of the tribe. At least for what was left of the people after the deaths brought by the ships, the same ships that brought cannons and the mysterious treasure. And the beeswax. Good arrived with the bad. All had to be sorted. This was the way of life.

Jewell's grandfather coughed. She could hear him though she was a distance away. She knew the lodge inside smelled of fresh cedar branches that served as their summer covering, and lavender, the plant she now looked out over as she watched the ocean, green and purple blending into blue. Jewell was attentive to smells, scents, sounds, that told stories all their own. When people walked on the sands, a sound was made, said to be from the crying women who had died in the great towering tidal wave from years before.

Healing. Sounds healed. Herbs healed. White person's ways could heal too. When Jewell went to Astoria to see the woman doctor the week before, the place where she saw people was spotlessly clean and had a sweet scent of lavender. It was a good sign that the white woman knew about healing herbs.

Jewell had been led into the woman doctor's room, where a glass cupboard housed vials and tinctures and potions, some with a skull and crossed bones to indicate their danger. A whale oil lamp illuminated the room on that rainy day.

Dr. Bethinia, as she was known. She was a big woman, tall like the Chinook women who lived across the great river in Washington Territory. Jewell often longed for such stature as it could intimidate and allow her to speak before men especially who tended to discount her words—and sometimes her very presence.

"My grandfather has a cough that came a few years past and now stays like an uninvited guest."

"Your grandfather has lived many years?"

Jewell nodded.

"A long life often invites such visitors along with stomach trolls and bone sprites."

"And thought thieves."

"Yes, those too." The doctor had smiled and motioned for Jewell to sit, but she wished to stand to be closer to the woman's eyes. "For a persistent cough, I recommend a mustard press on the chest. He should stay out of drafts and the cold."

"This is true. Thus, no swimming in the lake." She knew this to be so but wanted confirmation.

"It would not be wise. Will he come to see me so I might assess a perhaps larger problem? Listen to his heart, hear him breathe?"

Jewell shook her head. "I am here to take back with me as much healing as you can give me so that I can serve him. I do listen to his chest through a rolled-up paper scroll. Sometimes his heart skips like water bugs at dusk."

"Aha. Well, let me show you how to keep track of his pulse. His heartbeat."

And the rest of the half hour the woman gave Jewell was filled with doing things she had never done before. Holding a wrist and letting it speak to her about her heart. Listening and counting breaths. Fortunately, she had been allowed to learn to read and to write so she made notes for herself. And then before she left, the doctor gave her herbs for the mustard pack and the biggest surprise of all, a thing called a steth-o-scope where she could hear his heartbeat and better listen to how his breath sounded.

"When his breathing is like the whale spouting, you must try to bring him here. Or come to get me so that I can determine what to do next."

"We can decide what to do next?"

The doctor nodded. "We will decide with him."

Jewell smiled.

She wasn't smiling now, though, with a fog rolling in over Haystack Rock and carrying the weight of what she must tell her grandfather. This year, he would not be able to swim in the lake to catch the ducks. She had decided this and the doctor had said as much, though she didn't know about the ritual. The men put feathers stuck in beeswax onto carved ducks. Then added feathers into the cedar woven hats so hunters could swim up beside the resting ducks lured in by the beeswax shams. The men reached out and grabbed the duck's legs, then throttled them quickly. These were young men's activities, no longer accessible to the aged like her grandfather. But elders often resisted reality, hanging on to the wispy memories of youth.

She had not told him yet. It was what he had always done, the sign of his continued strength. How could she deny him such an important event? She wasn't sure, but she had until the fall at least to tell him. For now, she would mix up her concoction of berries and herbs and make the poultice to try to lessen the coughing sounds that came from their shelter. And pray to the Creator that she did not need to bring the white woman healer there for decisive moments. It was said the woman doctor left her child behind in order to go east and learn the ways of white medicine men. One had to sacrifice for such knowledge. Family deserved sacrifice.

chapter
26

hat?" John frowned. "Say that again?"

"They think we should leave." Mary whispered so her parents wouldn't hear. "Do what we can to be ready for the baby on our own claim. It's quite strange, really. We can get a better tent, maybe." She pondered from the comfort of a rope bed. "I can be alone. Mid-postal route, the nights you're there, we can get a few hours of work in together." Mary watched her husband peel his white long johns down over his spiderly legs. Like many sailors, his upper body boasted muscles while his legs didn't. Still, he could do much of the work alone, but it seemed silly of him to choose that path. People would help. They just needed to be asked. "As I'm up to it," she continued, "I'll bore holes in the stumps and we can light the fires when you get there, let them burn through the night." The fires would keep coyotes and bears away, too, wouldn't they?

He'll have to teach me how to shoot.

"I'm, ja, I'm surprised that now they want us gone."

The baby began roiling around inside her as though she'd eaten rotten cabbage, but who could tell if it was rotten or not? They'd have to build a latrine or dig an outhouse, first thing.

"We'll get a guard dog. Leave the horses at my parents'. I think we can do this, John. It'll be like going to sea in a sieve, doing what others might think is impossible. I'll work on my target skills."

"A tent won't do much against a bear or a cougar, Mare. This happens too fast, I think."

"Hence the target practice. I love that word 'hence.'"

John patted the bed beside him. "I will talk with your father. He makes sense. Come along now. We'll make it work."

That last was his mantra. It wasn't a bad one, though his voice held strain. Making things work was what she'd always been about, too, and finding the path she was supposed to be on, even if it did seem an odd one.

The morning negotiations gave them until the first of May to move. John would purchase a tent and other essentials they'd need for camping—which is how Mary thought of it. The following morning, John brought her ginger tea while she was still in her nightdress, ribbons at her throat. This was a good time to bring up her tender topic.

"Might we ask at church about having a gathering to at least get a frame up? I think people would be happy to help. People get inspired doing for others, especially in a time of need."

His blue eyes blazed. "Nee. We do our own."

Mary noticed that when he was emotional, John's English became more broken, his accent more pronounced. When she got upset, her body knew before her brain did. Maybe he was afraid of what people would say about them doing this somewhat crazy thing, as though they shouldn't have married without all these pieces in place. As if life ever had all the pieces in place. It was a jigsaw puzzle without the guiding finished picture. Her tea finished, Mary braided her hair, watched John dress as she looked in the mirror. Mary turned to him. "I'm having an inspiration." A word Mary knew meant *the act of breathing in* as well as being at one with the Spirit. "That cabin we saw, nestled in the trees. Do you know who it belongs to?"

"That I don't. It looked empty."

"Maybe it isn't. Maybe they are our neighbors and maybe they'd let us pitch the tent on their property, where I'd have help if something happened. Like a baby coming. And perhaps I could help them too. Put up jams for them. Bake. We could haul the stove up in case they don't have one." A little exploring about their nearest neighbors was in order. "At the very least, their presence is inspirational, don't you think? I do."

"You swirl a dozen ways, Mare. A tent on our claim, then someone else's? Dragging people to help us build, intruding on neighbors." He shook his head.

She lowered her eyes. "I'm just being adventurous. Like the Jumblies. Their friends worried over them, but they endured."

She quoted the "Jumblies" poem.

> "'Oh won't they soon upset, you know!
> For the sky is dark, and voyage is long,
> And happen what may, it's extremely wrong,
> In a sieve to sail so fast!'"

"Ja, their friends expected an upset and here we are. You and your Jumblies."

"Despite the challenges, the Jumblies kept going like us, swirling faster and faster. But they made it, John. And we will too. I'll find out who those neighbors are and make our request."

He swung back, the movement startling as stumbling onto a bear. "Nee. Gerritses don't beg." He shook his finger in her face like she was a child. "You tell me childish poems, I tell you nee, like to a child. I expect you to obey. We agree, ja?"

Mary blinked. The baby kicked.

chapter
27

Herbert Logan rode south from Seaside. He'd been in Portland seeking financing. They gave him hope but he had nothing in writing yet. His goal was to begin by the spring of the new decade, 1890, just a year away.

He'd made the journey thinking like a tourist. Board the river-boat in Portland on the Columbia and sail west to Astoria, through the wild river beauty where eagles flew and white herons stood sentinel as the boat passed. Once at that fair city he took another boat across another stream, then south by stage to Seaside, the way most visitors would come with their satchels and such. Then an early morning rise—this time with horses and pack animals—down the coast to Cannon Beach. Through timber and around lakes and fallen trees and mud, the detritus of a coastal climate. It took three days from Portland. Too long for both commerce and the tourist trade for true development at Cannon Beach. His road would change that. It was his argument with the money men. It still hadn't broken through to a deal.

That evening, Herbert sat on the porch of his hotel, overlooking the sand and sea. His road would take hours off that journey so people would venture here for longer than the summer. They'd be able to go back and forth. One day, there'd be a train from Portland. There was already track being laid between Youngs Bay south of Astoria and Seaside, if only there were backers to finish that. And there'd be stagecoaches and wagons on his Elk Creek Road.

He wished Olivia was here to experience this beach, these bird tracks beside the sea. She'd liked watching for birds in Devonshire. He recalled fondly their walks together—until they were no more.

He sighed and went inside, picking up his bamboo cocktail skewer and a bit of beeswax. The bottle he'd chosen for this project had two flat sides, perfect for display, but made his work to collapse the sails to get them inside a little more challenging. It required the total focus—putting a ship inside a bottle—that he sought. The tasks and the precision required him to set aside the memories of Olivia, his outrage at his brother, his father's betrayal, and the anxiety of the future. She would tell him—if she were here—to "stay in the moment, Herbie." *Herbie.* She was the one who had started to call him that, and much to his mother's chagrin, he often called himself by that name too. Except on legal papers—he had plenty of those piling up along with his worry. "I'm shoveling doubt as though it was horse pucky," he mused out loud, then chided himself on using the American slang.

He worked for an hour or so on his ship until the whale oil lamp dimmed. His eyes itched. He put the tools away in a wooden box and set the unfinished glass bottle on a shelf. Its presence reminded him of all he had left to do. But he had present-moment issues to address. He stepped out onto the deck.

A gull landed nearby and squawked at him. This one had distinguished itself from the flock with its damaged wing but could still fly. The healed injury made him cranky, though how could one really tell with a raucous gull? "I've some dried bread for you, Sam." He'd given the bird a name. "I'll get it for you if you'll but wait a moment."

Inside, Herbert rummaged through his pack until he found the stale piece of bread he'd kept for Sam. Back on the beach he tossed it to the bird who gobbled it up. Within seconds Sam was joined by a chorus of pals who opened their beaks and harped until Herbert went inside and found good bread. Just one biscuit, that's all he'd give up. He went back out, tossed the bread into the breeze and a couple of the gulls gathered them up midair. They were a noisy convention clamoring for more. He ended up giving them all that he had baked, just for the joy of imagining businessmen congregating with the same level of enthusiasm when he returned next week from more meetings already scheduled. A seagull congregation of investors. He could only hope.

He was about to turn in when he heard a horse whinny outside. He looked and his old pal Joe Walsh tied up his horse, removed his floppy hat, and brushed it on his knee. Joe, who had come to America when Herbert did, was a good horseman but drank more than Herbert or anyone else he knew. And sometimes, in his garbled English, he dropped bits of wisdom as he did this evening after Herbie invited him in, fed him, then filled him in on his financial contacts.

"If you can't use your *affluence* to get others on board, you may have to retort to a toll road."

His *affluence*? *Retort*?

"This is the American West. People don't like to pay tolls," Herbert said. The idea of a toll road reeked of failure to him. How could he tell Olivia with pride if his investment was in the hands of sheepherders and ruffians arguing about a fee? Herbert's family in England already thought of him as a failure by mere order of birth, as though he'd had any say in that. But he couldn't be a failure for Olivia. He led his friend inside.

"They like tolls more than getting the government to pass bonds and pay taxes to build the road." Joe tipped up his stein, then wiped the foam from his mustache-less upper lip with his wrist. "Aye, your investors might be holding out until the government does care about inland roads. But why should they? Everything they need at the coast comes on boats to Portland or to and from San Francisco. Roads are second thoughts." The coastal communities from Tillamook and Nehalem north to Astoria were ocean-dependent and tide-determinant. They had more in common with California cities and even the Sandwich Islands than the interior sites; the nature of the sea, mountains, and treacherous trees controlling their access. Joe might be a lush, but he had some insight. A toll road. Disgusting. Herbert had to raise the funds.

"Investors cared enough to authorize the overland route from Scholls Ferry to Tillamook," Herbie said. Maybe some would invest in the Elk Creek Company.

"That's a terrible road. Twenty percent grades. Deep canyons. Up and over those Coast Mountains. And you arrive at Tillamook's cow pastures."

"It doesn't get people into Cannon Beach any better either. But it does say there were people willing to invest in such a long road. That's hopeful."

"They collected tolls, that's all I'm saying." Joe poured himself another shot glass of whiskey. "And eventually the state incorporated that road into its system. Taxpayers are paying back bonds for forty-five miles for the rest of their maze." Joe burped.

Days.

"If you end up collecting tolls, the money will come to you. But the effort to maintain it, well, you'll use up all those coins is my guess. I'd say approach the legislature now, get them to authorize a bond, and then plan to troll the crazy tourists who are willing to make the trek." Joe grinned.

"You forget that we remittance men aren't citizens of this country. I don't have a legislator's ear." Only the financiers of Portland and Astoria had such access. Like James Austin. Maybe he had some clout. Herbie would have to work harder to persuade people to part with their pounds. Dollars. If he could squeeze just a bit more out of that cigar-wielding banker, they could begin. They'd recoup their investment through the commerce that followed the road to the golden sands of Cannon Beach. He had to make them see that.

chapter
28

Mary's wrapper fluttered in the wind behind her as she rode Prince toward the Batterson claim. John had taken Jake for reasons she didn't know, perhaps because he felt some guilt over gifting her but then taking that more sure-footed horse for himself. Most of the time. She hoped that Mr. Batterson, her old teacher, was at home and that Merritt would be too. John would be back tomorrow, and they were taking things up to the claim.

Her thoughts bounced up and down like the teeter-totter at the school. She was still trying to understand her mother's evicting them yet felt excitement about the Gerritse family finally being on their own. John had agreed they had to go, but then he'd barked at her like he was her parent instead of her partner when she proposed easier ways. Despite the optimism she displayed to John, she was a little anxious about making it work.

A pair of mallards flew overhead and the bay became a hotspot of activity at their landing, ruffling the water, stirring up a fishy scent. Tuna boats headed in with their catch. Oyster farmers checked their crop. When she'd felt a little morose in the past, she'd make herself notice little moments of joy, and here was an entire seaside palette being painted before her.

She reined Prince into the Batterson yard. Prince didn't flinch at the scarecrow's hat flying off in a gust. She patted his neck while beside them hogs grunted in their pen in the early morning, waiting to be fed. Merritt tackled garden weeds beside his dad. He stopped when he saw Mary approach, hearing her before his father did.

"Mrs. G! Oh, wow, that there baby's gonna pop out onto the saddle, you ain't careful."

"Aren't careful," his father corrected as Mary pulled Prince up beside them. Prince stood with one leg at ease.

The boy's energy made her smile.

"I'd dismount," Mary said. "But getting back on Prince has its difficulties as you, Merritt, have observed."

"Merritt ought not to be expressing all his observations." Will wiped his forehead, replaced his floppy hat. "Congratulations are in order, I see."

"Yes. Sooner than expected. We didn't get to that chapter on biology when I was in school last."

Her old teacher laughed. "Not a subject the school board would approve of, I suspect." Her mother would have grimaced with Mary's comment. "At least you have knowledge of calves and pups and such." Mr. Batterson cleared his throat. "What brings you here, before breakfast? Would you take tea with us?"

"Thank you, no. I've had my tea and milked my father's cows already. But I've come to see if you'd consider having Merritt milk our cows with my father."

"Planning ahead? When is the baby due?"

"August. But we'd need Merritt starting tomorrow at the evening milking. John and I are heading to our claim. Homestead. Whatever it is."

"Good to hear you got the cabin built."

"Ah, no cabin."

"Your mother will miss you."

Mary didn't respond to that. "Merritt could bring a few extra coins to the Batterson purse." She felt more embarrassed speaking of money than about reproduction. What would her mother say to

that? "And I think he'll like the cows. I've made pets of a couple.
They follow me like dogs."

"Your pa will miss you too," Mr. Batterson added. "I'll consider
it and let him know."

"If we could afford it, we'd compete with my father for Merritt's help on the claim. Someone to keep me company when John's
gone, at least until our family expands."

"John's going to keep the mail route?"

"I can come visit you, Mrs. G." Merritt had removed his cap
and brushed down the cowlick of dirt-brown hair. "I'd like to see
a big ol' fat bear. You got bears at your claim?"

"I don't personally want bears to hang about." She shivered
her shoulders.

"Why don't you get Mrs. Gerritse a jug of water, Merritt."

The boy put up his hoe next to his father's and walked to the
well. For a moment Mary was alone with her old teacher. They
had a view of the bay, but Mary couldn't look at it from this fine
homestead without thinking of Lucy Batterson and her escape
back to California. Mary couldn't imagine leaving John, but then
one ought not to judge. Family circumstances changed in a flutter
of a hummingbird's wing.

"Am I to understand that you have no structure on your claim?"
Mary nodded.

"And you're moving this week? Is that wise?"

"It's what is. I'll be fine."

"What if we got a crew together to build a cabin. People like
to do that."

"John has forbidden me to make the request. He's . . . stubborn
that way."

Prince stood, head low, shifted which leg rested. He made no
fuss when Merritt held up the jug of water and Mary drank.
"Thank you, Merritt. John says ours is a preemption claim."

"That allows that once you've proved up the site, built that
house and barn, and stayed six months, you can purchase the
land at a certain government-set price. If he isn't yet a citizen—"

"He is but we don't have the papers yet."

"Then when you do, and when he's put up proper buildings, then he can apply ahead of anyone else to purchase the property at that minimum per acre set by the government."

"So, it isn't free land."

"Not anymore, no."

"There's a cabin nearby. I had hoped there'd be neighbors where we could pitch our tent, but that suggestion pierced his pride."

"The Dutch can be stubborn. My Lucy comes from that line."

"One doesn't have to be Dutch to be obstinate," Mary said. "Koppig. That's what John says he can be. *Pig-headed*. I can be too."

"It's the other side of resilient. If you decide to have a cabin building, you let me and Merritt know. We'd be happy to help."

"Don't hold your breath. John has his point of view and he rarely changes it. Let us know about Merritt's services." Mary pressed reins against Prince's neck, preparing to leave, when Will spoke up.

"About that cabin. It's very likely no one is there. On my days at the courthouse, I get all kinds of information about abandoned claims. I could check for you, but you could just move in."

"Live there? Without consent from the owners? Wouldn't that be trespassing?"

"The odd thing is that because someone leaves before they've proved up their land, it really isn't theirs. It's the government's again. I know at least a dozen newcomers who have moved into and resurrected an abandoned claim. Some paid back taxes and work it." He shaded his eyes with his hand as he stared up at Mary. "So far the law hasn't seen inhabiting an abandoned cabin as trespassing. There is a little risk that the owners will return, but by then you'd have your cabin built. It would all work out fine."

John's favorite phrase: It'll all work out fine. "That'll be something to sweeten my husband's tea with."

If he didn't spit it out at her being disobedient.

chapter
29

Amanda took the biscuits from her oven. She had a fine cookstove with a section that heated water and an oven that baked evenly so her biscuits were browned on the top yet light and fluffy in the center. She had Salal berry jam she set out on the table. Mary loved that kind of jam. She was doing everything she could to smooth the rancor her insistence of Mary and John leaving had brought. The air when all four of them were together was as tight as a rope around a piling trying to hold a boat from bobbing out into the bay.

Now that they planned to leave by week's end and into a tent, remorse settled on her shoulders. What would be the problem if a Fisk family member came to their door while Mary was here? She was a married woman now, starting her own family. And except for saying she wished she had a sister, she'd expressed little interest in who her grandparents were. Amanda wanted to keep it that way. Of course, there was the question of how it had all transpired and whether some smart lawyer might try to get money from them for leaving New York with a child not officially adopted. She rarely let herself believe that Minnie's mother had changed her mind.

Amanda burned her finger and licked at it, then lifted the hand pump to run cool water over it. She was so grateful for a well. Mary and John would have to haul water. Guilt stung like a bee.

If that Fisk family member tried to tell Mary that she had relatives in New York, she and her husband would just deny knowing anyone. Wouldn't that work? Maybe she'd been hasty.

She'd done everything she could to deny and forget things from the day it became possible for them to take Mary with them. She sucked on the burned finger.

Mary had just turned three but still sucked her thumb when she came into the Edwardses' lives. Amanda couldn't believe that the Fisk woman—a neighbor up the way—was telling her she simply couldn't keep Minnie. There was the older boy, maybe two years beyond Mary's age. She simply couldn't imagine that a mother would give up a child she'd raised until she was three. They hadn't wasted a day once she told William they could have the girl, but Mrs. Fisk wanted them gone "right away" as her husband was uncertain about giving Minnie away. "He may come after you, so I'd leave quickly," Amanda had been told.

And they had. Packing, scurrying, sorting. As they left the house, Mrs. Fisk had waddled down the road to them, waving a paper, but Amanda had urged William to push the carriage forward, leaving the woman behind. They might have stayed in the little river town of Redwing, Minnesota, but then a few years later, a Fisk did find them, did knock on their door. It had been terrifying for Amanda. And within the week, they again left much behind and joined with another group traveling by wagon to Oregon.

Amanda's burnt finger throbbed. She put butter on it, then found a cloth, ripped a small section, and wrapped it. Did Mary have a memory of her real parents? She wondered about that with her husband that night. They lay beside each other in their bed. They'd been whispering ever since Mary and John's wedding and were even more careful after they'd told Mary and John they needed to leave.

"You'd think so," William told her. "But our memories don't always hold us hostage. Mary's memories might drift right out to sea. Most of all, I hope she knows that we love her. I hope she remembers that." Her husband sounded wistful, and Amanda knew he had gone along with her insistence of sending them to their claim, but it hadn't been a happy choice for him.

"Have we lied to her by not telling her about her actual family?"

"We are her actual family, Amanda."

"Are we doing to her now what her other parents did to her in New York? Sending her away?"

"No. Here." He handed her a handkerchief and she blew her nose. "We will still be a part of their lives, if they'll let us." He was so quiet she thought he'd fallen asleep. Then, "I wish you'd waited until the babe arrived, though."

"I couldn't bear to have her deliver here and ask me questions about what was happening to her with no way to answer."

William wrapped his arms around his wife. "You'd find a way to give her all she needs, Amanda. You always have." He sighed. "Who knows, perhaps being there on her own and then with John is exactly what she needs now."

"I'll pray that it is. And it does keep her safe, sending her off. If she found out now that her mother didn't want her, that might cause her harm, maybe even bring the birth on early." However would Amanda live with that guilt?

chapter
30

Your biscuits are the best, Mama." Mary reached for the jam and spread it over the butter she'd already put onto the pastry. Her hands shook a little. She was about to do something that might end up humiliating her husband and might be better done with just the two of them. But the presence of her parents she hoped would increase the pressure on John to do the right thing. He looked tired and he had another two days of mail delivery before being able to return to work on their claim.

"You have the recipe for those pastries," her mother noted. "I always add a little extra buttermilk."

"I'll make these once we . . ." Mary made a dramatic pause. "I'll make these biscuits when we move . . ." Another dramatic pause. "Into an abandoned cabin that is adjacent to our claim."

John's fork stopped halfway to his mouth. "What—?"

"Before you get started, John. Will Batterson said that people all over do it. They occupy. You know, fill up. He said he'd heard of lots of places where that kind of neighborly sharing had worked. Once we have a structure, well, then we can move into our own."

John put the forkful of trout in his mouth, chewed, then said, "And what do we do if the owners return and find us occupying their house?"

"We thank them. Offer rent. And we do what we were going to do, live in a tent until our house is finished."

"That's a wonderful idea," her mother said. "Isn't it, William."

"Trespass? Nee. I have been grateful, ja, that we stay here and ask again that your mind changes and the child is born in dis house."

He'd stepped right over her argument. "Occupy, not trespass. Maybe an empty home adjacent to our claim is a gift from God," Mary said. "Wouldn't we be fools to turn down such a treasure?"

"It really is best that you have your own place," her mother said. "More jam? In fact, your father and I think it is by far the best solution, even if you're living in a tent."

"I'll think on it for a day or two." John avoided Mary's eyes.

Mary sat up straighter. "We're not ganging up on you, husband. I just can't imagine bringing our baby into a tented world because you're too stubborn to accept a roof over our heads already prepared. I will live in a tent since we have to leave, but at least consider the alternative." Mary's voice sounded firm even to her. "Remember the Jumblies going to sea in a sieve?"

"That nonsense poem."

"It's about taking risks and growing taller. They went to sea in a sieve but to keep dry, they wrapped their feet in 'pinky paper all folded neat.' That's all I'm saying we need to do too. That cabin is our pinky paper. But either through our generous community helping us build or by risking offending a potential homesteader who hasn't returned, we're off on the sea, John. In a sieve. But we aren't foolish, are we?"

"I have heard of others doing such." Her father reached for the mound of butter.

"Have you, Papa?"

"I thought of doing it myself, but we were able to get a homestead grant. We had to stay five years and then get a patent on it, not have to buy it. It was a gift for being a citizen."

"Ja, I'm working on that. I expressed my intention to become a citizen four years ago. It takes time to get papers."

"Maybe I could take out a homestead claim. I'm a citizen." Mary hadn't thought of that.

"But you aren't twenty-one years old." Her father patted Mary's hand. "I think moving into the neighboring cabin is a good solution. We can help this very weekend, can't we, Mother? And if someone is there, we'll just carry on to your claim and set up the tent."

Her mother nodded, offering a half smile before rising from the table to start to clear it.

"Ja, then. I let you know. No more talk of it, ja?"

It didn't exactly feel like making a decision together, but waiting might be the glue to join their ideas. Mary's stomach churned, but she didn't get nauseous. Their baby approved of waiting, it seemed. So could she.

chapter
31

I t is to help your cough, Grandfather. Remember?" Jewell set the potion beside his bed.

"I remember doing many things with you, Granddaughter. Many visits to the mountain. Accepting the clams the Creator placed in the sand. You have been a good companion for this old man."

"You're not that old!"

"Aha. Now you tell yourself stories." He patted her hand. "Maybe we should play 'feed the baby.'" He laughed, pretended to slide a big spoon into his open, toothless mouth. The effort of raising his hand to his mouth appeared to exhaust him as it dropped down onto his chest. He was lying slanted against a down pillow, had been all morning.

"If that will make you take the syrup, yes."

He sighed. "Maybe today we see how this old man is without the trappings of healers."

Jewell had been making the poultice and giving him the syrup she'd made at the woman doctor's direction for several weeks, ever since they'd been back at Ecola Creek. He did sound better, but she hadn't yet told him that swimming in the lake would not be wise. Maybe he already knew it, as he had not mentioned that favorite activity.

She could tell that today was different. He had not resisted her treatments before and she'd seen progress. He was able to tend to the lodge but didn't feel up to going out with Jewell when she gathered the items needed for her baskets. She also prepared the weir alone, the one they'd put in Ecola Creek to gather salmon. She dried the catch alone, too, as Nehalem women did, putting a stick through the filets and angling them toward the fire she built on the beach.

"Please, take the syrup, Grandfather."

Her grandfather sighed. "I'm tired, little one. Maybe it is time to let the Creator create something new here, a man passing into the Beyond." He tapped his heart.

"Don't say that!" She'd seen him resisting the evidence of his mortality, but now it was she who clung to his living. "You don't want to leave me all alone."

"I do not want to leave you at all," he said. He coughed and grimaced, his face taking on a painful visage. "But to resist a passing is to deny the rhythm of the universe of which we are a part. Life begins, travels paths it did not expect, hopefully leaves a blessing, and then departs. You are my blessing, Jewell. I am ready to leave you behind as a gift to this world."

"I hoped the white doctor's medicine would relieve you of the cough and give you more time."

"But I know I will not be able to swim to hunt ducks."

Jewell gasped. Had she let those worries slip? "It was the white doctor's concern."

"And yours, my granddaughter. I understand. Time is a toll road. It takes its toll whether we wish to pay it or not. I wish to rest now with no more poultices, no more syrup." He patted her head as she bowed beside him, tears wetting her cheeks. "Let me hear the birds sing, the gulls call, the waves send their kisses to the sand."

"Don't give up!" She couldn't let him die. She would try something else, something the white doctor might give her. But she couldn't leave him to make the trek north to gain that knowledge. Maybe she could ask the white doctor to return with her if she went quickly. Maybe she could stop Mary's John on his mail route and ask him to tell the woman doctor to come to Cannon Beach. *Cannon.* "Don't you want to see if the cannons return after the next king tide? Don't you want to see if more beeswax appears? Grandfather?"

He had a smile on his face, but his breathing slowed. She reached for his hand. It was cold though the inside of the lodge was warm.

"Grandfather?" she whispered. But only she heard her words.

chapter 32

I bring presents." John didn't know how to apologize except by giving gifts. Had he seen that in his own father's behavior? If so, it had come to him by watching, not by ever having received a gift from him personally. Fists had been how they connected until John ran away. "Here you are, Mary. This'll be your guard dog when I'm not with you."

They were at her parents' place, and John carried a small brown-and-white puppy into the kitchen surrounded by cooking smells, the dog calm in his arms despite Shep's sniffing at her feet.

"She's adorable." Mary cooed. He'd made her happy.

The dog's long tail wagged from its skinny body, even as John handed it to Mary from his arms. The dog sniffed at Mary's chin, looked up at her. Curious, but it didn't lick.

"She'll be your inside pup. Name is Nellie."

"She looks like a Nellie. You said presents. As in plural."

"Ja. Just a minute." John left and returned with a leash on the end of which was a yellow long-haired dog the size of a pony. "St. Bernard," he said. "He'll be your outside dog. Name's Max."

"Oh, Max." Nellie leapt from her arms and ran to the larger dog, jumped up with front paws on Max's side. "They know each other. How sweet."

"Settlers near Seaside are leaving. Said they needed homes for these two dogs. I figured they'd be perfect for you. For us. When I'm gone, you'll have company."

Mary patted the thick fur of the St. Bernard whose tongue hung out in what John thought was a happy pant.

"Nellie lay across the saddle horn and Max trotted on behind. Prince didn't mind a whit."

"Let's get them some water." Mary waddled to get a bowl.

"They'll both have to spend the night outside," Mary's mother said. "Shep will have a fit if we let them in here. He's just finding out how nice it is to be by table crumbs. I don't think he'll want to share his space."

"It's only for a couple of nights, Amanda," Mary's dad remarked. "Shep and the rest of us can handle that. I wouldn't want them to try to return to their home, and I hate to see a dog tied up."

"Of course, William."

That was the end of it. John liked how his father-in-law could manage his family.

"And I've decided," John said. "We'll become occupiers. It'll be our pinky paper as you say. No sense in turning down a roof over one's head." He wasn't sure why it was so difficult to accept help. Maybe because he'd never be able to repay people for their generosity. But he could pay rent, so he was occupying but not taking advantage.

Mary kissed him, right in front of her parents. She hadn't ever done that except at the wedding after they'd cut the cake. Relief washed over him like a summer shower lowered the heat. It wasn't as though they were accepting actual help, just being opportunistic. And if the pinky paper got wet and disintegrated, he wouldn't be taking the blame alone. Mary was a forgiving mate for such as that.

Mary's parents helped them load the canoe. They didn't have all that much to take with them but enough to make the cabin theirs. That was Mary's hope. She loaded the clam bucket the neighbors had kept filled as they'd promised at the party. The Contrary Mary quilt—which is how Mary had renamed the Contrary Woman bedspread—she stuffedin a wooden box protecting glass things, a lantern, and a precious candlestick that they'd gotten at the wedding party. Jewell's blanket she wrapped around herself, the only "overcoat" big enough with her body full of baby. The summer air felt cool and misty. A new adventure always excited Mary, but this one held trepidation too. What were they going to find at that cabin? How would she manage all alone? Nellie lay awkwardly on her lap—what there was of it.

The tide took the crafts upstream, where John and Mary docked the canoe at the bank before the cabin. Close up, Mary could see that it needed work. Maybe more than a little. But she was up for the task. She had to be.

"Why, it's a perfect little place." Her mother stared at the structure.

Mary stared too. It wasn't that much better than the tent, though it had windows. And when they stepped into the cool room, the isinglass let in light. She smelled dampness. Leaves cramped in corners.

"It will be a challenge, ja." John put his arm around Mary's shoulder.

"Be careful what you wish for," Mary whispered. She straightened her shoulders. "Let's occupy!"

They unloaded the boats, and the men set about firming up the cabin's corners, then replaced a plank in the floorboards. Mary was pleased it had planks and not dirt. The four of them worked silently but well together. Mary's mother brushed cobwebs from the walls while Mary swept away dust and dirt. She brought a bucket of water from the Nehalem River a few yards distant and scrubbed the fireplace opening, then looked up through the chimney and was happy to see sky and not a bird's nest.

Whomever had been here had put money into the two rooms. She wondered what had kept them from coming back. She hoped it wasn't another Batterson departure following the death of a child.

I'll stay no matter how.

The roof had held, with moss growing onto the shakes. There

didn't appear to be any signs of leaks. Lots of mice droppings told Mary they weren't the only occupiers. They probably needed a cat more than two dogs, but she'd never say that to John. She knew what his gift-giving meant. There'd also been bear scat she hadn't brought to his attention. Now that they were here, she wouldn't let a peep of concern leave her lips.

"That's about all we can do," Mary's father said. He brushed his hat on his knee, shaking away half a sand dune.

"The duck-down mattress will make you as snug as bugs in a rug," Mary's mother said. "The rope mattress looks sturdy. You should sleep well. No need to count sheep to fall asleep."

With the tidal waters still up, her parents returned in the boat as Mary waved wistfully, scratching Max's head. Their family stood alone in the deep forest. Their latest adventure had begun.

This is where the fat meets the skillet, Mary thought the next morning as John waved goodbye and rode away to pick up the mail route. He'd be back midweek, so she had two days—and her first night alone—to manage. She took her time, drank ginger tea she heated in the pot on the andiron. John had filled the bucket and she'd boiled the water last night. With the dogs at her heels, she walked outside. The morning was glorious with shafts of sunlight filtering through the trees, the gurgle of river water a serenade. A whoosh overhead made her duck and then laugh out loud as a blue heron dragged its legs against the sky. "Oh, baby, a blue heron. Maybe it has a nest nearby. I'm sure it means good luck." She'd make up that myth even if it wasn't so. She'd have to ask Jewell.

Finding a wooden rake the owners had left behind, she began scraping an area that would become her garden. She had seeds in paper cones she'd plant and hope the potatoes and carrots and onions would grow. She didn't stop until she felt hungry, and by the sun, she thought it must be midday. The baby hadn't complained, and she wasn't bored a moment.

John had felled trees and the rounds were piled high, so Mary split a couple for firewood, then built a fire in the fireplace where she hung a cast-iron pot on the andiron and set the three-legged spider into the coals. Cooking in this more primitive way was a challenge, but they'd decided not to bring the stove. She happily chopped carrots and cut up venison into the soup bowl; added water and herbs her mother had given her. Then she made her way outside again to inhale the afternoon, listened to the whirring of insects, saw elk scat close enough to the house they could have rubbed their antlers on the door. This place truly did occupy her spirit. Why had she ever doubted that this shelter was a gift? Or that she was strong enough to make it alone.

She'd barely sat down on a round she'd rolled next to the house when Max began to bark. Nellie, inside the cabin, barked up a storm, too, and sprinted out the open door. Mary stood and looked to where Max glared, his shaggy coat raised.

Bear! It wasn't moved by the dog barks. "Shoo! Shoo!"

The dogs lurched and stepped back, barking, barking but not leaving her to chase it.

She ran into the cabin, catching her breath on the porch post, then grabbed John's gun, and shaking like a baby rattle in a toddler's hands, she lifted the rifle, tried to keep it steady as it gyrated in her arms. She aimed, closed just one eye as her father had taught her, and pulled the trigger.

Ping.

It wasn't loaded! Her heart beat at her ears as the bear advanced.

No! No! No!

Now Max barked deep woofs, his lips black against canines. Nellie yipped. Mary's thoughts tumbled.

Bullets. Where were the bullets?

What could she throw at it? She raised the rifle over her head. "Go! Go!"

Max leapt from the porch then, barking and howling as the bear turned tail, crashing sounds growing smaller like a long echo in a canyon. "Max! Come!" If he caught up with it, Max would lose. His gift was as a guardian. If only she'd had a loaded gun.

"Good boy." The dog appeared through the trees. Nellie, quiet now, trotted to him.

She patted Max's head, checked him over. "First test and we passed." Sort of. She rubbed her belly. She'd find those bullets—if John had left any for her. She took a deep breath. She might not tell John about this encounter. No reason to worry him. This was going to work out fine.

Dusk settled; a heavy darkness roiled over her in the shadow of so many trees. She ate her soup, then wrote in her journal (retrieved by John months before from Herbie's), set water out for the dogs, then read a few pages of *Jane Eyre*. Even though she knew the ending, the suspense brought chills to the back of her neck. "I mustn't let my imagination rule the night," she told her child. This was the true test then, this first night alone. She put the book away, blew out the lantern light, and with hands across her belly, spoke prayers of gratitude for shelter and the safety of family. She slept.

A scratching sound woke her in the dark.

At the door? On the porch. The bear came back? What if the owners have returned?

She lay still.

Just Max rolling over. Maybe Nellie with her long nails. Should she light the lantern? Not unless Max barked.

She steadied her breathing. She mustn't let small sounds scare her. She'd talked John into this occupied cabin. She had to learn to live with it all by herself.

chapter 33

J une arrived like a long-awaited-for friend, and Mary and John settled into their weekend routine. Mary augured holes in stumps during the week, and on the weekends, they burned them. She had made great strides as a lone homesteader and had walked the perimeter of what she thought was their land, had taken the canoe down once to visit her parents. Sounds in the night didn't faze her, especially not after the morning of the first night when she'd discovered elk tracks close to the porch posts. She was glad she hadn't opened the door to see what was out there!

Another morning, she'd been surprised by a load of lumber arriving by boat with Herbert Logan at the helm.

"Lumber?"

"Your dear John ordered it." He looked around while two other men in boats behind the lumber unloaded it and carried it to the claim. The pile of boards would encourage their building project for certain.

"I hear you encountered a bear."

"I'm not sure I can bare to see another bear. I barely scared this bear off." She grinned.

"I say, you do live an interesting life."

"I do." She wouldn't tell him of a day when her skirt caught fire and John had rolled her in the dirt to put it out. That had been a dreadful day. Her legs still stung.

She offered the men food, which they declined, wanting to return before the tide changed.

When John arrived the next evening, she treated him with special attention, grateful for his commitment to getting the cabin built. "The lumber was a pleasant surprise. I didn't know we had the money."

"Ja. Herbie give me an advance on wages."

"Wages?"

"I will work for him to build the road, when he has finances in order."

Her stomach soured. He'd been negotiating things—without her. *Choose your battles.*

With them apart so often, he was bound to make decisions without consulting her. She hadn't been upset when he bought lumber (rather than building a log cabin that would be cheaper, if not as pleasant) so she shouldn't be too upset that he had a plan for after the cabin was built, a plan made without her.

After eating, they talked about the baby and John's commitment to work on Herbert's road when the financing came in next year. He'd give up the mail route, he told her, but the pay would still be steady, and while he couldn't come home as often, it wouldn't be for long, just until the first stage came down the Elk Creek Road. He'd join the crew once the house was finished and the baby safe in hand and Herbert had the money he needed. "We have a good future ahead," John said.

"Yes, we do."

But something still soured her stomach, gave her pause she couldn't explain.

The future would take care of itself, Mary decided. They were all writing a new chapter in their lives with its good days and bad. What mattered was not that there were unpleasant chapters, but that they were writing this story together.

chapter 34

Some chapters have endings unintended. Mary thought of those words later. Today had been the first with John no longer carrying the mail and instead working full-time to build the cabin. Having the occupier house had been a boon to their progress and she'd sent him to the claim with a kiss and a promise to bring lunch in a bucket.

The log rolled out of the fireplace with a hiss. Mary heard it, grabbed a towel to beat it out, but only caught the cloth aflame. She kicked at the log to force it back into the fireplace, but it struck the lantern. Her skirt caught fire. She beat it with her hands, surrounded by smoke and the smell of spilled, now-flaming kerosene. *No! No!* She rushed outside, coughing, batting at her skirt to put out the flames. *The rake! Toss dirt! Water from the river?* She turned back to see the cabin engulfed.

Mary bent over, one hand on her knee, the other holding her belly as she gasped for breath. She stumbled toward their claim. "John!" He probably couldn't even hear her, the forest swallowing sound. "John!" The dogs raced before her. Smoke drifted overhead.

"What's happened? Is the baby . . . ?" John ran toward her, lifted her shoulders. He looked up as he held her. "Where's the smoke from?"

How to tell him? "A log rolled out from the fireplace. I . . . I tried to shove it back, but it caught fire to the towel that I threw when the flames burned my fingers. It must have knocked over the oil lamp. I tried stomping it out, but that sent embers toward the woodpile in the corner. The wood was so dry it sparked right up. Oh, John."

"Come, come." He fast-walked her toward the smoke, pushed her to sit, then pulled her upright, helped her move toward the cabin until they stood in front of the flaming structure. John grabbed a Pulaski to dig dirt he tossed at the flame's edge. It was too involved, too hot to get closer.

"It's all aflame. I'm so sorry." Mary turned, heaved, smoke choking her.

The dogs circled them, Nellie giving chirping barks. Max quiet, standing beside Mary, who shivered now despite the heat from the fire.

Old and dry wood, the roof collapsed inside. Unsuccessfully, John tried to move the canoe away from the side where he'd set it up on boards. Mary had painted it; the paint acted as an accelerant.

He ran to the river to scoop up water that did little to help. The roof and walls had caved into the center with water splashing around the outside. There were no Sitkas or firs nearby. The original owners had cleared a large swath of land, perhaps for this very purpose—to control a fire. Mary, too, grabbed a bucket, tossed water where the porch had been.

"It's a lost cause," John said, standing back. Heat engulfed their faces. They both coughed. He put his arm around her.

They stood unspeaking, the fire consuming their future the only sound.

"We go to your parents. Is all we can do, ja?"

Mary nodded.

The tide had gone out so even if they'd had a boat, they wouldn't have been able to use it to go down the river until early morning. So they began to walk the riverbank, dogs panting.

Her legs ached. She needed to rest. Maybe they should have gone to the claim and fixed up a branch lean-to for the night.

The tent they'd left at the cabin, so it had burned too. Still, they walked. They stumbled. Dusk threatened. Exhaustion dropped a cape over her shoulders and she sank onto the bank.

"Look." John pointed. "There's a boat tied up across the river. Must be people somewhere nearby . . . Hello, the boat!" he shouted. "Hello! Hello!"

Mary tried to shout, but her throat ached. She tasted smoke. Her head hung heavy as a cannon. The dogs barked, thinking it all a game.

Someone came through the woods. "He's seen us . . . We've been burned out," John shouted. "My wife, she's with child. Can you help us get to Nehalem?"

The man was tall, dressed in workman's clothes, his beard bear-like, covering half his face. "We can do that. But must wait for the tide."

"Yes. Thank you. Thank you."

Mary held her belly. John plopped beside her. All they could do now was wait.

It was months until Christmas, but Mary couldn't get that other Mary out of her mind. How exhausted she must have been. How grateful for that stable. *This* Mary feared she would fall asleep as soon as she stepped inside the boat.

The dogs lay along the muddy bank, letting the coolness soak into them. They all smelled of smoke. Mary's eyes smarted; coughing continued as they watched the slow rise of the tide. Eventually, their rescuer reappeared with a light. He stepped into the boat, put the lantern on the middle seat, and paddled across.

John grabbed the hull to steady the craft. "Come, Mary."

Mary carried Nellie as she approached the boat. "May I?"

"Yeah. The big dog can swim?"

"Max can handle the current," John said.

John helped Mary step in, then followed her. "I can row, sir. No need for you to do such work. It's enough you share the boat with us."

"I have the oars," the rescuer said. "And we go across to my cabin. Make the trek into Nehalem in the morning. Too late now."

"But it will only take an hour or so," John said. "We don't want to put you out any more than necessary."

"Aye. But I'll get you there on my terms."

The tone of his voice held a tinge of dread to it—or perhaps it was only the fatigue talking to her, her body as heavy as a whale.

Maybe this was why John was reluctant to ask for help. You never knew what price someone might exact for their effort.

chapter 35

F. Herbert Logan. That was the name on the contracts. Herbie held the long papers in his hands. He looked out across the creek, drank his cream tea to celebrate, though he allowed himself only a snippet of satisfaction. He sighed, threw a biscuit out to Sam, who swooped down to the sand to pick up his bounty. Ah, the carefree life of a bird!

Back inside Herbie put the contracts into his rolltop desk. Getting that piece of furniture to Elk Creek told a story of its own, a story that would serve as dinner entertainment when the hotel was finished. Once people came to stay. If they ever did. Time to deal with the disappointment. He had a contract alright but not enough commitment to fund it. No road this year. He toyed with asking his brother but didn't want to hear how the great heir wasn't made of pounds and his little brother needed to step up and do for himself. As if his brother had done so. He'd just been born first! Herbie calmed himself by taking deep breaths of sea air. Sam screeched at him for more biscuits. At least he had his hotel.

But even that effort caused consternation. He had to consider the competition with James Austin's inn that was full steam ahead, his accommodations south by Arch Cape. It was a strange arrangement

141

that required delicacy, as Austin was also an investor in the Elk Creek Road. Herbert supposed it was good that they needed each other.

He finished washing up his Spode plate and would have liked to have a visit with John Gerritse on his occasional stops as the mail carrier. But John had let the contract go to someone else while he readied his claim for his bride and the infant expected. The current mail carrier didn't often stop and preferred Herbie go into Seaside for his mail. Once there was a hotel—or two—he fully intended to request his establishment be the legitimate postal station. His would be the first building travelers spied at the end of the twisty road. There'd also been some days in the past month that the carrier had missed, even waving as he moved south. And he certainly hadn't brought any human cargo out of Portland with him, no one to rent his rooms.

Once the road was finished, things would change for the better. He pulled his pen and ink from their drawer and began his next letter to Olivia. These missives were becoming his journal. He'd write a draft and then transfer it to the paper he would seal and send. He'd describe the terrain, the way the sunsets set the sky on fire or how the wind dried your eyes some days, and how other afternoons there'd be no wind at all. Stillness. Quiet, broken only by an occasional gull. But lately, he'd also been sharing how he felt about her and his longing for her to come to America. Just as a friend.

> Because the very best days are when I hear from you or when I write to you. I pray you don't mind the many missives I send your way, always hoping they'll invite a response from you, my dear Olivia.

And then he'd tell her of his latest efforts with the road, describe the beach, ask after her health and happiness. He had decided long ago that it didn't matter how she responded; it only mattered what *he* did. Writing to her eased his mind. He sometimes found insights in what he told her that clarified his next steps. All the while, he truly hoped she'd consider making the long voyage to America.

She hadn't ever written back.

He told himself that she *had* sent letters but somehow they hadn't arrived. That's why who delivered the mail was so important. That's why the road truly mattered. The mail was the link he so needed. A link with her, his brother's fiancée, though she'd once been his.

chapter
36

The rescuing boatman rowed silently, skillfully, beaching the wooden craft against the riverbank. It was a short row across the river, but Mary shivered in the cool June evening. John jumped out and reached back for Mary's hand, helping her forward. His palms were calloused. He'd worked so hard. Mary wondered what was going through her husband's head. She was such a trial to him. The fire ruining what had been the perfect arrangement. She was so stupid to try to put the flames out with a towel, as she only spread it further. Just as when her skirt had caught fire and she'd batted it with her hands rather than rolling in the dirt. She had so much to learn, so many split-second decisions to make, then having to live with the consequences. She'd been so stupid.

John steadied the boat while their rescuer tied it up to the dock. She leaned against John, so tired, with a niggle of anxiety about what they had gotten themselves into now. Their rescuer had taken so long from the time they'd shouted his attention until he brought the boat over. They had nothing for him to steal but he might not know that.

"The missus is ready for you." The boatman had a swatch of

black-as-coal hair that covered one eye. Were his words ominous or just sharing information? *He's probably fine, a gift in the midst of darkness.*

The rescuer's wife greeted Mary, clucking her tongue while she took Mary's hand and steadied her in through the door. Nothing chilling about her! Mary's tiredness caused her to exaggerate worries, something good to know about herself. She'd never been this tired, this discouraged. Except when she'd waited that long morning to see if John survived, when they'd been pushed up against Hug Point days before the wedding. She'd been alone then; here she had family.

A cat stretched on the back of a horsehair couch. A table set for four. "Goodness," the woman said. "You be carrying. Peter did na say such about ye. Come, sit down." Mary collapsed onto the couch. "We don't want that wee one arriving afore its time."

"The baby isn't due until August." Mary took a deep breath. "Thank you so much for letting us be here until we can go back to Nehalem, to my parents."

"In the morning. You rest here tonight."

Mary looked at her fingers. Soot-covered; her skirt blotched with ash. She guessed her face was smudged with dirt and grime held hostage by sweat. The woman offered Mary a washbasin, soap, and a rag. The rough rag pinked her skin, cleansing. The woman busied herself putting supper on the table. She threw bones to the dogs outside where both Nellie and Max had curled up on the porch. John and the boatman sat silently, smoke from their rescuer's pipe gifted the air. They had shelter. Her baby was safe. That's what mattered.

She was glad there was no mirror to shock her. Mary's mother would be horrified at her state. Maybe they could find somewhere else to stay besides begging her parents. Find another cabin to occupy.

Oh those poor people! She and John would have to build two structures now, replacing the one she'd burned down.

She finished washing her face and hands, set the basin to the side. "John?"

He left his silent chair and used Mary's rag to dip into the soapy water. "You missed a spot." John dabbed the washcloth at Mary's forehead. Her eyes puddled with tears. She should have let him wash first. He had done the most work.

Mary sat down at the table as directed, the sizzling deer meat cast a savory scent amidst the smokey smell on their clothes. Her chin dropped and she nodded off to sleep.

"Best you lie down." John pressed her shoulder awake, then she followed the woman into a room where she sank onto the bed—their rescuer's bed. She didn't even undress.

The rescuer's wife—Marta was her name—gently woke her in the morning. "We will wash your clothes. Here is a wrapper for you." Again, tears fell. "Come. Eat now. For your baby."

They should leave, and yet she wanted to delay having to ask her parents for help. Her fatigue made the decision.

John was given clothing to wear while his blousy shirt and jeans were washed. It was no simple gesture, washday being ripe with potential dangers of hot fires, boiling water, and just plain hard labor.

A squall poured rain on this washday. Mary's offer to assist was declined. Barbs of the troubled future pierced her thoughts, stealing her from appreciating the kindnesses around her.

"Tomorrow, you have a place to stay?" Marta asked.

"I hope so," John said.

Mary slept most of the day, Nellie at her feet while Max joined John and Peter, their rescuer, returning to the site of the fire to make sure it was out. The rain from the night helped that. She dreamed through the second night, running scenes one to the next. Then on the next morning Marta announced that all was ready. She handed Mary a bucket of lunch.

"You take the boat," Peter said. "Bring it back when you come the next time. I imagine you continue to clear ground on your claim?"

John hesitated.

"Maybe we aren't meant to prove it up." Mary answered for him.

"Ah, no." Their host shook his head. "Discouragement is not where you go from this episode. We will see you again. We will help. You let us know." Peter smiled.

Mary wondered why she'd ever been frightened of him. Maybe because her mother was wary of strangers. John had said nothing about what their future on the claim looked like. Maybe they'd walk away. He'd be hesitant to leave her alone now; a woman who made poor decisions.

Beneath a storm-threatening sky, they set off in a borrowed boat, Nellie at Mary's feet. Max ran along the bank beside them, wind ruffling his hair. She felt refreshed. Gratitude washed over her.

"'They went to sea in a sieve, they did.'" Mary recited while John rowed, the swish of the water against the oars, a rhythm to Mary's words. "Then there's the verse where people are worried about them, remember that? 'For the sky is dark, and the voyage is long.'" She growled the words for emphasis. When she'd spoken that verse before, he'd treated her like a child.

"And so it is," John said. "I prefer your poem, 'We stay no matter how,' ja?"

"You remembered." The shiver that went through her wasn't fear this time but giddiness. "'And in twenty years they all came back, in twenty years or more. And everyone said, "How tall they've grown. If we only live, We too will go to a sea in a Sieve."'" Mary giggled. "Holy Jumblies. Despite everything, they inspired people!"

John rested the oars on his knees. "I hardly think we'll be someone's inspiration."

"Why not? Look at our rescuers." She stroked Nellie's head. "They've grown tall in my mind, taking total strangers in and giving up their own bed for us. Telling that story, how people help each other, that can be an inspiration. We can pass that on. And they asked for nothing, no tit for tat. I think that's what grace is. Gifts without expectation."

"Ja."

"And now we can only hope my parents will be as welcoming."

It took but a few hours moving downstream on the Nehalem for them to reach the dock near her parents' farm. Nellie scampered ashore, and John helped Mary out. He tied the boat as Max sniffed around them, panting. He smelled of smoke.

"Do you want to wait here while I go talk to your parents?"

"No. Let's do it together."

Mary held her stomach as she waddled up the bank and onto the road that paralleled the river. John held her hand. It spoke of how vulnerable he must feel. She squeezed his fingers back. They were in this together.

chapter
37

Jewell knew she should make the trek north to the tribe of her grandfather near Astoria. She should share the news of his passing, tell the story of how she had washed his body and wrapped him in an elk skin and sang the mourning songs over him. In recent years, they had traveled with that burial hide, never knowing when the burial clothes would be needed. She had sprinkled lavender oils on his body and over the elk hide. Then unlike the Nehalem tradition—more like the Tillamook—she pulled him into their canoe and faced it west so his spirit would find the easiest route to the world beyond. She knew she couldn't lift him up into a burial tree, which is what would have been his preference, she was sure. She would have had to ask for help to do it that way and such asking was difficult. Neither could she bring herself to burn their hut as was the custom. Maybe later.

She sat looking out at the ocean as the waves rolled in, a small fire burning at her feet. Behind her, the Ecola Creek flowed, its personality changing the way people sometimes did: rushing, strong enough to carry a canoe of goods and people, inviting salmon upstream, then quiet, nothing more than a sliver of water, a blend of salt and fresh, mixing with all that is new yet eternal, awaiting the return of the tides.

Which creek was she? It had been her desire to become a healer like the Anglo doctor, but that purpose seemed less important now. Her grandfather was gone. All the medicine in the world, whether of her people or the white doctor, would make no difference to him. The desire of her heart had disappeared. Caring for others, that purpose remained, but it was that small sliver of a stream now, not that which could carry her forward. She turned toward the creek that she and her grandfather had shared. The muddy creek banks mocked her.

Beyond she saw a pale light in Mr. Logan's cabin that was looking more like the hotels she saw in Astoria: a big structure. A long porch. A road would be carved out of the trees making it easier for people to come to this Crying Sands Beach. Maybe the people who came would be in need of a healer. Or maybe such a healer would not be her.

That night she slept alone in the rush-mat home she had shared with her grandfather. She heard the wind push against the structure and fell asleep imagining the interesting things the beach would give up. The beach was a changing pallet that made walking along it a new route every day. It made walking there a prayer.

As dawn peeked over the trees behind her, Jewell remembered her grandfather. And then she listened to her heart. Somewhere someone was calling her for comfort. She wasn't certain. But she'd head south toward Nehalem where her friend Mary lived. Perhaps with a friend, she'd figure out her next steps.

chapter
38

John had come to the bend in the river, or whatever one called a turning point. He'd get the contract back and he wouldn't just carry the mail, he'd work at Austin's hotel when he was overnight in Seaside. When he was too tired going over Neahkahnie Mountain, he'd count on Prince to keep going while he slept in the saddle. And on weekends, he'd clear ground with Mary so they'd have a garden. He might even sell some of the produce along his mail route. He'd do whatever it took and work on Herbie's road when the entrepreneur finally had enough money to start cutting trees for it.

But first, they had to face Mary's parents. Or rather, he did. He wasn't showing himself as the best provider, but God willing, he'd have another chance. He didn't want Mary to carry the blame for the fire. Accidents happen. He'd told her that but wasn't sure she believed him.

"Let's stop and see the horses first." Mary tugged John toward the barn.

"Ja. I miss them too." Anything to put this off. "One day, I'd like a stable. Rent horses out maybe."

"You've never said that before. That would be wonderful." She squeezed his hand. "Of course we need people around to rent them. But I can see riding on the sand just for fun, not to get from here to there. It's . . . romantic."

"Is it? One more reason why Herbert's road must be built. So people come."

Prince nickered at the sound of their voices and Jake stuck his head over the gate. Mary patted the big animal's neck, cooed to him. Baldy slept with his head hanging, matching how John felt. He was most concerned about Mary.

"How are you feeling, Mare?" Her face, backlit by the sun, was drawn. Her hand rested on her belly.

"I'll just be glad when this is over with. If they won't let us stay . . ."

"Then we'll take the tent offer from Peter and Marta, and we'll sleep on the forest floor like we were kids."

"I think I am just a kid," Mary said. "Seventeen isn't very old."

"Or we could go on to Herbie's. You can stay there while we get neighbors to help build the cabin."

She turned to him. "You'd do that?"

"Should have done it before." It was a hard thing to acknowledge, needing someone else. But he had responsibilities he hadn't had before. And for the first time he understood that his own father would have benefited by accepting help. Besides, a partner as good as Mary deserved a man who could change.

chapter
39

"Come in, come in." How had Amanda deserved this? How many times in the weeks since Mary and John had been gone had she cried to her husband, "Why didn't you stop me from sending them away?" She had spoken prayers, repeating them five, six times like a mantra before going to bed. "Keep them safe. Keep them safe." And now, here they were, their presence a relief from the guilt that had poked her shoulders as she baked biscuits or weighted like a rock when she washed sheets. There was no need to worry about strangers. Mary had a new name. That Fisk would never find them. "We were just talking about you. Well, we're always talking about you, wondering how it's going, aren't we, William?" Amanda looked beyond them toward the boat. "Where's your canoe?"

"We've had problems, Mama." Mary's voice broke.

"Hush, now. It can't be so bad. You're here." A child's tears never stopped piercing a mother's heart.

"Barely." Mary reached for her hanky, sniffed. Amanda pulled her into a hug, rubbed her daughter's back. Her hair smelled smokey. "You tell them, John."

"Ja." Her son-in-law lowered his eyes, shifted his weight on his big brogans. "The occupied cabin burned. And the canoe."

Amanda gasped. "Everyting is gone, ja. Some neighbors took us in and that's their boat. We must return it."

"But you're alright?" William rose from his chair.

"Ja."

"You're destitute," Amanda said.

"No, they aren't," William corrected. "They have family."

"We shouldn't have sent you out there. It was so selfish of me." She looked at Mary. "I know, I know. I'm like a kite rising, falling, then up again." She sighed. "We . . . exiled you—"

"Not exiled," William said.

"We were not hospitable. We thought we were doing the right thing, supporting your independence. But by the grace of God, we get another chance." She clapped her hands.

"We will ask at the church, ja. They help us put up the cabin?" Mary smiled at her husband.

"Yes, yes." William patted John on his shoulder. "Good for you."

"Ja. A stubborn man I am. We will have a house building and our baby will be born in his own home."

"No need to rush. Goodness." Amanda felt relief, joy. Her selfishness and worry had drained away like a waterspout on the bay. "It's a time to celebrate. That you're alive and the baby is alright too. He is, yes?" Mary nodded. Amanda would get a midwife to answer those vexing questions any new mother would ask that she couldn't answer. "Let the dogs inside," Amanda said. "We'll have a party." How things could change with a fervent prayer.

PART II

chapter
40

A firm knock. Mary started to open the door but her mother stopped her. "Let's see who it is first. One needs to be careful." Mary wondered if her lack of hospitality skills came from her mother's reticence toward neighbors. In the three weeks since she and John had been back, Mary's mother's old wariness had nosed its way in, though otherwise their time together had been surprisingly comforting.

"It is Jewell," came the voice on the other side of the closed door.

Mary swung the door open and grabbed her friend in a soft hug. Her family hadn't seen Jewell for some time. "We missed you at the celebration."

Jewell sashayed through the room to greet Mary's mother. She had a gentle sway that Mary envied, especially when her own walk rivaled a duck's. Or as big as she was, a goose's. One month to go by her calculations.

"I have come to see how my friend is." Jewell pushed her single braid onto her back. She wore a beaded belt around the waist of her calico dress.

Mary rubbed her belly through the blue-dyed linen wrapper

that was the only garment she could get into. "You can see. How are you?"

"My grandfather has passed into the Beyond. I had planned to come here soon after but returned to Astoria to tell our people. This took many days as I heard the stories about him I had not been told before." Mary motioned her to a chair. "But then it came to me to come here now. To see how you were. I did not know that you carried new life."

"You wouldn't believe all that's happened since our wedding. It hasn't even been a year. We've made good progress on clearing the site and are getting ready to build up a home and then have this baby. Can you stay?"

"For a time."

"Then you can join us for the cabin raising."

Jewell nodded. "This is so."

John had returned to the mail route and along with Mary had organized the group of men and women who would be helping build their simple cabin. The big day was scheduled for tomorrow, giving them time to recover from yesterday's Fourth of July celebration, the first with Mary being Mrs. John Gerritse, the first with her as a soon-to-be mother. Her pregnancy colored everything with lovely rainbow hues.

John had secured and had delivered upriver more lumber and shake shingles for the roof. Mary had accepted quilts and dishes and other essentials that neighbors brought over after they learned of the fire.

"I do have to tell you that the lovely blanket you gave us, well, it went up in flames. We had a fire. I should have left your gift here with John's blanket."

"You carry many 'shoulds,' Mary. 'Shoulds' are heavy as a whale."

Mary's mother asked, "Have you eaten?"

Jewell smiled. "I know when I see you, Mary's mother, that food will appear soon after a hello is spoken. I am fine. I had fish. You will soon be a grandmother."

Mary was impressed with how easily Jewell turned the conversation on to others.

"Yes. Isn't that something? But first we have to get Mary and John into their home and settled." She put eggs into the washbowl for cleaning. "What is it?" Her mother turned to a sound Mary made.

"I . . . I've water where it shouldn't be." Mary stared at the floor. Fear more than pain flowed through her. "But it's too early. Mama! What should I do?"

"Get Mrs. Effenberger! Quick!" Amanda pushed William back as he sauntered through the door. "The baby is coming early. Go!"

"Should I get John?"

"Later. Go! Now!"

Amanda returned to her daughter. "Try not to pant." Wasn't that so? Or should she pant? "Think of . . . milking cows. Or . . . Oh, Mary, I wish I knew what to do for you."

"What did you do? Oh, oh, oh!"

"Why I . . . William will be back with Mrs. Effenberger soon. She didn't expect to need to be here until August."

"It is good to squat," Jewell said. "Baby can reach for the outside."

"No. Lie down. I'm sure that would be better."

Jewell stepped back. The girl knew her place at least. Amanda held Mary's elbow and walked her to the bed. "Let me get clean sheets, Mary. Can you stand?"

"I will hold her." Jewell wrapped her arms around Mary.

"Yes, thank you, Jewell." She should comfort her own daughter but instead fluttered around the kitchen.

"The baby is early, Mama." Mary panted. "Is it supposed to hurt this much?"

"Maybe too much celebrating at the Fourth of July picnic. All that food and the music."

"I didn't even dance, Mama." Her daughter grimaced.

She was right. Amanda had sat beside her daughter during the outing, her eyes wary. There were many new families settling between Tillamook and Neahkahnie Mountain. But no stranger had been overly interested in the Edwardses or Gerritses. The fireworks over Nehalem Bay had been glorious, even if they did set Nellie into a barking frenzy. No one minded as a dozen other pets joined the chorus. Young Merritt Batterson had stopped at their blanket spread between seagrass and the dunes to say hello to Mary and John. Even Herbert Logan had chatted with them for a time, talking about his road company. There'd been no one around saying they were friends of the Fisks, or worse, a Fisk himself. Mary had not indicated that she remembered she had an older brother and this was good. It would only cause distress if she did. She hadn't brought up the photograph Mary had seen either. Amanda had gotten rid of it.

"Ow! Ow! Oh, Mama. This hurts."

"I know. I know. Yes, pant like a dog." Amanda finished changing the sheets. It was what she knew to do, which wasn't much when it came to birthing a baby. It wouldn't be long before her daughter figured that out. Only Mrs. Effenberger could save her child now. And Amanda as well.

Jewell rubbed Mary's back in a healing circle. She was accustomed to others telling her what to do even though she had wisdom passed down from her grandfather. But when it came to babies arriving, it was the wisdom of aunties and the ages she relied on, as she had never brought a child into the world. She had thought her own healing skills would be blankets of comfort to the old ones, to grandmothers and grandfathers. But here the Creator had given her a task, or perhaps an opportunity, to be of service in a new way.

"Oh, Mama." Her friend Mary moaned as she sank onto the bed. "Tell me what to do. Not that I'll be able to follow your directions. I'm birthing a contrary baby coming too early."

"Let me hold your hand, Mary." Jewell reached for her friend's fingers that grabbed out like someone drowning reaching for air. It didn't seem much, but sometimes just touching another in a time of trial could be enough. Jewell began a soft chant. Mary's mother frowned, but Jewell did not stop her singing. Music always gentled the spirit. Building a family was a natural thing, this birthing. But even natural things could have problems. She prayed this would not be such a day.

chapter
41

Mary was both relieved and disappointed, not sure how one could hold both emotions in her heart at the same time. But her heart was bigger now. A small bundle had expanded it. The day before, Marybelle—whom they'd call Belle—had arrived but not before Mrs. Effenberger burst through the door, Mary's father behind her.

Mrs. Ef—as Mary called her—helped with the delivery that had taken over the hearts of everyone in the room, her mother the first to hold the naked babe. Part of Mary's own body had torn as the little one made her way into the world. Mrs. Ef sewed the tissue, answered questions. But Mary needed time to heal, thus causing the disappointment in the midst of newborn joy.

"It will be better you stay here with the babe," John told his wife. "There's plenty help, ja?"

"I suppose there is."

She wouldn't be up to laying cedar planks or pounding precious nails into boards. Others would cook for the crew that would raise up their home. Mary was most sad missing that. She liked to serve their friends, liked a party atmosphere.

Belle had arrived small and a bit cranky, pulled from that warm womb a month early. But Mrs. Ef was the perfect midwife, along with Jewell, calming Mary's concerns while offering encouragement to do what only a mother can. Mary had a million questions, but Mrs. Ef told her she would find the answers to most of them inside herself. Mary couldn't see how that might work, but she trusted the woman. Her mother was reticent to give answers to "How do I get her to nurse?" and "What's that?" when something expelled from her body.

"The placenta," Jewell told her. For someone who had never had a child, Jewell knew things.

It had also been a joyous occasion once Belle was placed on Mary's breast, soon able to suckle. Could there be anything more glorious than nurturing an infant from one's own body? Perhaps watching John hold his firstborn—a sacramental occasion that filled Mary with the awe she'd felt when humbled by the sea on a glorious summer day.

After shedding a few tears, John handed the baby back to Mary's mother. "A towhead, like me. You did good." He sat beside Mary. "By tomorrow there will be a house for us to move into." Pride filled his voice. "We go now. Raise up our home."

Her father left with him, and Mary had only the memory of their earlier efforts she'd made toward getting their home ready. Just the week before, she and John had harnessed Jake and had him tow the cookstove along the river to the house site. It had been quite an ordeal and Jake finally just sat down on the uphill drag. When he did, John walked to the stove and saw that it was full of mud gouged up as they'd led the horse forward. John and Mary spent the next two hours digging out that mud so Jake could make the final trek. "A smart horse," John noted, wiping sweat and grime from his forehead. Mary wasn't much help, but she hauled water for Jake, her boots making steady sucking noises along the riverbank, and she dumped the pails of mud beside the trail. The cookstove soon sat beneath a tree, a tarp over it as it waited for its home.

Just as Mary waited for her house, for a baby. *Maybe that exertion brought Belle early.*

It didn't matter. The baby was fine. The stove sat ready. They'd achieved their goal that day, birds twittering their applause. And on the day Belle was born, July 5, they cherished an achievement more monumental than delivering a stove.

But on the morning of the sixth of July, Mary was left behind, missing the next adventure in their going to sea in a sieve.

"We have to be there, Mama. We just do."

"This does not seem wise, my friend," Jewell said. "Give your body time to heal."

"I think it's fine." Her mother crossed her arms over her chest and glared at Jewell.

Mary expected an argument from her mother, not from her friend.

"Let's load your chowder. It won't go far but it'll add to what the women took up earlier. If you have to be somewhere else, Jewell, we'll understand."

"Come with us, please," Mary said. "You're family."

Jewell hesitated, then nodded agreement. "I will carry the food and stay out of the way so your mother can help you and her grandchild."

Still uncertain of her mother's irritation, Mary got up, cuddled Belle, and with the tide being right, Jewell rowed the women in the boat to join the crowd building Mary and John's house. A warm breeze caressed her face.

"We're going home," she whispered to Belle.

As they approached the site, Mary heard the sound of voices in comradery and joy.

"More shakes," from a roofer.

"Got some nails over there?" from a man framing.

"Who's got the tin sink? Let's get it set in this cabinet. You make that, Joshua?" The chatter carried on, like the hum of bumblebees doing their work.

"I'm so glad we didn't miss this." Mary blinked back tears.

Here with the help of their neighbors, the Gerritses would begin their next journey in their little sieve. Only one window would be carved out of the walls, but they could hold the door open to the breezes on many days, letting fresh air and light in. Mary thought of their friends doing that—letting in light.

"Are you hurting?" Jewell asked as Mary sat on a pillow on a stump, watching men work. Her mother set the Dutch oven of chowder to heat in the fire.

"Just happy."

A cheer went up with the roof complete. Several men carried in the cookstove—minus the mud. And when Peter and Marta brought a table and four chairs and placed them on the dirt floor, Mary rose to step inside. Emotion overflowed as tears. Again. What was wrong with her? Crying at the sight of a chair. She shifted Belle's weight in her arms, cooed to that perfect face.

"This winter, I will put cedar planks down," John told her, patting her shoulder. "The table will be level then. The stove too."

"It's fine. It's wonderful." With Belle between them, she turned to her husband's broad chest and sobbed while a community stood behind her. The women applauded, the men dropped their heads and smiled.

Wiping her eyes, Mary told them, "You've made a house and a home. A piece of you will always be with us. We are so grateful. When John completes the plank floor, we'll hold a dance and party until the tide rises to take you all home."

"We'll be back," one of the men shouted. "For your chowder, Mrs. Gerritse, more than the dance."

Mary beamed. She'd done her part too in making this cabin a home. And with their friends, they'd all grown taller, just as all Jumblies knew how to do.

chapter
42

The Gerritses moved in the next day, and the following week, John returned to his mail route.

"I wish you didn't have to go."

"Ja, I know. But until the road work starts, this is what I can do to fill our purse. We have to buy flour and bacon for the winter."

"I wish I could do something to contribute."

"You take care of Belle. That's enough."

"I might plant a garden even though it's late." Her seedlings next to the occupied cabin had been crisped in the fire. "Onions could produce. Carrots too. Mama has starts."

"Ja. You take care of that." John held the baby while Mary prepared a corn porridge. Maple syrup, a luxury housewarming present they hadn't touched, sat in the center of the table. A treat for John's last night before leaving. The dogs lay on the dirt floor, Max now spending time indoors too, though he shed and blond dog hair drifted in the air.

Mary hesitated, trying to decide whether telling John something of import would make him worry or suggest she was weak. But they were a couple and couples shared things, didn't they? No, she'd keep this to herself. No need to express discomforting things just before he had to leave. She kissed him goodbye and bravely sent him on his way.

Alone with Belle and the dogs, Mary pulled up her brave pantaloons, as she called them. She and Belle entered their own adventure: a routine of morning Arbuckle's for Mary and nursing moments for Belle. She fussed and Mary wasn't sure that was normal, but she walked the floor to help her calm, then built the fire up to warm the cabin, singing to her daughter. When Mary went out to split wood, or raked a garden plot, she propped Belle onto a puddle of pillows to watch, but mostly the child slept. Mary hoped that was normal. Actually, wielding an axe and hoe proved relaxing, sweat wetting her hair damp when she finished to survey her success.

She should have accepted Jewell's suggestion to stay awhile to put off her being alone with the babe. Her mother, oddly, hadn't offered, and Mary didn't want to ask. Being alone with the baby was something Mary knew she must get accustomed to, but it scared her.

Max barked, stared at the door. *Bears snuffling at the cabin's edge?* The sounds stopped. Her imagination was too vivid, for she could find a scary explanation for every sound. She lit the lamp, checked on Belle, then wrote letters to her parents, telling tales of her daughter's antics, which weren't many at this point since she slept most of the time. John could deliver the letters without having to pay for stamps.

At first light, as she listened to her baby breathe, she prayed a prayer of gratitude. She rose, baked, heated water for Belle's bath, then took a bath herself and finally washed diapers in the remains. As the week progressed, Mary made new gains. When Belle developed diaper rash (could it be from those diapers not getting washed first?), she scorched flour in her cast-iron spider until it felt like satin in her fingers. With a little water she made a paste and dear Belle wore her concoction that cured the rash.

"What do you know about that," Mary told her daughter. "I'm an alchemist among my other many talents." She knew her words kept her from the worry that she wouldn't be able to keep this cheerfulness up once snow fell. Brave is a short sentence in a very long paragraph of life.

But they did sustain a pattern those months. Midweek, Mary fixed a grand spread for John and they had the weekends for shared tasks and tender moments. They built a chicken house together. John wanted to fell more trees and Mary handled the reciprocating saw with him. They crafted a lean-to for the horses so Prince could be out of the weather when John spent the night. It was a long boat ride to Nehalem so most Sundays they stayed home and read the Bible together. Later, John napped and played with Belle. It was only when he left on Monday that Mary felt her stomach clench. His last kiss of the morning was more of a piercing of her heart than the filling of that empty place in her soul.

On a Thursday in late November when the aspen had all but lost their fire red, Jewell arrived. "I felt a call to come. I missed my friend."

Mary hadn't seen her since the house-raising. Jewell flipped her braid to her back and smiled. Then she cooked soup and corn bread for supper. In the evening, the two girls—women now, having taken on new responsibilities and dealt with significant familial changes—shared stories. Mary couldn't believe how much better she felt having a woman to talk to. Belle with her button nose and porcelain skin seemed to like Jewell's presence too. She smiled her toothless smile when Jewell shook a deer hoof rattle in front of her. And when she slept, her long eyelashes resting on white cheeks, Jewell and Mary kept talking.

"I can find the feathers," Jewell said. "Sometimes the beach gives up beeswax. But I cannot carve the ducks. Maybe only my people use them to trick the ducks flying overhead. Maybe selling them to the white duck hunters is not a future way to earn the coins needed for the white man's trading posts. Maybe they would not hire a woman guide to show them lakes and rivers speckled with ducks and geese."

Mary turned the carved duck in her hands, holding it almost as tenderly as she did Belle.

"It will not bring me much money," Jewell continued. "And selling them will be hurtful. I should have given them away when he died, as is our custom." She held one of the carved ducks. "But I couldn't let them go then. Now, I must."

Mary couldn't imagine giving away precious things of someone who had died. She'd want to hang on to the halter John had braided from fine horsehair that he'd given her as a wedding gift.

"You could learn how to carve other ducks and save your grandfather's. Or carve something else. A puffin perhaps."

"Puffins would not attract ducks." The women laughed together.

Belle woke and fussed.

Mary picked her up, jostled her. "She's already eaten." She paced, embarrassment rising at her ineptness as Belle cried.

"Did you watch your grandfather carve?" *Distract*.

"The wood spoke to him. He would walk along the sand and choose from what the sea gave. I am not sure wood talks to me."

"If you have his knives, you could begin." Mary paced.

Jewell nodded agreement. "He kept them in a buckskin wrap. I have them."

"Learn as you go. That's what I'm doing." She bounced Belle. "Though not very well as you can see. Sometimes she cries like that and nothing I do helps. I'm not very good at this mothering."

"I have something for you." Jewell went outside, then brought in a cradleboard shaped like a canoe with an aspen bow and calico sides to lace over the child.

"It's beautiful." Mary nodded her chin toward the gift. "Let's put her in."

The child fit perfectly with a moss pillow beneath her little legs, and another under her head. Jewell laced her inside the cocoon; Belle quieted.

"I'm amazed. Thank you so much."

Jewell smiled. "I thought my journey was to heal my grandfather, but maybe my heart is meant to heal others."

"I was awful glad you were there when Belle started her journey."

"Mrs. Ef showed many things. These will help the next time I am near a birthing woman."

"Much as I love this little girl, I hope your next birthing woman isn't me! I should have asked Mrs. Ef about how to manage that."

"My grandfather used to say to not judge a life by the steps taken but to take each step one at a time and savor what hill they take you up. Enjoy the view at the top, look back only for a moment, then move forward. There is always the other side."

"Well, it's true that once you climb up the trail on Neahkahnie Mountain, you don't think of anything else but staying on it and not falling off. It's when you're at the top that the view overtakes you, though. Spectacular."

"We must find the spectacular, as you call it, in the sunrise and sunset and all the moments in between."

Belle woke with a grin.

"The smile of this child. It is a sunbeam to warm you even when the skies are whale gray over turbulent seas. You can still sail."

"I'll remember that when things get tough," Mary said. She hoped she would, though it wasn't only her child's smile that promised strength but the presence of her friend. She needed to remember that too.

chapter
43

The snow fell in early December and Mary welcomed it as a diversion from the steady rains. The downpours raised the river to the edge but then receded, leaving muddy banks behind along with the scent of wet leaves and salt. A bright sun followed the snow this day, and she bundled Belle up and with the dogs began a trek toward Marta and Peter's home, imagining the joy in seeing them. They would ask her to spend the night—if they were there. She hadn't thought of that. She had Salal berry jam to share. Time with friends mattered, she realized. It was the fuel for being alone.

But before they were a mile down the path, they encountered slick mud. Mary slipped, dropped Belle, the bundle landing in muck. "Oh now, baby. Are you alright?" Belle cried out but gratefully, the cradleboard Jewell had made protected her. They turned back. "The snow has started to melt," she told Belle. "The ground doesn't freeze here like it did in Minnesota." Back at the cabin, she unwrapped the muffler from her daughter's face. "We used to hitch a tarp to a calf's tail when we lived in Redwing and let it swirl us around, dumping us in the snowdrifts to great laughter." Mary had liked Minnesota, liked that her father let them do such things. They never told her mother about those risky adventures. Maybe they'd given her the strength to participate in this one.

Belle fussed, little whines like an unhappy cabin cat. Had she been injured when Mary fell with her? Mary walked the floor, wondering if her daughter could sense her own disquiet.

Then that night, like every night, Belle would sleep while sounds kept Mary awake. She hovered over the silent baby. Her breathing was normal, there were no bruises. She looked angelic. "No worse for wear, little one." She thanked God for that.

When John came that week, she told him about trying to make that trek and her memory of Minnesota. "Did I ever tell you that my father made shingles during those winters?" She scraped her frying pan of a quiche-like dish she'd read about in a lady's magazine her mother had. "He made a good living at it, I think. I remember the piles of wood chips." They'd peppered the white snow like freckles and smelled fragrant.

"Did he?" John ate quickly. She noticed that he did that, rarely leaning back to let the food fill him up. He'd then head right out to work. She could hardly complain about her fears or loneliness when he worked so very hard. They were making it. That's what mattered. She relished the night in the warmth of his arms and watched bravely as he left the next morning.

The following week, John arrived a day before expected.

"A surprise," Mary laughed. "I don't have a good supper planned."

He took her in his arms. She sighed.

"Belle and I eat sparsely when you're not here. Well, I do. Belle has a full meal whenever."

John kissed her and released her, stomped the snow from his boots. "I have a change of plans." He stood before the stove, warming his back. "George Luce. You remember him?" Mary nodded as she diapered Belle. "He took the mail route for me when we built the cabin."

"I remember."

"Well, he's in dire straits and I thought maybe it was time for me to spend the winter with my wife and family. It'll help him out to carry the mail, and I have a couple of thoughts for how we can fill the purse from here, for the next three months or so."

"Oh, John!" She felt her heart lift.

"Your mention of those shake shingles. Lord knows we've plenty of cedar rounds and I can make a shake bench. There's plenty of demand. I asked Herbie about it. Plus, those nights I worked for Austin at the hotel, I've been saving those coins. What do you say to that, Mrs. Gerritse? Would you mind a man around more?"

"I say," she mimicked Herbie's English accent, "you've grown as tall as those Jumblies did. I'll need a ladder to kiss you."

That winter, John hunted and Mary helped dress the elk. While the meat dried, he made shake shingles from the many timber rounds he'd felled. They had plenty of deer and elk for food and John had time to play with Belle while Mary cooked. He watched his only child bat at the dogs who let her. She'd roll onto Nellie, who sniffed then laid her head back down before the stove, eyes watching. John fashioned his shake bench, then a cradle. He rolled a stump beside the house to act as a place for Mary to clean fish he caught, and when she asked him to watch the baby while she heated laundry water, he did. He actually liked it, though he wasn't sure he'd ever confess that to his former shipmates. Didn't seem very manly to like cuddling a babe, smelling the lavender Mary put in her bathwater. He should make signs announcing that a child had blessed their home, just as they did in Holland when a newborn arrived. That should have happened when they were busily working on the cabin raising. He'd remember for the second child.

They had a quiet Christmas planned when Mary's parents arrived to share the small space, trim the tree, and fill the cabin with smells of cinnamon and spice. They laughed together with dominoes as witnesses.

"Mary tells me you're making shakes." His father-in-law smoked a pipe while the women looked over quilt pieces Mary's mother brought to work on.

"Ja. Filling the purse."

"I found it a soothing thing to do too. It would kill my back, though. Take many breaks, son."

"That I will, sir." He thought of his own father and wondered how he was. Maybe he should write to him. As if he'd notice that he hadn't.

For the New Year celebration of the new decade, 1890, and again at midmonth, for Mary's birthday, they took the boat to Mary's parents'. They returned to their claim in February, and together they built a split rail fence, hoping to bring all the horses there. Mary was certain that having Prince and Jake around would be a good thing. She was a hard worker, his wife. She knew how to pound pegs and saw boards. She could burn out stumps too, and now wore a pair of his old pants so as not to catch her skirts on fire. Sometimes a light snowfall made everything look pristine and clean, and they'd sit on the porch with knitted mitts on their hands and drink coffee and hot chocolate, Belle bundled up, nestled in either his lap or her mother's.

At night, they read the books, or rather Mary did, John's English not being so good.

The chickens Mary's mother gave her for her birthday became an irritant to John. Their predators were many and one had to remember to put them up every night.

"Their enemies come by land and by sky," Mary teased as she helped John hang leather hinges on the chicken coop door. "Skunks and hawks. The days might be just as dangerous as the nights as owls brazenly fly around and cause a ruckus. Max can only add to it with his barks."

One moonless night, John had to just imagine the carnage as he stood on the porch in his underwear, holding a shotgun he shot into the dark.

In the morning, John and Mary stared at the empty pen, feathers blanketing the wet ground. "It's an eggs-aggeration that chickens are easy keepers." Mary sighed. "I do like their companiable clucking."

"I'll get you more. We'll try covering the pens with fishing nets."

Later that day, John took a load of his shingles into Nehalem for sale. People put them not only on their roofs but on the sides of their homes to thwart the rain, and the ocean's wind. When he returned, Mary fixed porridge she'd feed to Belle after John had his fill. She had dried berries to add to his and poured the tiniest bit of syrup from what they had left. His wife had a sweet tooth. He needed to acquire a cow. "I didn't get so much for the shingles, Mare. We will have to do something else, ja?" He'd best tell her that he'd taken the mail contract back. He dreaded the look on her face.

But she adapted, and then in the company of March winds, John said, "It looks like Herbert's road plans are coming through." He used a casual voice. He'd been trying to find a way to tell her. "Once we start the road, I won't do the mail contract again. You understand. We talked of this before, ja?"

"There goes my free mail to my parents." She laughed as she served him tea.

"I never considered your letters as part of the mail, Mare. Just carried postage between family members because I was going there anyway. It would have been illegal not to buy a stamp and have the postmaster lock them up."

"I know. It was like writing in a journal. I'll have to write letters to myself." She made a face at Belle, who laughed from a high chair he'd built for the babe. They tied her to it with a dish towel around her tummy. "At least we can have you midweek, can't we?" Belle squeezed an egg noodle in her chubby fingers and laughed. His daughter already had a tooth.

"No. That will change now. I won't be coming midweek. I'll be working on the road. Full-time. It'll bring people to Cannon Beach. Form a better route for the mail. It'll be good for all of us. A few months of fine wages too."

Belle squealed a happy chirp. Mary lifted her from the chair and plopped her on her hip while she stirred a bubbling soup.

"It's only for the spring and summer." He raised his voice so she could hear him as the spoon scraped the pot. "We'll have it built by fall and then things will change for everyone."

"Will they?"

"I'll have enough money so that we can buy our acreage out-right. Get cows. Have a real farm like your parents have." His last year's effort had failed miserably beneath a wet summer and fall, but they'd put in the six months thanks to Mary's staying on the claim.

She handed Belle to him, hands on her hips. "I have never un-derstood why my parents chose to try to carve a living out of dense trees, rainy winters, mud, and bogs. They've worked more than ten years to have what they have, John. I really wonder if we can do the same here, farther from markets than they are."

He scowled. Was she challenging his judgment? Hadn't they gotten on well all winter?

"You don't tink we try to farm then, ja?"

"I don't know what I think. It just came to me. I'm like that, expressing my opinion even if it isn't thought out. It makes me . . . adaptable." She looked into his eyes. "That's a worthy virtue for a wife, don't you think?"

"Ja." She could be sarcastic, his Mare—was she being that now?

They had a quiet supper and then Mary said, "Is it possible the roadbuilding is not only a source of work for you but also for me?"

He frowned. "Why would you say that?"

"I have an idea." She fluttered her eyelashes at him. "Trust me, sailor. Don't you like surprises?"

The truth was, he didn't. And this woman, his wife, was full of them. What did she have planned now?

chapter
44

Dearest Olivia,

It's March. I pray we begin the road I've written to you about. We do not yet have all the money we need. I have borrowed perhaps beyond my capacity but I'm certain there will be returns enough. Sometimes just going forward sets Providence into moving. I want to avoid the toll road: so many farthings for a horse, so much money for a wagon. Requiring a toll is a statement of my failure. I don't really want to charge anything for those arriving by stage as it will be our mainstay. Stagecoaches bring fishermen. Beachcombers. Treasure seekers—I might even don my boots and search the hills myself! But I want tourists who will bring their families, fly kites, build fires on the sand, race the waves, and who will come back time and again. Making memories. That's what families need, opportunities to be together in memorable landscapes. I must quote our Lord Byron who noted, "There is pleasure in the pathless woods, There is rapture on the lonely shore." And you would likely quote a Scripture, about the Lord knowing my lot and making my boundaries fall on pleasant places.

I imagine your presence in this pleasant place, Dear

Olivia, making such a lonely shore more palatable. So know my invitation comes to you with the greatest of discretion. You could reside in my hotel and I would ensure another woman of stature would stay as well that you might feel safe. I would light my silver candlesticks at my dining table in your honor, granting you the respect due a future sister-in-law.

I will cease such longings now for fear you will be set off—a term once used here among fur trappers I am told who return to England but "set off" their Native wives. How very different our lives are here, Dear Olivia. How much your visit would bring to me the longings of England.

On a hopeful note, I have found someone to help me build the road. A Netherlander, John Gerritse, and a few other hands I've located will do the work. If only I had all the money secured for that seven-mile road. In that regard, I hope to return to England, seeking final funding even as we begin the work.

It is my great desire to see you while I am there. Perhaps you'll tell me if you've received my letters. At one level, I pray you have not for you have never replied. Perhaps out of respect for my brother you fear that corresponding with me would be unseemly. But I know you are betrothed to him. You will be my sister upon your marriage. It is to my wonderment why he has not married you yet. But then he was always obstinate. And I harbor the fantasy that you broke our engagement not because you no longer cared for me but because you, too, are a captive of heritage, your status requiring that you marry well so as to support your family and marrying sooner rather than waiting until I have made my mark. I know your younger sister must wait to speak her vows until yours have been said. I digress.

Please know of my great desire to see you if only from a distance.

Your forever faithful future brother-in-law,
Herbert Logan, Principal, Elk Creek Road Company

chapter
45

Mary said goodbye to her husband, letting him ponder on her surprise. After he left, she rowed the canoe to her parents' with Belle in the boat smiling up at her mother from her cradleboard, jabbering a language known only to her. Jewell had also sewn trade beads no larger than a grain of sand onto the body of the leather lace straps in the form of a seashell, the intricacy of design a marvel. Belle gave her a one-tooth smile, grabbed her little palms together. She wore red knitted mittens to keep her hands warm in the March weather. Mary had dyed the wool herself. She'd left her hands outside the cradleboard so Belle could bat at the shells hung from the bow.

Jewell had been a precious guide to mothering, even though she wasn't one. How to hold the baby facing away sometimes to calm her. How to place a towel over her face while she nursed to help her focus on latching on to her mother's breast and suckling instead of letting her eyes wander around the room. She was growing in her understanding of what Belle needed and grateful she could provide it. So now, Mary felt confident enough to do what she'd been considering.

The wintering with John had emboldened her. She liked hearing his stories of adventure on the trail, of his dreams to have a stable where people rented horses to ride once they began to come to Cannon Beach. She liked his stories of delivering the mail, meeting people, sharing news. Mary realized she could be a good mother, but it wasn't all she wanted to be. Her own mother had stayed at home and done everything to make her father's and Mary's lives easier, but Mary didn't think she was made of that stuff. She liked adventures. Her mother had found her place caring for family. But Mary was different, and she had decided through the winter that it wasn't bad to be different.

Max ran alongside the canoe on the riverbank as Mary rowed. He barked at the blue heron who startled above them heading for the bay. Nellie quivered at the boat's bow. She didn't like the unevenness of the canoe moving on the water. Belle seemed to like the motion as she giggled. Reaching her destination, Mary docked the canoe, lifted the baby and cradleboard, and secured it on her back. Max barked his excitement of something new.

She had irritated John by not telling him of her surprise, but if she could secure Herbert's consent for her idea, it would be harder for John to disagree on the merits.

An arrow of pelicans flew overhead as she approached her parents'. She shivered in the cold. Maybe taking Belle all that way wasn't a good idea. The weather could change quickly.

"I'll borrow that Baldy horse of my papa's. He's slow but steady. You'll ride just fine in your little board." Jewell had told her to talk to Belle not as a child speaking to a doll but as though she could understand, like talking to a sister. "But my mama will likely say that an overnight journey isn't good for a baby. What do you say to that, Miss Mary Belle?" Mary called the dogs, then made her way up the bank. It was good to listen to an inner voice, Mary thought, do a little something out of the ordinary that called for a bit of bravery. She prayed that inner voice had her best interests at heart.

It was William who came laughing first through the door. "Look who's here, Amanda. It's our girl and our grandbaby. Just thought of that, why they call them grandbabies." He chuckled as he lifted the cradleboard from Mary's back.

Amanda didn't hide her frown. She did like Jewell, but there should be a distance. Indigenous people were, well, different. That cradleboard was but one example, wrapping a child, keeping it from kicking its legs and strengthening its limits. She may not know much about infants, but she did know *that* much. Why, such swaddling could prevent muscle growth and keep a baby from learning to walk, she was sure of it.

William gazed at Belle in that board. "How nice of you to come visit. And you picked the perfect day." He was always so cheery. "The wind has made its peace and gone to sleep. For the moment."

"Oh, wow!" Merritt slipped in behind William. "Look at that baby grow. She's big as a yearling piglet."

"Not quite pork size," Mary said. She stretched. The cradleboard must be heavy as Belle at eight months certainly wasn't.

"Whataya doin' here, Mrs. G?"

"We've planned a little outing to Cannon Beach and decided to stop by here first for Belle to see her grandparents. But I've had second thoughts about going over the mountain and spending the night with an eight-month-old. So . . ." Mary flashed that smile that Amanda knew her father couldn't resist. Well, she couldn't either. "Papa and Mama, would you be willing to have Belle for the day and tomorrow? I plan to surprise John when he rests halfway between Seaside and Tillamook."

"We'd love that," William answered for her. "Wouldn't we, Amanda? I've missed the little tyke. I always like having a babe around."

Amanda wondered if that was a poke at her. They had only Mary "around." Though he'd never expressed disappointment in her, only in the sadness of the circumstance of her miscarriages, those babies who came but didn't stay.

"What about feeding her while you're gone, Mary? And is it wise to leave a child overnight without at least one of her parents? She'll miss you."

"I'll miss her too, but I think it'll be okay." Mary took Belle from the cradleboard, handed her back to her father. "I'll leave milk, but she drinks cow's milk with maybe some cornmeal soaked in it. She eats real food. I'm not sure she gets enough from me, though Merritt here thinks she's piggy-like." Mary ruffled the boy's hair. "You've stretched up too, I see. What are you, eleven?"

"Twelve." He beamed.

Amanda looked at Merritt, hoping he hadn't really understood this talk of breastfeeding. She was relieved to see he'd moved his attention from the child to the dogs.

"I'm sure we'll be just fine." William again. "Won't we, Amanda. You've been missing our girls. You said so yourself just last night."

"Yes, yes. Of course. Let's round up some lunch and you can tell us why you'd leave your baby behind." Did that sound judgmental?

"Let me tell you while I feed her."

"You go into the bedroom to do that. Be private. I'll fix up lunch, then you can tell us all."

Amanda worried about her daughter's decisions. It seemed she was sometimes oblivious to propriety or danger. She supposed it was good in some ways. Otherwise how would Mary have stayed alone on that primitive claim? It was just that the girl mustered up courage for the strangest things. She could just imagine what adventure she was up to. At least she chose a safe place to leave Belle. She was grateful for that. And like William, she did enjoy having a baby to spoil, one whose life she'd been a part of from the beginning. Maybe she could influence this child to not grow up to be a contrary Mary. Yes, this would be an opportunity to shape Belle's days.

chapter
46

John plodded along the Front Road moving the mail forward. They had more than six months on the claim, enough to "prove it up," as the government said. They'd built a cabin, a lean-to barn, a chicken house and fence. Once proved, they could buy the land at the government rate. John still kept the horses at Mary's parents' now that he was back delivering mail—until Herbie gave the word about the road. John patted Prince's neck. They'd soon be at Herbie's place. He was grateful the mail contract came up again since the roadbuilding had not yet started. Delivering mail was a hard job, but it paid well, and they needed the money. But more, he realized he didn't like to be cooped up with a wife and baby around the clock, much as he loved them both.

It was also pretty clear that Mary could handle the claim on her own, even with Belle. She was a natural in the woods, collecting small specimens of plants she'd dry and either press between the leaves of her books or serve to spice up a meal. At night, if Belle was still awake, she'd bundle the babe up and take her out onto the porch to "feel the night breathe," she'd say. Or to catch the stars "blinking their good-nights" through the trees. Mary had a way of seeing the world in both its smallness and what she called its "breadth." He'd misunderstood her, at first thinking she spoke of pastries. He hadn't told her that, embarrassed at his limited English. She was a teacher too. John couldn't have asked for a more cordial woman. Even when he informed her that he'd taken on the mail contract again, she didn't whine nor whimper, instead teasing a surprise.

"Bring me a trinket from Seaside now and then," she'd told him. "Or the newspaper to line the shelves with, once I've read it."

He thought of her sweetness as he approached Herbie's Elk Creek Hotel from the north and squinted. Was that Baldy tied up at the rail? What was that plodding horse doing here? Mary's father must have ridden him. Was something wrong? Was he here to tell him bad news about Mary or the baby? And why not ride Jake? Another horse hung with a tired head, resting, with one leg bent. The halter rope touched the ground. He apparently wasn't tied, just willing to stay there. That horse looked familiar too.

In the background the ocean breathed itself into an incoming tide.

John spurred Prince around driftwood. At the sight of the other mounts, Prince had picked up his pace. The others whinnied. John dismounted, carrying the locked mailbag with him. "William Edwards," he shouted as he came through Herbie's door. "What are you doing here, sir?" He searched the room for his father-in-law.

Joe Walsh, Herbie's fellow remittance man, sat in a chair, his legs splayed out, his chin on his chest, hands clasped over his belly. John could smell the liquor from his stance at the door. Joe must be sleeping it off at Herbert's tonight.

"Papa isn't here. It's me!" Mary stood at the table where it appeared she'd been watching Herbert work on his ships in a bottle. She grinned that grin that always made him faint with love. But this time he resisted that emotion and let the confusion then anger rise up through it. What was she doing here?

"Where's Belle?"

"She's with my parents. I rode Baldy here to meet you. Aren't you happy?"

"This is your surprise? I don't much like the idea of you leaving our Belle behind."

"You do it every day," Mary chimed back.

"Nearly finished, I am," Herbie said. He put up the tools he'd been using—the thread, glue, a little handle with a bend on the end that reminded John of one of Mary's crochet hooks. Joe Walsh slept through it all. John suspected that Herbie was interrupting the tension between him and Mary rather than actually being finished with his ship in a bottle. John had seen dozens of sailors do that work. It had never appealed to him. His fat fingers dissuaded him but also he was a man of big movements. Horse training. Strapping down mailbags. Being jovial with sometimes drunken sailors or calming belligerent recipients of undesired mail.

"Let me fix us some vittles," Herbie offered.

"Oh, let me," Mary said. "That way I can show you what I'm capable of."

John frowned. That was an odd thing for his wife to say. He remembered the mail. "I do have a letter for you, Herbert, ja? When I saw your name, I held it out before the bags were locked. One day I hope there'll be a postal office here. They should call it Cannon Beach when it happens. Cement the name in the sand like the cannons. Any sign of them of late?"

"Not a sighting. I appreciate your allowance, John, saving me the trip to Seaside."

Mary bustled behind him in the kitchen where she cooked, smells of bacon and eggs wafting over him. She was a good cook, he'd give her that.

John pulled the letter from his blouse, handed Herbie the envelope sealed with wax and a crest. "Fancy," John said.

Herbie sat down. "It's from my brother. I told him I'm coming to England, to talk about family investments." John never liked bringing bad news through his deliveries. Maybe he should have had Herbie ride to Seaside or Tillamook to get it so he wouldn't have to see that sadness in his friend's eyes. Family. It could be a trial. John looked up at Mary, who shook her head no. Was she saying he should stay silent?

"I hope it's good news," Mary said. She finished setting the table, then turned back to flip the eggs in the cast-iron skillet, pepper the potatoes. This was fun, cooking for more than just herself and John. And it was a good distraction from the variety of emotions flashing over John's face like a spring squall one always hopes will be quickly followed by a sunbreak.

"It rarely is good news from my brother." Herbie stared at the envelope. Took a deep breath, then opened the letter. A paper fell out and floated to the floor near Mary's feet.

She leaned to pick it up, handed it to Herbie, who accepted it absentmindedly while reading the letter that accompanied it. He cleared his throat. "Aha. Verily. A mixed blessing, indeed."

Mary exchanged looks with her husband as she put the platter on the table in the center of four places of Wedgewood plates. Herbert had lovely silverware too. A bit tarnished. Mary thought that was something she could remedy. John's scowl hadn't lessened. She was in trouble, but she just knew she could cajole him into a better mood. She had before. She had really thought he'd be happy to see her.

Herbie put the letter into his vest pocket. "It seems a bit of celebration is in order. Let me get the silver candlesticks."

"Did I hear celebration?" Joe Walsh scratched at his mustache and unfolded himself, fully awake. "You're the pillow of the community, celebrating at the drop of a cat. And a soft touch ye be too."

Herbie laughed while he rumbled around in his sea chest, pulled out the candlesticks. "Unfortunately, I have no alcohol with which to lift a toast. I find the liquors make my legs ache more. I'd say even weaker, and I have no need of a creeping paralysis with this important venture facing me. Challenging me. Us."

"I have some spirits," her husband said.

"John!"

"Just hauling it for potential medicinal purposes, Mare."

"I've got a wee bottle on me horse. Let me go get 'er." Joe stood tall now, a little bowlegged, but he appeared to Mary to be stable. He blinked rapidly. "Back in a jiffy." He burped, hit the side of the door as he moved through it.

"I shall go with you," Herbie said.

"I'll do it. You gentlemen sit down to eat before it cools off." Mary took Joe's elbow and the two walked out the door. She hoped by the time they returned, John's demeaner would have improved. Maybe her coming here hadn't been a good idea at all. She needed to listen to that inner voice a little more carefully.

chapter
47

las, this is what is.

Herbert swallowed, pursed his lips as he reread the letter, waiting for Mary and Joe to return. He didn't want John to see his concern so he turned his back. The document Mary had picked up from the floor was a banknote for additional pounds, enough to begin—if not finish—the road. The precious road he had hoped one day Olivia would ride a stage down and fall into his arms. But from his brother's letter, it was clear that would never happen. Instead, a date had been set for the wedding, and if he accepted the banknote, he was also agreeing not to contact Olivia again. Contacting her was the highlight of his solitary life even when she had never answered. Could he forgo that small pleasure of writing to her? *That large pleasure.* Maybe he'd keep writing but not send the letters.

He'd accept the note, though. What choice did he have? Going to England now made no sense. He shouldn't have delayed.

"Your food is cooling," Mary said as she returned with Joe walking taller than before. "Joe couldn't find his wee bottle, so we'll do with fresh water from your spring." Mary gave a sidelong glance to her husband. "Let's bless the food. Will you, John?"

Herbert folded the letter. He hoped John hadn't seen him nearly crumble with its contents. Herbert set the candlesticks on the mahogany table he'd had shipped from San Francisco. He sank into his chair. "We are celebrating my brother's remittance of enough pounds to begin the clearing for our seven miles of road. Fresh water is indeed the best liquor for such a venture." He motioned Joe and John to sit. Then Mary.

John prayed, and Mary added, "Amen. Let's have our vittles before they spoil."

Herbert lit the wax taper and John talked about the beeswax candles the Spanish had required their priests to burn.

"Good for us," John said. "It's always a treat when wax from the ship shows up. Sure would like to see those cannons again too. Maybe this time someone can haul them out of the sand to above the tide line, so they stay put."

Mary passed the salt. "I'd like to live closer, to be here when they reappear. Maybe one day." It was always good to have hope.

"You might be an old woman by then." John winked at his wife.

Herbert hadn't considered that the cannons would be much of a draw, but everyone liked a little mystery, a few surprises. Austin had said one of his reasons for planning to build his hotel was to be here when the cannons showed.

Herbert dished up the potatoes with their savory scent. He inhaled. Mary was probably right about moving closer. The Gerritses would be good neighbors if they did.

The food was tasty. Mary had added some spices she'd apparently brought with her. The bacon spoke for itself, fixed crispy as he liked it. And the eggs were as orange as a blood moon, the sign of a well-fed hen. Mary also put out huckleberry jam, finding a tiny silver spoon he must have had in the back of a drawer. His bachelor status loomed obvious. Mary had polished the spoon, probably using the vinegar in his larder and a bit of sand. There was plenty of the latter around.

While they ate, Mary entertained them with stories of Belle or the dogs or even more, the horses. She had an affinity for the equine. Herbert knew that from the time of their miscalculation at Hug Point. She was a good storyteller too and had cajoled John out of some sort of funk he'd been in since his arrival. Maybe it was the food being blessed. Herbert's Episcopal upbringing suggested that prayer mellowed the angry spirit.

"Then one night when I imbibed a bit too much, my old horse just stood there. After I slid off onto the soft ferns on the trail." Joe Walsh began his own storytelling. "I waited there, I don't know how long. I could hear the waves, feel the breeze, and smell the bracken and the horse, of course, but just didn't have the convention to get up. Eventually, the good Lord sent along a Samaritan who helped me onto me horse. 'Do you know where you're going, mate?' they asked. I tells them, indeed I do. But I didn't. Still, no matter, my old mount took me right to me door where I slid off again. But I was at me home. When I came to in the morning, I thought maybe me dear horse had unsaddled hissself and put hissself up in the barn. But he was moseying near the fence line ripping at weeds. What a pal!"

Herbert had heard this story a hundred times, but Joe always added a little twist. This time it was his belief the horse could unsaddle itself and put itself up for the night. Friends. They'd get him through this sense of loss as deep as the sea.

The meal finished, Herbert stood, ready to announce his bedtime and show the others where they could lay their heads when Mary asked if he might sit down for just one minute more.

"Well, of course, Mary." Herbert sat. He really wanted to nurse the wounds of his brother's letter, remember his glorious days walking the formal gardens with Olivia before his father's death and the inheritance going to his brother. He had come to the States to earn enough to make his own mark, hopefully turning it into something that would make Olivia willing to immigrate to America. But his brother's letter had been clear: the date was set. She'd said yes. At least that was what his brother claimed. If he deposited the pounds, his love was lost.

"I thought that might work," Mary concluded.

"I don't think so." John's voice was gruff.

"What? I'm so sorry, my dear Mary. I'm afraid I was distracted."
Were the two of them readying themselves for an argument? Didn't
they know what a gift they had in each other? He'd ask Mary to
repeat herself. And he would focus, put the longing into another
place—with the help from even troubled friends.

chapter
48

"O ur Mary," Amanda said. "Always a surprise, isn't she?"
She held little Belle and bounced her on her knee, securing
her head, though Belle held it up by herself quite well.
Was that unusual for an eight-month-old? Or just typical? Until
Belle turned three, Amanda had no experience about how babies
grew and changed. "Look at you. Look at you." She baby-talked
and the infant giggled. "Yes, you, little Bellie. Look at you." She
snuggled her face to the child's, who twisted her head. Didn't she
like being that close?

"That there's a baby girl!" Merritt touched her little pug nose
with his fingertip.

He was gentle with the child and made it a treat after helping
William milk cows in the morning to play with her. Amanda had
been surprised by his interest, but then she didn't know how they
could attract older-brother kinds of people.

William put his book down. "She's a joy. A little hint of ginger
hair like her mama has."

"Like sprouts in a spring garden." There were too many for her
to count. "It'll fill in. I wonder if Mary's hair curled like that as a
baby." She caught herself, looked at Merritt, but he hadn't seemed
to hear. "I don't see how Mary can leave her even for overnight."

"She wanted to surprise her husband." William was a hopeless romantic. "He won't be staying here tonight, I suspect. John will head straight to Tillamook, then back toward Seaside."

"I hope he brings my order of potatoes. I wish they could make a living on that claim, but they're so far from the pasture on the mountain. I hate it when you have to bring cows through the fern tunnels." She shivered, remembering the one time she'd helped bring cows home and had felt suffocated by the thick ferns. "We're lucky that you selected such a good place for us."

"Oh look, she's fluttering her eyes," William said.

"Just like Mary did before she fell asleep."

William stood behind his wife while she swayed the baby back and forth on her knees. "Maybe all babies do that flutter." Belle fussed. Amanda rocked harder, but it only made the child cry out.

"Here, let me." William lifted the child and put her in the cradle he'd made. The gesture caused Amanda to take in a breath at the separation. She was being silly. This baby wasn't going anywhere. She was here to stay. No need for Jewell's baby board either.

"When'll that baby be able to put herself to bed?" Merritt asked.

"No time soon." William tucked a blanket at Belle's neck. He kept his hand over the child's heart, patted it gently. Why did the child behave better for him than for her? William had been more successful with Mary too, now that she thought about it, getting her to follow routines.

"Time for lunch," Amanda announced.

"I thought you'd never say. This bigger baby in your life is hungry. You, too, I bet, right, Merritt?"

Merritt nodded. The Edwardian clock chimed one, well past lunchtime. Amanda scurried to steam the blue-necked clams William had dug that morning, her heart beating faster with being behind, not having time to scrub and clean as it was important for her to do each morning. Her feet felt heavy as rocks and she moved off-balance as though coming out of a dizziness. Following a pattern calmed her. The baby interrupted that routine. But wasn't that what babies did, remind grandparents that what they thought was important just wasn't?

She took a deep breath, watched as her husband and Merritt dug into the steamed clams. Belle snuffled like a baby kitten as she slept. Maybe having her around would bring a new kind of balance to Amanda. She could hope so. Mary just didn't know what she was missing.

chapter
49

Mary's heart picked up its pace.

Her voice quivered.

John had heard what she said and had frowned, but Herbie, the patron she wanted to hear from, was distracted. She took a deep breath, preparing to repeat herself, when Joe's loud snore gurgled up from his bulbous nose. That remittance man had fallen asleep as soon as he'd finished his supper.

"I say, Mary. If you were speaking to me, I'm afraid I missed it. Let me get Joe settled in the bed and I'll come back, and we can chat. John, would you lend a hand?"

Mary watched her husband on the opposite side of where Herbie lifted Joe's elbow. He was upset, she could tell by the set of his jaw, but he nevertheless helped his friends. She should have chatted with him beforehand, gotten his agreement. But the truth was, she needed Herbie to see that it was a good idea in order to help her convince John—in case he didn't.

She washed up the dishes, put leftover potatoes in Herbie's chiller, and carrying the lantern, took it out to his spring. The moon had risen and she could hear the incoming tide with its mesmerizing touch of sea to sand interrupted in rhythm by a thundering plunge of the waves. She never tired of the sound. It always humbled her to be such a small spot in the vastness of the universe. It's ever-ness reminded her that the tides had been coming and going for eons, giving her hope even on the darkest of days that life continued, steady but with natural disruptions.

She walked back into the hotel and picked up the broom, sweeping up breadcrumbs. She'd take them out in the morning closer to the water and throw them up at the seagulls. She loved doing that but not close to the house as Herbie said those seagulls could be a nuisance. Once he had paying guests in his finished hotel, he didn't want gulls bothering visitors. She had told him that guests would love that the birds came so close, pecking bread off the driftwood porch railings, but Herbert pointed to the white blotches of "used biscuits" that he had to wash off after a stint with them. "What at one time seems charming can become an irritant," he told her. She guessed that was the way of life, if one didn't find a way to change one's attitude toward the irritating parts.

"Now. What was it you were so earnestly telling me, Mary? I'm sorry I was distracted. Just a difficult night, I'm afraid." They were all three sitting at the table now, hot tea before them.

Mary looked at her husband, took a deep breath. It was a risk, she knew. But she also knew that being on the claim alone with Belle for the rest of her days was not what filled her bucket. She was a good mother—but would be a better mother if she listened to what she felt was God's guidance to do good and to follow her heart. "I have an idea for when you begin work on the road."

"Go ahead." Herbie patted his vest as though looking for his pipe, seemed to think better of it, and gave his full attention back to Mary as he rested elbows onto the table.

"You'll need someone providing food for the road crew," Mary began. "And I thought I could be that person. I'm a good cook as you can see. I know how to fish and trap, and I can supplement dried food with fresh that the men will surely appreciate. I can move the camp as needed with Jake or Prince, whichever horse John hasn't brought in to work on the road." She wanted to ask John which horses he would commission—or if he'd acquire others—as part of the clearing work. It would be hard on the animals, and she hoped they'd have plenty of horses to keep trading off, so any one wasn't overworked. She knew how to make soothing pastes for saddle burns or harness abrasions, but that wasn't what she thought was her greatest asset for the roadwork. But if she stopped to discuss the horse supply, the men would move away from her purpose.

"Jewell's summer camp isn't far from here and I could solicit her help too when she's there. But I think I'll be fine managing on my own. Like in the books about the Old West I've read, I'd be your chuckwagon cook, only for road builders instead of cowboys." She nearly chirped with enthusiasm.

"What do you think, John?" Herbie turned to her husband.

"No, now, I'm making the offer," Mary said, directing Herbie back to her.

John's face turned red.

"But of course I wouldn't do such a thing without John's approval." Mary smiled, licked her dry lips. "I just wanted to know if it was even feasible before I chatted with my husband about it. No sense getting into a . . . discussion that might prove . . . intense that had no hope for resolution." She had dropped the word "quarrelsome."

Her potential employer looked at John. "Well, of course it's feasible. Indeed, I will need a camp cook. But I had thought about a Chinese chef from Astoria perhaps. Their families are still in China, so no separating them to worry about."

"I wouldn't be away from John."

"But Belle," John said. "She can't be out there in a tent."

Mary wanted to say that she surely could, but it would be difficult to accomplish the work with a baby about. And she liked seeing that John put Belle in a prominent place. "We'd see her on weekends, of course. She's eating oats, not dependent on me. And cow's milk. She'd be happy with my parents. You've watched how they dote on her. My mother is . . . blissful when Belle's there. Papa too. Maybe they'd bring her for visits. They'd be happy and you and I would be together and we'd have two incomes to help us fill the purse. Not just for our claim, John. But for building up the occupier shelter I burned down. I know that disaster has cut your mind like a razor clam."

"She has some strong arguments, John." Herbie made everything sound important. "The road company could use someone like Mary."

"And you've talked with your parents and now Herbert before you even mention it to me? A wife does that, what kind, ja?"

His English was fractured, so Mary knew he had skipped from the heart of his anger to its origin: being hurt.

"I haven't spoken with them, John, not before talking with you. And Herbie. It's almost as though I've been replaced by my Belle in my mother's eyes already, she's so besotted with our child." Did she really think that? She did. Mary smiled at John. "I wouldn't join you until April."

Herbert tapped his finger on his upper lip.

"And of course he wouldn't hire me without your consent, would you, Herbie?"

"No, that I would not. I'm an innovator but not a fool." He smiled at them both. "But I do think it's feasible. Not with any lady, but Mary, I say, you're quite the stalwart woman, if I may use that term. A woman any man would be proud to stand beside."

Mary thought he looked wistful when he said that, and she wondered again about the letter he'd just gotten. Did it have to do with a longed-for stalwart lady to stand beside him?

"What do you say, John? Do you want you and I to speak of it separately?"

"Don't see how it would make any difference. You've covered all the bets."

Had she humiliated him by not talking about this first? She was sorry if she had. She'd make it up to him.

"I was a bit afraid you'd say no, and I didn't want to have that sadness without even a chance to have Herbie say yes, if that makes sense."

John brushed a crumb Mary had missed into his palm; knocked it on the floor. She'd sweep again later.

"Ja, I marry you for your sauciness so can hardly be upset when you display it."

"My sauciness? That's perfect then, as that's what I'll be doing for you all—making up sauces."

"Hunger makes the best sauce. My mother used to say that," Herbie said.

"Not having you with Belle is a bother, though. Seems like a young one needs its mama every day."

"Many infants are raised by other than their mamas. That's what nannies are for, isn't that so, Herbie? English nannies are often famous characters in books." And then Mary's memory flashed on that photo where a child stood isolated, a woman sheltering a boy. There was something familiar in that photograph. Was it the woman? Was she a nanny or a mother? Why was her mother so upset when she looked at the image?

"Mary?" John touched her hand.

She'd lost her train of thought. His touch brought her back. "And they turn out just fine, children raised by others. What do you say, John? It's only for a few months."

He stayed silent for a long time. Mary sighed. She'd offered an adventure that kept with their mutual goals, she'd expressed her expectations and her needs. At least she hoped she had. But apparently it wasn't enough. She rose to put the snuffer on the candles in the silver sticks to save them. She turned up the wick in the lantern. Herbert did pull out his pipe now, tap it and suck on the stem, the tiny sound the only *wheeze* in the room. What would she do if John denied her? In marriage could only the husband decide? She hoped if that was the case that she'd married a wise man and not one who saw a deity when he looked in the mirror each morning.

chapter
50

They snuggled at Herbie's hotel while she tried to explain to John how she didn't mind being at the claim but not for always. She tried to share with him it wasn't that she couldn't be alone with Belle but that she felt a need to be part of something bigger and she wasn't always sure what that was. She could only card and spin and plant so much. But being the road crew cook thrilled her. "That's a funny word, isn't it? Being thrilled by the possibility of hard work."

"I don't know of women who pursue such," he said. The sea sang through the open window. "But it was a thrill for me to run away to sea as a boy. And the mail route. It has its moments of thrill." He said "tril," still working on his pronunciations.

"On the mountain?"

John turned over to face her, pushing back her ginger hair with his calloused fingers. "Yes. I took a spill a while back. Jake kept his head and prevented me from sliding over the edge and I pulled myself back up."

"You never said."

"I didn't want to worry you. To add to it, the Tillamook People were burning up the slope. I felt all manner of peril. That's how to say it, yes?"

"The trail can be worrisome. But there is danger everywhere. One can't keep the fear of it from doing our duty."

"It is a duty to deliver the mail, but I don't know if duty calls for you to cook for a road crew. Being a mother and father is duty." John turned onto his back, hands behind his head. "Delivering mail is just a well-paying job."

"But what you deliver is important, for people, for the community. I'd like to try that sometime, deliver the mail."

"Oh, Mare. Now that's an argument you'll have to make long and hard before I'd let my wife do such dangerous work."

"It was just a thought."

"Ja. But one to not dwell on." He sighed. "We give the cooking a try. See how it goes. It would be nice to snuggle with my wife after a long day." He kissed her, then was soon asleep, leaving Mary to consider if delivering the mail might well be a task in her future. But a task wasn't an obligation as duty demanded. First, she needed to prove herself to Herbert and her husband that their faith in her as a cook was warranted. And she had to get her parents on board. That should be a piece of cake, as people said. Carrot cake, one of her specialties.

Mary rode beside her husband on Baldy until they hit the mountain trail that required single file. The ocean breeze threatened Mary's straw hat, and she pushed the butterfly hatpin deeper to keep it atop her head. They were above the hawks that dipped and dropped below them. On the upside of this section, the grasses pushed against the morning wind. Just below the trail, on the slope before the drop-off to the sea, birds flitted low over the ferns and brambles and stubby trees that hovered at the edge. It was always a difficult part of the journey, this trail, but there was no better view of the sea than from here. John had shouted his "hello" and waited for a response before they'd started around the ridge. They were early and the sky had cleared of the morning mist.

On the far side, starting down, mud formed, and once again Mary was grateful for Prince's sure-footedness and this time,

Baldy's plodding demeanor. When they could ride up next to each other, Mary chirped, "Herbert looked excited as we left, didn't he?"

"Ja."

"Don't you wonder what else was in the letter? I mean, he had the money for the road, what he'd been hankering after for years. And yet his eyes were sad." She paused. "Maybe getting what one wishes for in the end isn't always the great reward. It takes away the hopefulness."

"Or changes it. I suppose I feel a bit of that with my wife deciding not to be a wife at home but working on a trail."

"I see your worry, John. But you were never going to stay put on a claim. You were roaming from the time you were a lad and far from home too. I don't have quite those wandering legs, but I do like adventure. It pleases me to do something for others, like helping with the road."

"Being a good mother does for others."

"I can do both and our Belle will figure it out in time that she has more than just a mother and father in her life. She has a grandma and grandpa and one day a brother and sister and each brings something new to her family. I don't think that's a bad thing."

Baldy lagged back, depositing horse apples on the trail, and Mary spurred him forward to catch up to John.

"If you really feel that I shouldn't do this, or if my parents decline to care for Belle, you know I won't accept the position. You know that, don't you?"

"Ja. I know. But in future, even if you think I won't agree, you must confer with me first, ja? It is courtesy. Wife to husband."

"Yes. I agree. And before you take on a mail claim or decide not to, you'll talk with me, isn't that so? It is only fair, John."

"But sometimes a decision must be made. What then? When we two might disagree?"

"First, we pray," she said. "Then we listen and hope we hear more than just the tide rolling driftwood around."

"Ja. That we do."

They quieted then, each privy to their own thoughts. Mary

worked in her mind the arguments to use with her parents. How well they'd managed with Belle overnight would be the true test. If they said no, she had a backup plan. Jewell came to mind. Mary hurried along, giddiness riding with her. Her husband had called her saucy with hopefully the right blend of spice.

chapter
51

I t's difficult to understand," Amanda said. "Isn't it, William? I mean, abandon Belle just to cook for the crew?" She set the teapot on the table, didn't care that Mary might be offended.

"It'll help us with our finances," Mary said, not waiting for her father to respond. "And I like being helpful."

"You have always been a help with the chores," William said.

"I never got along with bovines," Amanda said. "Even in Minnesota." But it wasn't the cows—it was what she remembered when she thought of them. How afraid she'd been with William in the barn and she and Mary at the house. Anyone from New York could come and snatch Mary back. Might the Fisks be searching for a grandchild to claim? "Maybe little Belle would enjoy the summer outing *with* you, Mary. Nestled in the trees, working toward the sands of that cannon beach." And be far from where anyone could find either of them. No. The Fisk family wouldn't know about a new descendant.

Mary frowned. "It would be difficult to have her with me. She's crawling and those little knees wouldn't last long in forest duff. Plus, it'll be a fair amount of work fixing two big meals a day for the crew as well as a lunch. And I can help with the horse teams too. They'll need several to scrape the road, won't they, John?"

"You're good with this, John?" William asked.

John inhaled. "Ja, I understand Mary's vanderlust, maybe I call it. And I get the pleasure of her company." He smiled at his daughter. "I know our Belle will be in good hands."

"It's only for a few months, Mama. I intend to prove to them that I can deliver, the way John delivers the mail, through hailstorms and gale winds."

"Delivered," John corrected. "I let the contract go once we build roads."

Amanda was never more certain than at that moment that Mary had been birthed by someone more bold, more outgoing than she would ever be. Maybe that had been part of the tussle she and Mary had had through the years, such different personalities. What adventures would she come up with as a mother? A wife? A woman? Amanda would do everything she could to let Mary and Belle know they were loved and that Amanda would always be there for them. Wasn't that the greatest gift of family? All this other talk about adventure, that was nonsense if you asked her. But no one had.

chapter
52

The Elk Creek Road activities began beneath blue coastal skies. Herbie marked the day in the new decade. He and a local man had surveyed the road and marked with red paint the trees that would have to be taken out. He'd decided early on to remove as few as possible, as the firs and cedars were tall and wide and required time and extensive labor to extract. Instead, there would be many turns and twists going around trees and removing bracken and brush. Men from around the region signed on for the work, and after the first few days, John proposed a bet: an English pound for every turn in the road more than one hundred. Several workmen had taken the bet and laughed—in the beginning. The days were long and often hot, and the men washed in the creek before supping on Mary's evening meal or waking to the smell of fresh fish, eggs, and pancakes too. She packed a light lunch of bread and cheese wrapped in swatches of calico they popped into their pants, advising the men, "Don't let your horses pull them from your pockets."

Herbert limited himself to two letters a week he wrote to Olivia. He put the postage on them as though he'd mail them. But to honor his forced agreement with his brother, he didn't send them. He put them on a shelf next to the candlesticks. Telling her about the trials and triumphs of the project strengthened him. This road was likely the masterpiece of his life. His leg aches and occasional paralysis—worse when it rained—reminded him that his days were finite. He focused on his road. He knew it wasn't his, exactly, but his heart and soul were more wrapped up in it than any of the other investors. Some, like James Austin, had the resources to build a hotel at the southern end of the beach and, like his Elk Creek Hotel, it would be ready when the road was complete. Herbert sold lumber for such construction so he could hardly complain.

Herbert had secured several teams of horses that came from Nehalem and Seaside and the new settlers on Neahkahnie Mountain. It was good work for many trying to make a go of it as dairymen, vegetable farmers, and loggers, of course. There was something magnificent about the way the teams, often one behind the other with land scrapers, sculpted out the road, foot by struggling foot. And twice a week he wrote of these moments to Olivia, knowing she'd never read his thoughts but with the hope that perhaps after his death the letters would be delivered to her. He'd have to put that into his will, he supposed, not that he could expect his brother to honor that request. Something more to do. But first, finish the road and then the additions to his Elk Creek Hotel. He had the structure complete but needed to furnish all sixteen bedrooms to be ready for guests. He allowed himself to be excited about the rooms having themes, something Mary had suggested. He'd written of that to Olivia. He'd have one with wallpaper he'd ordered to replicate the flowers and birds brightening the parlor walls of Olivia's family home. Maybe one day, she'd feel at home here if she visited these golden sands.

The road activity ushered in Mary's launch of herself toward purpose and Cannon Beach. It was where she'd longed to be since she first saw the waves roll onto the sand. Crying Sands, Jewell called them. If not living at Cannon Beach, she longed to at least be a part of that place in some way, and now she was. Life on the North Fork was fine, an adventure, but she dreamed of living where she could hear the waves at night and help build a community too. Now she could do both.

Mary, with the budget Herbie gave her, bought local produce. The road was a boon for those raising chickens and selling butter and eggs. She often baked biscuits on top of her Dutch oven over an open fire. And Herbie's stove allowed her to fix a few pot pies of chicken and crust. Mary used the bottom of an Arbuckle's Coffee can to cut the dough and sometimes biscuits. Herbert wouldn't have called them biscuits. To his British sensibilities, biscuits were like American cookies or crackers, not flaky little puck-like pastries that the workers split open and piled high with butter and cheese or Mary's jams. Sometimes she served them with gravy thick and flavorful, nestled beside eggs. She baked the biscuits weekly while she waited for supplies at the Elk Creek Hotel. But she also spent hours fishing, shooting ducks, then plucking the feathers for pillows and comforters while soaking the meat in a salt brine, readying it for supper. In the pathless woods, she picked currants and new sprouts of greens that she mixed with her sauces.

The pleasure of her purposeful roaming and the knowledge that she was a part of something important made her feel full as one of those hot-air balloons she read about. She did miss little Belle and felt guilty for not wanting to give up this adventuring, as she thought of it, just to stay home with her baby.

What kind of mother am I?

What had Jewell told her once? To shed guilt from her shoulders she should make a personal change. Well, she'd make notes in her journal to share with Belle, which she did while she waited at the hotel for the egg farmers and the sack of flour being delivered by the postman. She wrote so Belle would know what her parents did to open up the beach for families seeking respite from a world beyond them, all to access the golden sands and be humbled by the ocean, its waves and tides. She supposed some might say it wasn't much to contribute, but Mary saw it differently. John would remark that was no surprise. She saw many things differently.

She kept the journal not with her but on one of Herbert's shelves, next to a pile of letters he was apparently waiting to mail,

208

perhaps all at once, to someone named Olivia. She liked the idea that Herbie had a secret love somewhere across the "pond," as he often spoke of the ocean separating Britain from America. She hoped one day he'd tell her about the woman. Mary did like a bit of gossip, though it was never mean-spirited. She just liked stories, she supposed. And made them up for Belle if she didn't have someone else's to share.

It was on a warm morning that Mary had a few words with the mail deliverer as he rode toward the Elk Creek Hotel. Prince nickered to the postman's horse and Max barked his arrival too. The postman was late on his way to Tillamook, he said, but he wondered if she might not have a spot of tea he could take to rest himself and his horse too. Mary obliged. She heated the water and the pot before adding the tea leaves. To save on Herbie's budget, she often boiled spruce tree needles. She loved the scent as well as the taste. They chatted about the perils of his route.

"It's tough work," he told her. "We are the heart of commerce. One of your biscuits, Mary? If you have enough." Mary handed him the pastry. "Keeping our eyes out for things to report back about, new settlers, almost like we're part of the census recordings happening this year," he continued. "Important work though it is dangerous. That it is, delivering the mail."

"So I've heard."

The postman had a walrus mustache, and crumbs from Mary's biscuits sat below his nose caught on the gray hairs. "Least when the road's finished, we'll have an alternative to the Front Road." He sipped his tea. "Guess I best be on my way," the postman sighed and stood up. "Thanks for the tea."

"Oh." Mary's eyes grazed Herbie's shelf where she kept her journal. "I wonder if you'd be willing to take these letters with you, save Mr. Logan from having to post them at Seaside. He's stamped them and everything."

"Why not? I get his tea and he gets my service."

She hoped Herbie would be happy she'd forwarded his intention without his having to make an extra trip.

chapter

53

Mary's heart squeezed in envy and joy when her parents brought Belle to Cannon Beach for the Fourth of July and Belle's first birthday celebration. The dogs bounded about and acted happy to see her. That was more than she could say for her child. Belle thrived, wearing her red floppy hat her grandmother had knit for her. She'd outgrown the outfit Mary had sewn and now wore a little sundress her mother had apparently crocheted. Even as Mary reached out to hold her child for the first time in weeks, Belle twisted back toward her grandfather, who reassured her, "It's fine, Belle Baby, your mama's got you."

Mary wondered if she did.

Belle squirmed in Mary's arms, her little face with pink cheeks turned often toward the sounds of dogs barking or gulls flying overhead, squawking at the sea, pointing at the sky. Their sound was more forlorn than Mary remembered. She had to reacquaint herself with her daughter, that was all, though when Belle fussed and twisted and put both arms out to her mother, Mary felt as empty as an abandoned pot left behind in the dunes.

"She took her first steps," her mother said. "I'm so sorry you missed that." It was the price one paid for adventure. Maybe she paid too much.

Jewell came to the event with several other Clatsop-Nehalem

people and the two women chattered like squirrels catching up. Mary ignored her daughter's penchant for her parents instead of her own company. Well, it gave her more time to visit with friends. Even Will and Merritt came, the boy remembering Mary's wedding song, breaking out into the chorus, "I'll stay no matter how." Mary blushed.

Real music came from a traveling fiddler, and as the night wore on, fires were lit on the beach and people danced in the sand. Some community souls brought fireworks they shot out over the beach to the oohs and aahs that rose spontaneously from hardened workmen and small children alike.

There was something peaceful for Mary, knowing that all over the coast and inland and around the nation, people celebrated the founding of the country with the explosion of colorful light in the dark sky just as her family did. Belle's first birthday rode on the tails of such an august occasion. Mary sat on the blanket, Belle asleep in her mother's arms, while Mary wondered: Would each year on Belle's birthday be a reminder to Mary that time marched on? And time carried the weight of regret with it. How one balanced the burden would determine how fast and far one could travel.

After the Fourth and Belle's birthday celebration, John found himself missing little Belle. He guessed that was the reason for the emptiness he carried. He hadn't missed his family when he left the Netherlands so he didn't recognize that longing. Still, he enjoyed the bantering between Mary and the workmen as they ate. They had made progress such that they soon approached Elk Creek, the terminus of the work. He felt a pride in his wife's skills. She was especially affectionate to him as well, singling him out for the biggest piece of fish or an extra chunk of huckleberry pie with a glob of cream she'd whipped up with her strong arms. In all, it had been a good season of effort and a part of him wasn't looking forward to its ending—except for having more time with Belle. And Mary. In their shared blankets at night, they talked about their future, opening doors to ideas they hadn't considered before. Marriage apparently did that, two committed people growing and changing and discovering futures they had never imagined before when they first "went to sea in a sieve." That Mary and her poems. Now she had *him* spouting those phrases.

In August 1890, the Elk Creek Road was completed enough to have its own celebration. It ended close to the front of Herbert's Elk Creek Hotel, on the north side of Elk Creek. Travelers would arrive at his establishment first, well before Austin's. That was fitting, Mary thought. After all, Herbie had put most of the money into the venture.

John had won his bet with the few takers, as there were more than one hundred turns in the road: one hundred eleven, to be exact. It didn't cost the bettors much and it was quite a story later, helping to celebrate the builders who had managed such a feat. There still wasn't a bridge across Elk Creek and there were dips and ravines where horses and wagons might get bogged down in mud. But it was a road that would save hours of travel time from Portland, Astoria, Seaside. During high tide, it also shortened the route beyond to Nehalem and Tillamook. There was even an article in the Portland paper about the road opening up at last to the most amazing beach on the north Oregon coast.

Dignitaries came for the August event, bringing a wagon or two down the road. Mary and other women prepared a lunch for the fifty or so people who listened to speeches and the stories the workmen told about their adventures. Mary's parents brought Belle again, who waddled in front of the hotel where the speakers sent their praises, Max walking beside the child wherever she went. Nellie leaned into Mary.

Before bedding down on the sand near the hotel, John and Mary snuggled with Belle between them in their bedrolls. Both dogs lay beside them. The horses were hobbled nearby, her little family, together.

With the Elk Road finished, they were about to enter a new adventure, Mary knew that. But they weren't sure what it would be. "Maybe I could work for Herbert at the hotel, be his cook?" Mary proposed. "And you could operate a stable for people to ride on the beach."

John laughed. "We need a few more residents in cottages or using the hotel before they'd need horses enough for us to make a living at it." He paused. "I can try to get the mail contract back." He pulled the blanket up around Belle as the night air cooled.

"But that means we'll be separated again. I've been thinking." Mary leaned on her elbow, her body a cover over Belle and close to John. "Maybe we should sell the claim. Buy another, somewhere closer to here, this beach. I've always loved it, John. We could have cows and sell the milk and cheese to tourists. And residents, when they come." John lay silent for so long Mary thought he'd gone to sleep. She spoke a little louder. "I realize something I didn't know before working on the road. I really need escapades, John. You probably understand that, sailing around the world."

"A man thrives on adventure."

"I think a woman does too. At least this woman does."

"This cooking for a crew, it was a temporary ting."

Ting. She heard the misspoken word. She stroked the cheek of her child, the being she'd carried and loved.

"Temporary, yes. But I loved it. Does that make me a bad mother?"

John took his time responding. Then, "Nee. You're a good woman, a good partner, a good mother."

Warmth filled her. "It's that I felt . . . unfinished, even with Belle when we were on the claim, only seeing people every now and then, you off on the mail route, having 'exploits.'" She emphasized that last word, hoping he would see what she was trying to tell him. Tell herself in the process.

"Ja. A husband wants a happy wife, and I did marry you because you saw things a little different."

Mary relaxed. "We'll think about what comes next then, together."

She lay back down, fluffed the quilt around them, smelled the sea air in her child's hair. She'd missed some moments watching her daughter grow, but she vowed to pay more attention in the future.

"Maybe the adventure now is raising a family," John said. His voice was soft. Belle snuffled in her sleep, an endearing sound.

Mary caught her breath. "Yes. But there is room for more." *There has to be.*

The little Gerritse family watched stars poke the night sky, making it look like holes in a giant black sieve.

Mary listened to the waves murmur. "Family first, now. I agree." She really thought she did.

Herbert felt a great sense of pride in the road's completion. He wrote of it in his Olivia letters that he now kept in a dresser drawer. He had noticed right away that the letters were missing and had asked Mary if she knew what had happened to them.

"They were there when the postman stopped by for tea. I . . . I handed them to him to save you the trip to Seaside. Should I not have done that?"

Herbert had caught his breath, but it was past doing anything about, those missives arriving across the ocean by now. There had been nothing romantic in them. They were an account of what turned out to be quite an amazing feat. The letters delivered in England were the result of an accident, nothing he had intended. He might let his brother know that, but perhaps he didn't need to. Olivia might not even read them. His brother likely intercepted them, asserting his right as her husband. The Gerritse marriage practices would twist his brother into a pretzel with their shared decisions. His brother as a husband would be as arrogant as an older brother. At least Herbert thought they were married by now. It was done. *What is, is.* Now his task was to put aside thoughts of an unrequited love—or one not allowed to go forward. The road was his love now. Maintaining it his new goal, his monthly remittance check, the kiss on his cheek, his fuel to keep going.

chapter
54

The road did bring commerce, Herbie was pleased about that. Busy people needed a place of respite where the sea pulled far and flat toward the horizon; then in its time returned to swell around Haystack Rock and, a bit away, Hug Point and a half dozen more rocks distinctive enough to carry a name. And with commerce came competition. Herbert knew that would happen when James Austin finished his hotel near Arch Cape, a land formation at the southern end of the beach.

The road contributed to Austin's success by being the means to bring their 122-reed organ to Austin's hotel. The wagon got stuck more than once, horses strained, their efforts leaving gouges that Herbie had to regrade and fill while Mrs. Austin held her cheeks in worry. "The tongues are very fragile," she told him.

"I say," Herbie said, "most tongues are." They got the organ delivered, though, and Mrs. Austin took the time to thank him with a fresh-baked huckleberry pie.

The Austin structure wasn't as luxurious as Herbert's spruce wood construction, but when Austin's opened in the spring of 1891, it featured Lydia Austin at the reed organ and every week thereafter through the summer, playing the latest tunes like "The Volcano of Delight" and "McFadden Learning to Waltz." There wasn't any room for waltzing at the Austin House, but tea and sassafras and listening fed the spirits of those who came to vacation. Herbie had visions of people building cottages they'd close for the winter and reopen to the sea mists come spring. Locals would know the tourists and welcome their return.

Friendly competition between the two hotels gave options for those drawn like magnets to the sea. Mrs. Austin hung flower baskets to make their establishment homey and covered a walkway to the ocean with shells. At the Elk Creek Hotel, Herbert imported wines and beers to give his establishment a more European bent. People could order up special-occasion moments to include silver servings and sometimes Herbert's candlesticks at their table. He introduced amuse-bouche, from the French, served before a meal, something tasty—and free. Mary learned after prodding him at the Fourth of July celebration that the word meant "mouth amuser." Mary laughed. "Ha. A new name for Joe Walsh's tongue-wrangling words."

"Indeed. Joe told me once to 'illiterate' the competition," Herbie said, "even while my competition was also an investor. Oh, and he said to me that you needed a 'champagne insultant.' And he hadn't even been imbibing at the time."

Mary threw biscuit crumbs to the gulls. "Have you applied to establish a post office at your hotel?"

"James Austin is more likely to get the postal designation as he is a citizen while I'm not."

And Austin did.

Once the Austin Hotel claimed the federal designation, the postman from Seaside and the postman from Tillamook would meet to exchange their mailbags and sometimes passengers at Arch Cape, bypassing Herbie's establishment altogether. Herbie was there at the opening to see James proudly stand behind the counter wearing an official postal service cap with the mailbag key on a leather thong around his neck. James even got to name the post office, and this Crying Sands Beach, officially as Cannon Beach. He had chosen the site he had because he believed that one day those cannons from the *Shark* would reappear. He often walked the streams after a king tide to see if they'd been washed up that far inland. He regaled his guests with the story and the possibility of them seeing those guns for themselves.

Herbie fumed after that ceremony. It seemed everyone had a dream, and finding the cannons was Austin's. It was another attraction for his hotel. Herbie would promote finding them for his guests as well.

As for Herbert's finest claim to fame—the road he'd built—it soon appeared that maintaining it was a much harder task than he'd imagined. The grades needed constant scraping. After a windstorm, there were often fallen trees over the roadways that had to be removed. People sometimes got their wagons stuck and they'd walk to get a team to come and drag them out. Not all that happy about it either. Because he was the largest investor, having put $1,500 into the road, he felt responsible for its maintenance. Not unlike relationships, Herbie mused, as he finished his latest unsent letter to Olivia. Maintenance wasn't thought of much in the joy of beginnings. But it was essential in all relationships.

Herbie's remittance check was first late and then did not appear at all. He had no illusions. By accepting the money from his brother, he had agreed not to write to Olivia. But he had—though not intentionally. His letters had been posted. His brother had responded by cutting him off as though he was a child who hadn't earned his allowance.

As much as he'd hated it, users of the road were going to have to pay a toll. His project would become known not as the Elk Creek Road so much as the shortened version: the Toll Road. Herbert seethed. It took the bloom from the achievement. Still, he knew it was the road that would grow the town, the road that was his legacy. Like a demanding wife, the turns and twists to Cannon Beach would keep him focused as he collected those tolls.

chapter
55

Johnny Gerritse was born July 10, 1891, at Mary's parents' place in Nehalem. A first son. Mrs. Ef and Jewell showed up for the delivery of a blond-haired, blue-eyed boy who looked like his father. No one had told Jewell, she just had a sixth sense about where she was needed, a talent Mary envied. John arrived a day later on the mail route and he kissed Mary on her nose. "A good job you did!" Then he had Mary make signs he took around Nehalem announcing *A baby Gerritse boy arrives!* "A Netherland's custom," he told her. Jewell left her parents sooner than Mary hoped, and within the week, Mary returned to the claim as she and John had agreed she would do.

Mary bit her tongue into silence when both children cried at once and wouldn't be comforted. What she wanted to do was to howl with them. "Lucky John," became Mary's mantra, though when her son reached to pat her face with adoration in his eyes, she thought, *Lucky me. John is missing this.*

"A mix-up at the original survey." John had ridden in, put up Prince, stomped his brogans on the porch steps, and fell into the rocking chair, his head back, floppy hat on his knee. "I can't buy

218

the land for the lower amount. And we can't own the land, we can't sell. All our work for naught. You say that word, ja?"

"Naught. Yes. But we can still stay here?" She couldn't imagine tenting with two children.

"We can never own this place, Mare."

They'd gotten a rug to put over the rough boards John had laid, and Belle played there now with Nellie, the dog's eyes bright, tongue out, waiting to snatch at the rolling target. Belle pushed the ball of yarn off while Nellie ran to get it, accompanied by the girl's squeals of delight.

"Maybe that was why the occupier's site had been abandoned, a survey mix-up."

"I think about what you say, to sell. But now we can't. I make a poor decision those years ago." He sighed. "I say we find another place we can prove up. Start over."

Even though she felt separated from adventure, to leave behind so many memories . . . "What happened to 'I'll stay no matter how'?"

"Ja, you wrote those words."

"And you sang them, more than once."

John nodded, held her gaze.

Why am I being disagreeable? He's doing the best he can. So am I.

Mary handed Johnny to him. "If we're leaving, let's pick a place near Cannon Beach."

Mary had cross-stitched a puffin on the pillow. John pulled it out from behind himself, punched at it. Johnny's little fists followed suit. "Ja. I find new work. We move when I find a job and place, better."

"Look for land near Cannon Beach?"

"Ja. I try."

Mary felt her spirits lifted. Something new on the horizon.

Later that evening after the children were in bed, John told her that they didn't have the resources to buy at that golden beach. "Investors even before the road was built bought up the prime properties. They sell to such as us, but we cannot afford for only a hundred feet of seafront. No one can make a living on that. Even renting it out to summer guests wouldn't be enough for a growing family."

So Mary waited to see what John came up with though she was like a horse held back, wishing she could be out there making things happen. She had nothing to offer but acceptance of what he proposed, all her energy going into her children. The chickens. The garden and gates, keeping predators out. Most of them. Not the ones that kept her off-balance with the weight of her soul wanting more.

John came home a few weeks later, having found them a place to rent near Stanley Lake, closer to Seaside where he had found work. "At least its near water," he told her. "It has a shoreline if not a beach."

Mary packed essentials into carpetbags, including John's blanket, and left a note of welcome on the table to whoever would occupy their home. Then with one child before each of them on horseback, the Gerritse family rode away, dogs trailing behind.

John took a job running a Seaside hotel while Mary stayed at the lake cabin. One big room, no leaks. She made an adventure of new views, watching ducks land. Belle squatted to make mud pies on the banks while Johnny blinked beneath his cap, watching the dogs splash. Mary hauled washtubs near the shore to avoid having to carry buckets to the cabin and built the fire beneath them. She had plenty of water close by to put out errant flames.

Mary thought of these months at the lake as nurturing roots, paying attention to what lay beneath that would one day sprout. She wasn't afraid here, had gotten used to all the new sounds. John spent most nights at home. During the day, she struggled with the babies, alone, but found solace reading bedtime stories to her children. A rescue trip to her parents would take hours.

"I have found a place," John said. She was too exhausted to argue. During a hailstorm, they moved into a cabin on 160 acres south of the Tillamook-Clatsop county line closer to Mary's parents.

"At least you listened," Mary told him. A small sandy beach wasn't far from the property near the mountain's base.

"Ja and I quit the hotel. Back to the mail and a midweek rendezvous. French word, yes?"

"Yes," Mary said. He held Johnny and they watched Belle run on the sand. "This will be a good place for us. It's a claim? Like before?"

"Some different. We prove up for five years, this one. Then it is ours so long as we stay here, never abandon even for a short time."

"We'll stay no matter what?"

"We'll stay no matter how."

On weekends, John worked to make their cabin more livable. And he hunted, selling surplus elk meat to help supplement the purse the mail route filled.

She knew John did his best to make things easier for her. On his one night midweek, he insisted she ride on the beach for a time of rest and checked the cinch when she rode. He put tooth powder on her brush before he left. But on weekends, he was preoccupied with necessary tasks on the farm. Fixing the fence for the three cows they had. Planting potatoes. Affection became more perfunctory than romantic. She made special meals for him that he sometimes noticed. Mary thought he must be tired too, but at least he got away, met with people. Refueled, she called it. She couldn't find her nourishment.

"I've taken a job on a ship." They'd been on the property over a year and John arrived one evening out of sequence for the mail route. "I'll come home for a week every three months. It's good pay. We make it work, ja?" John buttered a slice of Mary's bread, leaned against the table. He didn't look at her. "I'll earn enough to stay home eventually. Hey, Johnny, come to Papa?"

"Three months at a time?"

"Out of Portland to San Francisco. An old friend finds me the job. We're fortunate."

"Are we?"

They spoke in short sentences until he left, and Mary watched her family as though from a distance, an intricate sandcastle crumbling in the surf, with no way to prevent it.

In her shock at learning of his leaving for so long a time, she didn't tell him she was pregnant again.

chapter
56

The following year, on July 29, 1892, Leonard Roy arrived. His was the easiest birth Mary had had, which was good, as Mrs. Ef the midwife had burst through the door after the event. Amanda held the newborn. "I delivered her." Mary's mother beamed. Jewell smiled beside her. She had come to take Mary and the little ones to her parents' before Mary even knew it was time.

"All that practice makes perfect," Mrs. Ef said.

"Hopefully not permanent." Mary sighed. "We need to figure out what's causing this." The women laughed but Mary didn't.

John hadn't made it for Leonard's arrival. And despite living closer to her parents, it wasn't close enough for Mary with three children now under the age of four and her husband gone at sea. Her incompetence weighed on her like a whale on her chest, not just with the children but milking the cows or tending the chickens. She failed to appreciate the beauty of a light snowfall on the Short Sands Beach or the call of an unknown bird near the barn. And when John arrived the following spring for a short visit, she barely waved goodbye when he left yet again.

He had leave for Christmas that year and stayed to help Mary celebrate twenty-one years of age in 1893. The children were gifted picture books that the older ones devoured. The year wore on after John left, and she struggled even when he showed up for the Fourth of July and again in October when he brought her news of something about the stock market collapsing and how fortunate it was they had land to bring them wealth. "You are doing good, Mare. Proving up our claim." She did not feel wealthy or good. When he came the following spring, he brought her something called Coca-Cola, a refreshing drink he said was all the rage. And it did revive her after she'd milked their cows, washed clothes, fixed meals, put up jam, baked, and milked the cows again. When he visited—and that was how she saw his infrequent appearance—her husband became just one more obligation. He came, he left. This was her life now.

Somewhere in the spring, she began to notice that her clothes sagged on her. She started wearing John's old pants she could hold up with twine. She could feel herself wasting away, trying to keep the garden up and the children down for naps. She snapped at Belle, who got distracted looking at books instead of watching Leonard. What Mary really wanted was to sleep away the day. She took some solace in tending the horses, telling them her woes, but even that kept her too close to the children's unending needs. Yet she knew they were normal demands. Her prayers had no specifics. Just a lament and a plea.

On John's first leave for a time, Mary served him a dish of potatoes dressed with onion, egg, and oil, and the juice of a rare lemon she'd bought at Tohl's. She watched as John ate, chattering on about his adventures. He held his youngest, nearly two. What was his life like, missing this boy, these children growing, or did he miss them? He must.

They sat on the porch, the rocking chairs creaked.

"Maybe you could find something else, John. I know you work hard. But the mail route was better if not as lucrative. And at least we saw you." A March wind blew off the Pacific, keeping a flock of pelicans holding steady, unable to move forward. She understood their position.

"We are making it, Mare."

"You are. I'm not."

"Ah, but you're a good mother, ja?" He patted her hand, praised her resolve. "Everything will work out fine."

One morning not long after, Belle shook Mary's shoulders to wake her to Leonard's crying. A cow bellowed, and when she dragged her pants on, Belle said, "Johnny isn't here."

Where was Johnny?

Her heart pounded, her hands felt cold as ice. "Look after Leonard." She ignored Belle's look of worry, pulled a shawl around her shaking shoulders, didn't tie the laces on her shoes.

"Johnny! Where are you?" She prayed as she searched, whispered the running prayer of "Please."

What if there's a sneaker wave? What if he's fallen into a bog?

She would never forgive herself. "Johnny!"

Her eye caught a snap of blue in the distance. She stumbled toward the color through the dune.

She found him playing in the sand a good mile from the house. She grabbed his bony arm and shook him.

Stop it! It wasn't his fault.

She stopped. Had she spoken those words herself? As when Jewell appeared at just the right time, Mary felt a presence, halting her, letting her see the fright in her son's eyes. "I'm sorry. I . . . I was so worried." She pulled him to her, tears falling. "Why didn't you answer me?"

"I knew where I was, Mama."

Relief spread like warm water over her. Relief and something more.

Mary led her son home, fed and dressed the children, thanked Belle for waking her, milked the cows, then walked the children and the cows the several miles to her parents.

"I need help," she said.

Mary's father wrapped his daughter in a bear hug as she fell into his arms while her mother herded her children to a table and fed them. After supper, her father sat Johnny on a chair and cut his hair, the curls falling to the floor as the boy giggled at himself in the mirror. Mary's mother read to Belle with Leonard on her lap while Mary curled herself on the couch. Here, her children safe, Mary could see and appreciate the uniqueness of her little clan. Belle, the quiet lover of books. Johnny, the explorer. Leonard, the social butterfly who, young as he was, jabbered to his grandparents as though he had something important to say. How she loved them! How she felt overwhelmed by them. What a failure she was.

She felt more confident as a dairymaid than as a mother. She wished she and John were raising them together. Her prayers were that she could be as faithful to her family as the surf was to the sand. Dunes built up in the summer, were pulled back to the sea in the fall. It was a rhythm she had yet to find. In the morning, she donned her brave pantaloons. John might have trouble asking for help, but she couldn't afford to be so proud. She had children to care for. And herself. She must take more time to fill the pitcher from which she drew that care, before it became dry. She had no money to hire help. She would abandon the claim. John would have to live with her decision.

chapter
57

Mary wore a wool shirt with plaids and John's old pants and donned her usual straw hat, then rode Prince up the coast to find Jewell. Friendship would soothe her soul. She found her bent over a fire near her newly built cabin up Ecola Creek. Jewell had made portiere curtains of periwinkle shells she'd collected. Sunlight filtering through the trees made the shells sparkle on the fishing wire hung over the doorway and single window.

"When we have a home on this beach, I'm going to make curtains like these," Mary said, fingering the small shells. "Maybe I'll use sand dollars."

Jewell served her huckleberry tea. Mary's eyes scanned the room as they adjusted to the darker interior. On the table sat a whittled duck half covered with tiny shells the size of a baby's fingernail. Jewell followed where she looked.

"Beeswax came to me," Jewell said. "From a ship that sank. I melted it and put it on this fresh carving." She picked up the wooden duck and handed it to Mary. "The wax keeps the shells in place. It is not finished."

"It's beautiful. I never would have thought to press shells into wax like this to make them look like feathers." Mary handed it back. "You can sell these. In Astoria. Or to the Portlanders. For their cottages." She took a deep breath. "Maybe John can sell some off his precious ship."

Jewell frowned. "I hear sadness in your words."

Mary sighed. "Marriage isn't what I thought it would be." She felt guilt about leaving the 160 acres, guilt about needing help with her children, guilt about not appreciating all that she had. She didn't know how to tell her friend any of that. Nor how to make a different change to send the guilt packing.

"Take the duck. Finish it with shells from your beach. Then give it away."

"But if you complete it, you can make money from it . . . sell to travelers on the Toll Road."

Jewell smiled. "They are too tired of the many turns to look for things they do not need. But maybe when there is a trading post on Cannon Beach, maybe then my little shell-covered ducks will float on mantels above fireplaces. But this one, it will be ours together."

The thought of that lightened Mary's mood.

"They will not draw any birds to the river or the lake. But they give me joy."

"And that is worthy," Mary said. "I don't seem to find joy these days nor make anything except babies."

"Babies are more worthy than carvings." She pushed the duck toward Mary. "You and Belle and maybe Johnny will find shells and remember a happiness. Of pressing them into the wax. Soon little Leonard can help. And the new one."

Mary gasped. Yes. There'd be another. She hadn't wanted to admit it even to herself.

chapter
58

Mary spent the night with Jewell, tossing in her sleep. She admired her friend's ability to see what wasn't readily seen. In the morning, after a piece of fry bread settled her stomach, with the unfinished duck in her bag, Mary saddled Jake. She could check the cinch herself and did. She didn't need John. She could make her own fire, a small flame to light a way but not burn. She could manage both wax and wick.

She stopped to see Herbert, who stood beneath wind-twisted trees near his hotel.

"Lost in your thoughts?"

Herbert turned. "I like the view beneath these wind-bent firs and how they frame Haystack Rock. It's a good place for a blanket and lie-down too. I've hired a photographer to come so we can make postcards. Maybe we'll get people interested in marrying at the sea. I'm calling it the Wedding Trees anyway. For the arch it makes."

"You might get a whole boodle of people to come to a wedding. Fill your hotel right up." Jake shifted his weight, waiting.

Herbert had hired a Chinese cook, and his fellow remittance man Joe Walsh had moved into one of the rooms. Joe welcomed guests whenever Herbert was off at Astoria or checking on his mill at Seaside or managing road maintenance.

"How goes the toll collecting?"

Herbert grimaced. "I say, it is a troubling task. I don't like doing it at all. People grumble about it and forget how the road has made their life easier. Or it's their first time to use it and don't know how terrible it was before."

"If we lived closer, I'd collect for you." Mary paused. "Maybe a good sign would help."

"A wooden sign so I wouldn't have to keep repeating myself. Excellent."

"Just tell me what the fees are and I'll make one up."

"Let's go to the hotel and I'll write the rates down. Do you think you can have it by next week?"

"I'll make a point of it."

When she left the hotel with her assignment in hand, she felt a lightness. It didn't take much to put aside sadness. Little things mattered. Doing something for someone else might well be the key.

She stopped at the Austin House next. She hadn't seen Lydia since the funeral of her husband James earlier that year. It had been sad to honor his passing. James Austin had so wanted those cannons to appear on his watch. Sea air drifted toward the hotel, swinging the baskets of red geraniums. Mary opened her saddlebag, then went inside to the distant call of gulls.

"Do you have mail to send?" Lydia looked at the letter Mary held while putting on her postman's visor.

"I do. I hope it will inspire John to come home soon. It's been three months." She handed the letter over.

With her long delicate fingers that played the organ, Lydia whisked the letter into the bag with the small stamp. "All ready for the mail carrier, whenever he gets here."

"He isn't reliable?"

"Usually he is. One never knows the condition of the mountain trail or the tides."

Mary looked out at the sea and a sky as dark as dirt. "John used to talk about the trials when he had the contract." Mary wished he had it now. She'd at least see him weekly. Rocks near the hotel formed an arch that caused the locals to refer to this section of the beach as Arch Cape, but Mary was glad the post office remained known as Cannon Beach.

"I've wondered about being a mail carrier myself," Mary said. She wasn't sure why that bit of inner thought popped out.

"Have you? I imagine you've heard the story of Minnie West-man. She was written up in the *New York Times* back in '88."

"The year we were married. Did she deliver mail back East?"

"No. Right south of here, from the Siuslaw River over the Coast Range to Hale near Eugene. She was only twenty years old."

"How did she get the contract?"

"Her father had it. She carried it for him." Lydia leaned into Mary, with almost a whisper. "She packed a revolver. Had to." She straightened up and crossed her hands over her stomach. "Robbers prey on postal people. I guess they think they're still having to collect the costs from the receiver. But that was before stamps. And only postmasters have the mailbag keys, so it's futile to try to get something from the carriers. Then there's the unpredictable weather. It's quite dangerous, Mary. Not something for a mother to do."

"Maybe not." Mary looked at the dark cloud over the sea.

The women shared a little tea. She told Lydia of Herbert's plans to get a photographer to take postcard shots and they speculated on which places should be featured. "Haystack Rock for sure. Maybe Hug Point. Did you know they've dug footholds into that rock so if one is caught by the tide they can step and hug their way to the top?"

"I didn't know that," Mary said. "Terrible Tilly? We'd want a lighthouse photograph."

"Oh yes, even though it's at the north coast, the story of building that lighthouse will go down in history." Lydia adjusted her round glasses. "One thing about being a postmistress is that you get news from other places." She sighed. "It helps now that James is no longer here. The nights get very lonely. Well, you know about that with your John working away. At least you have the children."

"I do," Mary said and decided not to try to explain to this childless widow how the presence of the children sometimes made her sadder rather than less lonely. How could anyone understand?

Still, as she rode back toward Nehalem, dark clouds scudding inland, Mary found her spirits boosted by the possibilities. A few more cottages had been built. And she saw a whale breach in the distance, surely a sign that good things were afloat somewhere, even for those on a sieve at sea. She had a task to make Herbert's sign, and she had an unfinished duck with Jewell's directive to get the children to help. She had a way forward however narrow the path.

Mary finished the sign for Herbert and loaded it across Prince's rump the following week. The gelding was good that way, not shying at odd shapes or weights. Some horses, Baldy for example, acted like the sight of a kite was a vulture come to steal his hay. Trying to heft a deer onto his back was like she was asking him to carry a lighthouse. Horses certainly had unique personalities.

Mary's work had required a trip to Tohl's for black paint and her father's help to find the perfect board. She rubbed glass paper on the plank to smooth the edges.

SINGLE HORSE MULE—.25

SINGLE HORSE AND BUGGY—.50

CATTLE DRIVEN—.25

SHEEP AND HOGS—.10

FOUR HORSE TEAM—1.00

"Quite splendid, Mary." Herbert pounded the sign into the ground next to the gate he'd put in. "There might be a future for you as a sign maker. As we grow, every business will want a sign. I like that you put my name at the bottom—'H. F. L. Logan, Pres.' But maybe we could take off the top line that touts it as a toll road?"

"It is what it is, Herbie."

He sighed. "You're correct. There'd be controversy if we left it off." He said "controversy" the English way as *conTROVersy*, reminding Mary once again of how far from home he was. Maybe he was lonely too. Maybe, if she knew what was happening inside the hearts of others, she'd realize that everyone at some time wandered in a pathless wood. Everyone had souls that needed tenderness. Her task was how to rise above her own ennui and do unto others, not to heal them, but to walk beside them while the Holy Spirit lent his balm. Kindness, that's what she could give.

"What do I owe you for your fine work?"

"Nothing. I need to do for others."

John arrived at Mary's parents' home in June for a quick stay. "What are you doing here?" She had never told him they were living with her parents now. "I came all that way and saw no wife, no children. No cows."

"It was too much, John." She rubbed her belly absentmindedly. "A farm needs more than one when that one is also trying to tend to children."

He shook his head, lowered his voice. "Maybe we hire help for you. You have to go back, that's all I know."

"No, maybe you have to leave your ship. Money is not worth it."

"Well, not if you leave the claim."

"We are like pelicans held in one place in the wind. Neither of us will move."

"Ja. That is what is."

John picked up Leonard, tossed him high, then caught the boy as he giggled. Belle elbowed her way past her brother to get closer to her father, who plopped into the rocker on the Edwardses' porch. He talked to Belle rather than to Mary when he said, "I've hired on as quartermaster on the *Columbia*. It is a rise, that's how you say it? Raise? More money, more responsibility. Like before, I sail from Portland to San Francisco. I'll still come home every few months. Just like old times? Ja?" He smiled up at his wife. "But with more coins."

"Your joy is not contagious."

John's blue eyes held hers.

"I had hoped it would be temporary, your sailing away."

"It is a man's duty to provide, not to talk so much, ja?"

It was her duty to commit to the grand adventure of raising a family. "But could we not remain at my parents'? You can see." She stood in profile. "There is another on the way."

John grimaced. Then his face brightened. "A big family. This is good. But, Mary, we need to stay on the property or we will lose the claim. Your being there makes it possible that one day we own. This is goed, ja? Important work raising children and saving land. We each do our part."

Before John left, he moved his family back to the farm and hired Merritt to help with the chores. Merritt was John's plan.

At least the boy didn't need diapering.

Alice Hazel was born late in December as a storm howled around them. Mary delivered with three pairs of eyes hovering close. Otherwise, she was alone, since Merritt visited his father for the holidays. Everyone had somewhere to be.

chapter
59

There must be something wrong with her, but she didn't know what it was. She'd resolved in the new year to be more hopeful. She wrote things down—good things.

Healthy children.

Parents to help now and then.

A roof with no leaks, a barn housing milk cows, pigs with new piglets; the sea giving bounty in oysters and clams.

Horses to ride.

Walking prayers.

Most of all, a husband who loved her and worked hard to support them. She had no right to despair, and yet by March she'd abandoned her journal, no steam to write down Belle's cute sayings like "straw babies" for strawberries or make note of Leonard's antics that made his siblings laugh, if not her. *So much for doing better with baby books than my mother had.* Her poem-writing disappeared with tears.

Yet with John's March visit, he blew on a hopeful flame. There'd be an end one day. He'd have enough money to leave the ship and farm. She just needed to "stay the course. A nautical term but applies to marriage as well, ja."

She didn't think he realized that money for their purse was secondary to the glow of adventure the ship's passage carried with it.

"It has more responsibility," John told her at his leave in July. He'd be with them for the celebrations of birthdays and the Fourth festivities. And to tell tales to Herbie and make new acquaintances as more people settled in the region. "Quartermaster, ja, I must apply what I know of navigation and am responsible for corrections. Even training new recruits."

"I'm happy for you. A corner beam in the barn needs shoring up. Might you help with that before you leave?"

"Ja, ja, of course."

He'd let her sleep that first morning back while he and Merritt milked. But children paid no attention to time and had awakened her, seeking breakfast she'd served in a sleepy daze. She didn't feel well.

Now the children crawled all over their father as he sat at the table. They poked at his pockets for the trinkets they knew he brought them from San Francisco. "The washing equipment arrived?" John asked her. "It's brand-new. To make your work easier, ja?" His eyes met hers even while he held his hand above his head, teasing Johnny and Belle who reached for the leather bag, cheering as they grabbed it, giggling as they pulled it open.

Bop! Bop! Bop!

A clatter of marbles hit the plank floor, scattered under the table, around the chairs, struck the corners while John and the children laughed, scrambled to gather them up; laughed with joy, laughed together, the dogs barking, happiness rising to the beams.

Her breathing shallowed, she grabbed her ears with her hands.

"What's wrong, Mare?"

She shook her head, fled to the outhouse, then saddled Prince and rode toward the sea.

The morning after John left, Max returned with Leonard in tow—she hadn't even known the boy was gone. Then one cow made a run through a broken-down fence and Belle argued she wanted to just go to the beach and didn't want to watch her siblings. Merritt left before finishing the milking, too sick with the ague to continue.

Whatever John might say no longer mattered. She must keep her children safe. She could no longer do that by herself.

"Come along. We're going to Grandpa's."

And if her brood couldn't join her parents, maybe her parents would join them.

"I can't do it anymore, Mama." Mary sat at the table drinking dried blackberry tea.

Amanda patted her hand. What could she do for her daughter to keep her safe? That task of protection never left a mother's hands.

"My mind keeps this phrase rolling in like the surf: 'I have to go away. I have to go away.' The only time it seems to stop is when we're here and I know everyone is getting enough love from somewhere if not from me."

Amanda rose and picked up her porcelain rolling pin and walked to the cabinet dedicated to flour and pastry preparation. Her hands trembled as she lifted the doughboy's lid, then dribbled water into its flour well, a task so familiar her mind could wander. Was there a sorrow greater than watching your child in pain? Yes, losing a child, but this was a close second. Amanda knew she was about to make it worse.

"Can we come back here?" Mary said. "I know John thinks I can handle the farm, but I can't. Not and tend the children too. Poor Belle is having to act like a little mother, and that isn't fair to a seven-year-old. She's becoming contrary, just the way you said I was." Amanda heard the desperation in her daughter's voice. "Besides, we need to be closer to a school," Mary said. "Belle will have to walk two miles."

Amanda turned to her husband. "You tell her."

William Edwards cleared his throat. "We're selling and moving back to Scholls Ferry."

Mary swallowed back her rising despair. "Is it because we've put so many demands on you?" These babies, so precious, so needful, as all children are, were taking their toll on her parents too?

"Not at all," her father said. "We love having you with us. But my knees are creaking like an unoiled hinge, and bending under those cows isn't getting any easier. We cut back to two, but still." He shrugged his shoulders.

"I could do more of that for you. I could."

"Not your job," her father said. He patted her shoulder.

"I know. Being a mother is and I'm terrible at it." She bit at her cuticle. Her parents' silence confirmed her fears.

"Maybe you should move with us," her father said then. "John could find work close to Portland. Plus the farmland is so much better in the Willamette Valley than here."

Was that a possibility? "Truth is, I don't think John much likes farming. It's the sea he's drawn to—Hey, hey." Mary interrupted herself. "Don't push your brother, Johnny. Leonard needs to hang on to the chair to stand. But I don't much like farming either," she continued. "It's the sea that calls to me too, but more, the beach, the rhythm of waves, riding a horse along it." She heard Alice cry, wanted to carry on the conversation, but knew what her youngest child needed. "I've got to nurse the baby." She sighed. "It's time she was weaned."

"Yes, about time," her mother said.

Was that a criticism? Mary could no longer sort out neutral observations from critiques.

Mary nursed Alice and sang a song to Leonard, hoping it would put at least two of them to sleep. Johnny wandered over and leaned his head on her shoulder. She wiped his nose. Should she try to reach John to tell him? Would having Merritt there prove up the claim? In the early years, when her father had to leave their family to work at the Cape Meares Lighthouse at Tillamook, she and her mother had to remain, only visiting him now and then, her mother wary as a feral cat. She'd never understood that. It didn't matter. Her mother had done something obviously hard for her to do. Mary could follow her footsteps.

She would send a letter for John, but who knew when he'd receive it. These were decisions she would have to make without him, doing the best she could for her family.

chapter
60

I hate leaving you." Mary rubbed Prince's velvet nose as the horse yawned. He was relaxed, his head hanging low. "But Papa says there isn't a barn on the property, just a small lean-to for the team hauling us away. You understand? Merritt will look after you, you and Baldy and Jake." She hoped she was making the right decision. She could live without a beach ride on Prince, couldn't she?

"I'll ride them now and then, Mrs. G. Don't you worry." Merritt had come up beside her as she said her goodbyes.

"Don't let them pasture on the meadow on the mountain. I know it's good grass, but there's a steep ridge. It drops off and if they get to playing around, they won't be able to stop. I saw that happen to some horses once. The skid marks before they went through the fence haunt me still."

Merritt nodded, scratched Max's head. "He won't like being separated from Nellie, nor the crab cakes." The big yellow dog panted between them, pressed against Mary's legs.

"There's just no room," Mary said. Tears were her partner now; grief her constant companion. Except that, oh yes, there was another child on the way. That spark during John's March visit had established more than a hopeful flame.

"Best put that spinning wheel on last," William said. A vee of geese honked overhead, flew against the slate sky as they worked.

"Let me, Mrs. G." Merritt helped load the wagon, then waved goodbye to the family he'd adopted—as they had adopted him. With Merritt caring for the farm, John would see that she'd been a responsible wife, wouldn't he?

She didn't care if he didn't.

Mary's father took them on the road from Tillamook east over the Coast Range, toward the Willamette Valley. They drove through small villages, then, not far from Portland, turned south to Scholls Ferry. The older two children kicked their legs out, hanging over the wagon's back, holding on over the bumps in the road. It had seemed her parents were driven to get as far away from the world as possible when they'd traveled to Nehalem. Now, moving back, they smiled more.

The area they returned to boasted of tall timber and stumps, but also black soil close to the Tualatin River with neighbors nearby. Her father had bought a house with four bedrooms, some upstairs, some down. Belle started school and Mary found room to appreciate how Belle loved books—just as Mary did. She hadn't totally ruined her oldest child if she found joy in stories.

Mary did the milking, but there were only two cows now for the family's needs, not the seventeen they'd milked in Nehalem. William purchased beehives and Mary learned to harvest the honey, some of which they sold. Her father, always industrious, broke apart the growth rings of stumps, softening the fibers in water to weave baskets. Sometimes he felled young white oaks or willows that grew wild beside the river to make splints. Mary wove baskets too, the work calming, the over and under and through, like the strands of a life. It made her think of the unfinished duck Jewell had given her. Maybe here the children would help her press shells into the wax. Maybe here, with her children safe while she nurtured new life, she could also nurture roots while she waited for blooms.

As a present to herself, Mary wrote poems again, thinking of Jewell and the need to create something besides babies. She signed the verses "Mary Edwards." She thought she was on her way like the Jumblies in their sieve when they "sailed to the Western Sea, to a land all covered with trees." She put that poem to music and sang as she watched Alice spoon oatmeal into her mouth, the two laughing at a face covered with mush.

> "'And they bought an Owl,
> and a useful Cart,
> a pound of Rice, and a Cranberry Tart,
> and a hive of silvery Bees.
> And they bought a Pig, and some green Jack-daws,
> and a lovely Monkey with lollipop paws,
> And forty bottles of Ring-Bo-Ree,
> and no end to Stilton Cheese.'"

"What do you suppose they did with all that cheese?" Mary said. "And what's a lollipop paw?"

Nearly two, Alice turned her palms over and licked them.

Mary laughed, something she was doing more of. Could she rediscover family as the adventure of her life? Her children were thriving and so was she, tending her family—with help—while rediscovering herself in the comfort of words. As another poem went, "All is well with my soul."

And then on a September morning, she woke in a pool of blood. Searing pain. A rough ride in a wagon followed, someone helping to stop the bleeding. In and out of awareness. Fleeting prayers. Alone.

She couldn't feel her legs.

"My baby?"

Even without the nurses avoiding her eyes, she knew she'd lost her, her womb a hollow cave. The sharp pains in her belly had rescinded, giving her more time to wonder about not being able to walk. What did it mean?

Finally a doctor delivered the news. They could not save the child—and she'd have no others. "It will take time, but you'll walk again. That's the good news."

Alone in the hospital's whitewashed room, Mary awoke to the sounds of healing: rickety wheels on a chair being pushed; moans down a distant hall; the clickety-clack of the nurse's shoes.

The trek for her parents to visit in Portland was time-consuming and long, and children weren't even allowed in. She missed them. The fall rains kept the roads a sea of mud, so Mary spent days with only a doctor or nurse stopping to administer their healing tools, interrupting her sleep and her tears. *What will happen next? Maybe I'll just disappear here, never go home.* She had time on her hands, time to pray. Time to listen but she heard no answers.

"How are you this morning, Mrs. Gerritse?"

She didn't know the man who stopped at her bedside. He wasn't wearing a white coat, though his hair was white as sea-foam. He pulled up a wicker chair and sank into it beside her bed. "You've had quite a terrible time." He was a portly man who looked like his work was paid for with beef and potatoes. Behind round lenses were the eyes of a younger soul that defied the wrinkles recording his years.

"What have they told you?" he asked.

She hesitated. She'd said none of this out loud, let alone to a stranger. "That my baby died. That I almost did but for the prayers of my parents and a doctor close by who accompanied me to the hospital. I might still die if I don't remain quiet."

"Will you be able to do that? Remain still, in order to heal?"

"I . . . I don't know. I've always been busy, looking after my children." Her breath caught at the half-truth of her statement. A November sleet pelted the window like marbles rolling on a plank floor. "I'll have no more children. My husband doesn't know." What would John say when she told him?

"God uses all the seasons to heal and inspire. You might well be walking in a fallow field."

"I'm not walking anywhere at the moment."

"A time for everything, Scripture says. A time to tear, and a time to mend. A time to mourn, and a time to dance." He smiled. "There is also a time to remember promises and make them our own."

"Promises?"

"Like the promise that you shall love the Lord your God with all your heart and your neighbor as yourself. I've found that as a signpost for healing."

"I thought that was a command, one we humans fall short of."

He rubbed his chin. "I see it as something you can look forward to, loving God and out of that have the strength to love your neighbors. And yourself."

"And how would I do that?"

"My grandfather would say, 'On the tired feet of faith and the buoyant wings of hope.'"

"I hope my tired feet will hold me up again one day. So I can serve my family."

"An apt comment. The word 'family' comes from the Latin word *famalus*, meaning servant."

"Does it."

Her visitor smiled, then stood. "I must be on my way. But I leave you today with a verse my grandfather loved from Isaiah. 'Those who wait on the Lord shall renew their strength; they shall mount up with wings like eagles, they shall run and not be weary, they shall walk and not faint.' Trust, Mrs. Gerritse. You aren't alone. We are never alone. And I think you'll walk again."

He came every now and then. Mary looked forward to his stories from his grandfather—if that was their real origin. The hospital staff never interrupted while he visited. He didn't come on the day her child should have been born. She grieved alone. Maybe not, as he had reminded her.

"Do you think this is God's punishment for me?" she asked him one day. "For my being Contrary Mary, as my mother used to call me. For my failure as a mother and wife? For being so different."

"Not the God I'm acquainted with," he said. "We are harder judges on ourselves than God would ever be."

"Is that truly so? Oh, here I am being contrary with a man of the cloth. You are a man of the cloth, aren't you?" Mary looked at him from her bed. She continued to have to lie down. They were going to get her to stand soon—an adventure she both dreaded and thought couldn't happen soon enough.

"We're all 'fearfully and wonderfully made.' God loves a big, floppy family, full of uniqueness. He knows there'll be strains and gives us leeway to resolve them as best we can as we seek our purpose. His judgment is tempered with a love so deep we can never touch the bottom. It's a love you can trust," he said, his words both warm and wise.

She had hours to consider. Would her marriage survive this strain? Did she want it to? *I'll stay no matter how.* She truly didn't know if she could.

chapter
61

Mary sent word to John that she was returning to her parents' home. He was still at sea somewhere between Portland and San Francisco. On a March morning, she walked with a cane and let herself be flooded by a wave of welcoming children. Alice scrambled onto her lap, took her face between both her little hands, and smacked her on her lips. "Mama home." She saw the worried looks on Belle's face melt into a relief when she reached out her arms to her firstborn. Johnny held back, holding Leonard's hand until she urged them forward. "I won't break." She inhaled the lavender scent of Leonard's hair, cherished Johnny's cheek against hers, as smooth as a river stone but not as cold.

Her mother's hovering frown began to fade as Mary held her family. She was a young woman and her particularity of living had been giving birth as God had allowed. That gift had been taken away. Had she brought it on with her melancholy, her lack of joy in being a mother? She didn't know. These children, her parents, John. Family. They were gifts. She just had to receive them.

She was learning. Her body had mostly healed. Now it was time for her heart.

The wagon led by two horses pulled up in front of the Edwards home. William waved to the driver, whose hat hid his bearded face, but he must be someone her father knew, perhaps come to borrow the beehives. The two men bent in deep conversation when Mary turned away from the window, gingerly walked toward the door. The cane helped her balance. She turned back when she heard Belle shout.

"Papa! Papa!"

It couldn't be John, could it? The man was slender, not stocky like John was. But he wore a blousy shirt, white as a beach morning glory. Pantaloon pants. Sailor's clothes.

Mary picked up her pace, made her way down the steps, and reached the front door just as John leapt up onto the porch. Hat in hand, a beard with a tint of red covering his chin. It wasn't trimmed. He'd been in a rush. He lifted Belle, hugged his daughter with one arm, Mary with the other. "I've come to take you home, ja, if you'll let me."

"Oh, John. Where is home? I . . . I couldn't do it anymore. Merritt . . ."

"Ja. And your father says you nearly died. And I wasn't here." He set his daughter down, took Mary's hands in his. "You forgive me, ja?" She'd expected to ask him to forgive her. "We go back, together."

"I can't return to the farm without you, John. I can't."

"And so you'll have me. And should have had all these years. Especially with the lost child." He inhaled. "I've quit the *Columbia*."

"You're not going back to sea?" Hope spread like a river flowing across crying sands.

"We will do it different. We sell the farm, ja? I've found a place in Manzanita, south of the mountain but closer to Cannon Beach. If you approve."

"Close to Cannon Beach?" She could see Jewell more often.

"Ja. Manzanita. I'll stable horses at the beach to rent to travelers and tourists. We can rent out some for clearing ground. And . . . I . . . I've taken a contract for the mail again. George Luce—you remember him?" Mary nodded. "I'll pay him to take the route from Cannon Beach to Tillamook. I'll do Seaside to Cannon Beach, shorter, more time on the ranch. We can do this, Mary. We can."

That still meant there'd be two and a half days each week when she'd be alone with the children and the demands of the farm. She couldn't go back to the pattern that had brought her to despair. But maybe . . .

"Let's hire help," she said. "Not only Merritt for chores but also someone to look after the children."

"We'll talk later, of details," he said. "Let's get you packed up."

"No." She put her hand on his forearm. "We must talk now, tend to things together but before all decisions are made."

Her parents had taken the children into the house, so they had the front porch to themselves.

He looked at her, lifted her chin. "White streaks have found their way into your hair, Mare."

"With each child a little less rust and a little more white." She fiddled with a strand.

"It becomes you." He took her hand, kissed the palm. "We make a new start. No proving up. I look to money to serve my family when I need to give time and attention, ja."

"Yes." He was beginning to understand. She knew what she needed. She took a deep breath. "Instead of George taking the southern mail route, let me. We won't have to pay out wages. Maybe he can get the route from Cannon Beach to Seaside. But I'll take the trail from Cannon Beach to Tillamook and back. What would you say to that?"

"Up over Neahkahnie Mountain?"

"Yes."

"This does not fit into my thoughts." He paused. "You would need to go over Neahkahnie in all weather."

"I've pastured sheep there and calves. For my father."

John scratched his beard. Belle came back outside and hugged his hip and looked up at him and then her mother. She was silent, then slipped away, leaving them alone.

"No woman has carried the mail on the coast. Maybe not anywhere."

"That isn't so, John. Lydia told me about a woman younger than me going from the Siuslaw River toward Eugene, years ago."

"Maybe. But not up the coast with king tides or over the mountain in gales. The trail goes up 800 feet to the sky, Mary. I don't know about this."

"I know," Mary said.

"And what of the children?"

"A nanny. Jewell comes to mind if she will do it. The children love her already."

"The route is lonely, Mary."

"I wouldn't always be alone." Hadn't her hospital visitor said she was never alone? No one was. "People often come along with the mail carrier, you know that. I'd be doing something good, and we'd share the load. It would save our family." She whispered, "It would save me."

"We can talk on our way back."

"No, we need to decide now, because if I go back, we won't have my parents close by to help rescue us should you decide to return to the sea." Had she said "if"? *I'll stay no matter how.*

She chewed her nail.

"Alright. We talk now."

"We went to sea in a sieve," Mary said. John lifted her single braid and pushed it behind her shoulder. "Remember that final verse in that Lear poem about how in twenty years they all came back and everyone said, 'How tall they've grown!' They grew, John. Despite the trials and the scary parts. I want us to grow together and maybe we can inspire others to go to sea as we did, try something that seems good, even not knowing how it will turn out. And having the courage to change our minds."

He sat a long time. Then, "We give it a go. If we find good help for the children. And if you are healthy enough. The horses stay strong. If you have trouble, we make changes, agreed?"

Mary nodded. "One more thing . . ." She'd made her case. The rest was frosting on a carrot cake.

"Ah, woman, ja, what is it?" He leaned back, smiled though, a smile that rose to his eyes.

"I'll always get to ride Prince." She could hardly wait to see her horse again.

PART III

chapter
62

A few stars speckled the predawn winter sky as John checked the cinch on Prince, made sure the saddle set properly. He'd agreed to this but didn't feel secure in the decision. Still, it was a team effort, both him and Mary working toward the same end. This was what she needed. "You'll want to walk on the Neahkahnie trail, you know that? Get off of Prince."

"I will."

"And be sure to holler before you start out on the narrows." Would she listen?

"I will."

John patted Prince's neck. The wind picked up, carrying a hint of sea spray. Were clouds moving in? The temperature had dropped.

"Maybe I take the trail today. Wait for a better day, ja, for your first mail run."

"John. It'll be fine. Don't you always say that?"

He buttoned up her wool jacket. "Well, give me your foot, then." John made a stirrup of his two palms and Mary stepped into them, pushed her leg over the mail packs secured behind the saddle as John lifted her onto the horse. "I truly hope I'm doing the right thing here." He adjusted his bowler hat. "One night out, ja, then you are here with us. I don't want you stuck out on the mountain overnight. Cougars. Bears. Whatnot."

"So long as no worms wiggle down my neck, I'll be fine." She patted her trusty pistol and gave him the grin that washed his heart with love.

"You shoot at bears, but worms bring you to screams."

Mary laughed and shivered in exaggeration. They spoke of nonsense things as a drizzle started. Nonsense, to put aside the worries as they both ventured onto a new road. It had taken some time to move, then to hire a child keeper who arrived just as school started. John could tell Mary liked this Manzanita place. It was closer to the sea, but she said she loved it because they were all together here, in one place. She'd tried to talk her parents into returning but they'd refused. She understood.

"Prince and I have ridden that trail before, just not carrying the mail sacks." She patted Prince's roached mane. They'd docked his tail too, so the long strands didn't pick up mud or gather weeds. "I'll see you late tomorrow."

"Ja." John patted Prince's rump as Mary pressed her knees and the two as one walked north. John had picked up the mailbags at Tillamook and brought them to the farm. Now Mary would carry them forward to Cannon Beach and Austin's postal stop. The contract for delivery from Cannon Beach to Seaside was let to George Luce. John watched her ride until she was out of sight, then plodded back toward the house.

Rita should be getting the children up. There should be a coffeepot on the cast-iron cookstove, a Number 8 Standard he'd bought in Astoria and hauled down the Toll Road. He'd have his second cup. Both Belle and Johnny should be dressed, and there'd be the tussle with Leonard wanting to trot off to school with them, though he was too young. Rita hadn't been their first choice for looking after the children and handling the housework while Mary delivered mail, but they'd been unable to find Jewell, their Nehalem friend, to ask if she'd be willing. Not that she'd have consented to being the childminder, but the older children knew her, liked her. They were adjusting to Rita, who he feared might be more interested in Merritt's attention than tending their children. And because they'd hired a girl to help out, they couldn't afford Merritt but a day a week. But Rita lived at home with her parents and would stay just the nights that Mary was gone. Then it would be him and Mary and their offspring. At last. The family. A part of him thought it was all foolishness, letting Mary go off to deliver the mail. But with a woman like Mary, one had to be prepared to try a few new things. Her father had said she needed to be around people, which annoyed him. He was people. Their children were people, and she had difficulties with only them. She needed the accelerant of tales to fire up her days. Delivering the mail wasn't going to get her *that* many more encounters with people. But overcoming landscape challenges—and time with Prince—well, those might fill Mary up. He wished he could but accepted she needed something more.

"Mr. Gerritse, come quick." Rita stood in the doorway, a towel in her hand, a scarf wrapped around her dark hair. She'd already been tidying up after Mary left. That was good.

"What's the problem?"

"Leonard thumped Alice on the head with a big wooden spoon and she bit him back."

John picked up his steps. "Is she alert? Talking? Is he bleeding?"

This was just the sort of start to his day he didn't need. Alice came running out and he picked her up. She had a bump on her head. Belle and Johnny passed them by, waving cheerfully as they headed for school, bundled up against the now pelting rain.

He snuffled Alice's neck and she stuck her tongue out at Leonard. It might be a long day.

Secretly, John thought it would be fine if Mary had some minor setback that would make her change her mind, that the weather became an inconvenience, or she didn't get along with travelers wanting to tag along. Something that would make her decide that being a mail carrier wasn't for her and come back home to happily raise their children.

But he'd committed to this route. Still, it didn't stop him from missing the sea.

chapter
63

Yes! Yes! Yes!

Her spirits lifted like a hot-air balloon. Who cared that the weather threatened? What did a little downpour matter? Mary pulled her hat down so the sleet wouldn't blind her as they rode up the trail, gaining altitude. Without a corset, Mary's body felt freer too. Just as the mother and daughter who walked from Spokane to New York did, according to the newspaper article Mary had read about them. It was a new era for women, and she was right in the mix of it.

Poor Prince had to endure the rain without the benefit of a hat. He was sure-footed and steady. Could he feel her joy? Maybe a little trepidation rode with them. "I guess you know it's best we get over the hump," she told him. "Before we're into the mud."

Prince lifted his head, rattling the bridle rings. Mary took that as agreement.

On a clear day, the view over the Pacific from this point on the mountain captured the immenseness of creation, combining sand and sea that on any given day might be a shade of blue or green not found anywhere else. Painters must find the coloring captivating, blending to get the right hue, only to have it change by the next time they looked. Even in the rain, Mary couldn't keep the grin from her face as she wiped her cheeks.

"Anyone ahead?" she shouted into the wind. She didn't expect anyone to be foolish enough to be on the trail in this weather, but they might have started out and then got caught in it. She shouted a second time. With no response, she dismounted as John had told her she must—she would have done it anyway—as the trail narrowed no wider than a cradleboard.

Prince followed. Mary didn't look at the drop-off even though the heights didn't scare her. It was the mud she focused on, its slickness pressuring her and Prince to pay attention. Mary made note that when one's life was at a precarious edge, one couldn't think of anything else—or shouldn't. It required a kind of spiritual attuning that kept mundane worries at bay. Maybe that was why she so liked walking the pathless woods. It kept her in the *nonce*, a word Herbert had told her meant "in this moment," that place where the Eternal is met.

They eased along the mountain's flank hugging the uphill side, making the precarious section around the ridge without incident. Once the trail widened so they could again walk beside each other, Mary checked the security of the mailbags. She exhaled, not realizing she'd been holding her breath. The biggest hurdle, over. Until the return trip. But each phase would be different. It was part of the appeal. She mounted up to continue the two-and-a-half-mile downhill section.

She couldn't stop grinning.

At the Austin House, Mary shouldered the mailbags onto the porch, slipping past the basket of flowers frantic in the wind. No gulls cawed their presence. It was just too miserable.

"Here we go!" She plopped the bags onto the counter.

"Where's John?"

"I'm taking the route now." She stepped back, pressed her hat onto her head, straightened her shoulders. She surely shimmered with rain on her slicker and accomplishment on her face.

"Are you?" Lydia, slim as a hairpin, put her postal visor on. "I remember you saying you wanted to do that. I didn't think you would with your little ones so . . . little."

"George Luce will take the route from here to Seaside."

"Yes. I expect him this evening. I thought you, or rather John, might delay with the weather so disagreeable." Lydia turned the key she had around her neck in the lock and pulled back the waxed leather flaps. "Lots of letters," she said. "I'll get on sorting them. And after George arrives, I'll have a bag ready for Tillamook in the morning. Will you spend the night?"

Mary wasn't sure she wanted to have a girl chat with someone questioning why she wasn't home with her children. "I'm going to see if my friend Jewell is up Ecola Creek."

"We're calling it Elk Creek now. That herd came off the mountain and played in the surf a few days ago. Rushing in and out of the waves, like children!" She leaned in. "The tourists love them, but they can be a nuisance."

"I may be back." Mary waved goodbye, adjusted her stirrups, and mounted up on Prince. "Let's go find my friend."

But Jewell wasn't there. When had she last seen her friend? Before Alice was born. She never did finish the duck carving Jewell had given her to press shells onto the wax. At least she still had it. The unfinished craft had traveled with them. Was Jewell alright? She wouldn't know about the child they'd lost. And she didn't know of Jewell's losses either. All friends had them. "I have to do better," she told Prince. Friendships took tending, just as a marriage did. As a family did. Jewell was family.

Mary led Prince to Herbert's Elk Creek Hotel that evening where she'd stay the night. Joe Walsh and Herbert filled her in on the latest news from faraway places, a bonus for a mail carrier.

As they finished, she asked, "Have you heard from my Nehalem friend, Jewell?"

"I've not had the pleasure," Herbert said.

Talk turned to how Herbie busied himself now lobbying the state to make all the beach roads public highways. "And adopt the Toll Road as a public road too, so everyone would cover the cost of maintaining it through taxes. It would save my bacon," Herbert said, not elaborating. "I am thinking about making a trip back to England later this year. These maintenance costs." He shook his head.

"I'll be here to take up your porch," Joe said. "You won't need to worry about a thing."

"Take up my porch?"

"Or your torch. Yes, that's what I meant. I'll take up your torch to get things sorted. To our flavor."

Mary carried an inner flame of joy listening, being a part of news and views she'd never hear being at home. She could hardly wait to be the bearer of these tidings to her family. One more gift from being able to pursue a new adventure.

Mary loaded the mailbags onto Prince beneath a clear morning sky.

The entire journey as far as Manzanita proved uneventful. The tide gave way to her travel; seagulls swooped in celebrations of a perfect coastal day. This was what she'd imagined, doing her job with a glorious view. She wanted this first round trip to be without incident so John wouldn't have second thoughts about supporting their new venture mixing family needs and filling the purse.

She didn't go by the farm, went on south to the Tillamook Spit, past the Thayer Bank building in Tillamook, toward the lighthouse where Lizzie Biggs served as postmistress. The post office on the ocean made it easier for ships who had deliveries but meant more travel for the mail carrier with the overland route. Cape Meares Lighthouse winked its light, reminding her of the summer her father worked there. She couldn't imagine then that she'd be back as a woman carrying the mail to that very lighthouse.

Dusk settled, but it was only a three-hour ride to rest in her own little bed beside John and she could surprise them all. The children might be asleep, John, too, but she'd see them in the morning.

"Are you up to a night ride, Prince?" He yawned. "Ah, I woke you." Prince lifted his head and let Mary scratch behind his ears. She checked the cinch, secured the new mailbags, headed for home where she could celebrate with family the perfect ending to a flawless journey. "May there be many more just like this," she whispered. "Thank you."

chapter
64

Herbert glued the emblem onto his little ship in the bottle, the fifth one he'd finished. He planned to put a ship in every room in his hotel. He had eleven more to go. He adjusted the whale oil lamp. Though it was the height of the summer, the sky was a pallet for a roll of storms lining up beyond the shore. His hobby did help him forget his worries: his creeping paralysis, his lack of money, his failing vision. And he'd failed to get his road designated as a public entity. The new governor adored bicycles and had paths designated for them where riders could avoid startling horses. The Toll Road wouldn't be able to handle a bicycle with all its ruts and roots. But if it were a public roadway . . .

During his last visit to Astoria, he'd learned of a plan to allow citizens to bring things to the ballot for a statewide vote. It would take an amendment to Oregon's constitution, but if that happened, he might be able to get enough signatures on a petition to permit a vote on the state taking over toll roads, for the benefit of all citizens. He'd need a citizen to collect the signatures. That wasn't going to happen anytime soon, so he might as well stop hoping for it. As for the sawmill, he did get logs from land he'd invested in and they were processed at the mill, but he needed more development, more summer cottages built. The mill also had its maintenance issues and costs. He had to admit it: he needed the remittance checks his brother no longer sent. He was entitled to them, wasn't he?

It was time. He'd make arrangements and return to England to have it out with his brother. Not the most comforting future to think about, but one he needed to face. Perhaps he could promote his hotel and this Cannon Beach in England, bring European guests across that pond.

The possibility of a walk with his sister-in-law made him drop the emblem. Just thinking of her caused his hands to tremble. Maybe he and his brother would find a truce and they'd come visit here. Such joyous things had happened—though he confessed, not to him. Besides, why should his brother have the pleasure after what he'd done to him?

"You got to come! I've a whale of a story." Joe Walsh hopped onto the porch. He'd been off collecting mussels Herbie's Chinese cook could put to good use.

"I say, old friend, I'm not in the mood. I've packing to do, things to arrange. I'm going to return to jolly old England."

"Not for a while you won't. A whale has thrown up on the beach."

"I beg your pardon?"

"A whale! There's whale on the beach. If you come now, we can finish it and blunder the blubber for oil. For the machines at your sawmill."

"Render the oil. Yes, I see." It would be a boon to his bottom line to not have to ship in grease and oil.

"Come on. Can't look a gift fish in the mouth."

Verily, this coast could cough up treasures.

chapter
65

It happened, just before the July 4th celebration and all the birthdays, when Mary'd been keeping her route, trailing behind Prince, taking her time. Under a canopy of trees, a summer breeze brushed warm across her face, when for no reason at all Prince lifted his head and, in an instant—as though he'd been stung by a bee—he startled off the trail. Without thinking, Mary did the same, seconds behind him. Simultaneously, she heard the crack of the branch, and the crush of broken limbs hurled onto the very spot where she'd been standing.

"Whoa!" Her hands shook as she patted the horse's neck, her heart aflutter. Luck? Or maybe another of those moments she attributed to divine intervention. On her return trip, she'd bring a saw—unless someone after her got there first. Weak-kneed, she mounted up, a little shaky but grateful this hadn't happened on the narrow ridge. Should she tell John of her close call? No, he'd only worry.

She thought of all the smaller daily miracles she celebrated now too. The first bleeding hearts showing up in the swamps, blooming back away from the sea. The finely veined leaves of the cascara plant with its tiny red berries representing faithfulness despite the challenge. Even dead animals they encountered spoke to her—the carrion would feed the hawks and eagles and coyotes. Everything had its purpose. And mundane as it might be to some, delivering the mail was hers.

She became accustomed to knowing where the wild strawberries were likely to give up their "straw babies" and vowed to bring Belle with her on one of her trips to share that first taste. Daily, she thanked God that when she thought of her children now—which was often—it was with joy instead of weight, with anticipation instead of dread.

Arriving at the narrow section, she hollered as they approached. When she didn't hear a reply, she and Prince started forward, having gone several feet, only to be surprised as they rounded the ridge.

"Go back!" a man shouted to her coming from the other side. He led a horse, and another rider behind him waved her back. A third gentleman wearing a tailored suit sat atop a horse, both man and mount showed whites in their eyes, the drop-off but inches at their feet.

There was no way to turn back.

"This is a bit of a pickle," the lead man said. His horse touched Prince's nose and snorted. The man wore a bowler hat, and despite the pickle, he had a grin on his face. Mary calculated that it would be difficult for either party to try to back their animals to safety. She and Prince were the most likely candidates to be successful, Prince being sure-footed. But it was stressful on a horse to back on a narrow trail.

"Did you holler? I didn't hear you," the lead man said.

"I did. Did you?"

All three men nodded. Only one looked terrified, and Mary determined he must not be local. He proved her right when he spoke with an Eastern accent. "I knew we should not have taken such a road. You said it would be no problem. What are we going to do?"

Mary assessed their animals. They stood calmer now despite the pawing of one. That one swished its tail; sweated. Prince stood still as a straight pin. "Here's my suggestion." Mary adjusted her hat. "It may not look like it, but the trail is slightly wider where you are. You push your horses as close to the inner bank as possible. The misters might gently dismount and shimmy up a bit and hold on to the bank's grasses so the trail is totally the horses'. Then I'm going to bring Prince alongside your animals. He can step almost inside their feet. We'll be by you in a jiffy."

"Oh, Lord!" wailed the white-eyed man.

"You've done this before," the grinning man said.

"No, but a mail carrier is prepared for every occasion."

The Eastern-accent man moaned. "I can't see how that can be done. Wait! Wait!"

The lead man must have decided Mary's plan would work as he helped the fractious rider off his mount and began pushing his companion up onto the bank. "I can't hold on to grasses. My feet will slip and I'll fall. I'll end up with it right over that edge and take a horse with me. Please. Oh, God, help!" The third man patted his back as he pushed him up onto the bank, pulling himself up beside him.

"Send up that prayer and hold on." Mary kept her voice sympathetic to his fears while staying firm. Her heart beat faster but not in fear. The horses would hear hesitance in her words.

Mary heard whimpering as she led Prince close to the other mounts, their scent piercing her nose. She gently placed her hand on the lead animal, eased past him with soothing words. "It's alright, we're just passing by. That's right. You're alright. Good girl. Good boy."

She would not look over the edge.

Sound ceased but for the clop of Prince's hooves and her words to the horses. "That's right. You're good."

She passed the second.

And then the third.

"Hallelujah!" The leader shouted from behind her now.

She turned to pat Prince's chest, then watched the leader help the most vulnerable member back off the side of the bank, his legs wobbling.

"I will never come on this trail ever, ever again. And we're not even off of it yet!" He looked over the side. The grinning third man caught him as he wavered.

"You have very little distance to go," Mary shouted back over Prince's head.

"What's your name again, miss? And you're the mail carrier?" This from the middle man of the trio.

"Mary Gerritse. Mrs. Gerritse, and yes, this is my route from Tillamook to Cannon Beach. Who's asking?"

"Allan Slauson. I write 'Willamette Wavelets' for the *Oregonian*."

"You're Porthos?" She'd read his column now and then. "That's you?"

"Guilty." He grinned. "Alright with you if we meet up tomorrow at Austin's on your return trip? I'd like to write up this little encounter and talk with you about what it's like being a mail carrier of the female persuasion."

"Happy to help," Mary said. She waved them off and headed down the trail. "We're going to be interviewed, Prince. Won't John be tickled."

But he wasn't.

"There's no need for that," John said when Mary arrived home all abuzz. "No need for all to know a man has let his wife do such dangerous work."

"I thought you'd welcome it. He'll talk about Cannon Beach and people will want to come visit. It won't be about a woman doing a man's job so much. I'm sure it won't."

"When you took this on, I thought it would be the mountains and sea that would challenge, not some reporter messing up how our family has worked things out."

"He can only mess us up if we let him. Are you saying I can't do the interview?" He didn't look at her. "How we've worked things out might inspire, not disparage two who found a way to support each other. I think it'll show a strong man married to a strong woman."

Despite John's misgivings, he didn't forbid her, so Mary met with the journalist the next day. They sat on Lydia's porch, the sound of the reed organ drifting through the window. She'd enjoyed the interview, especially when Mr. Slauson told her she was quite a storyteller herself. "You ought to write some of these experiences down," he said. "I'm using your maneuvering things on that ridge as part of my article."

"Oh, I'm not sure there's much interest in the daily doings of a mail carrier, female or not."

"I bet I get a lot of letters about this story." He had an engaging smile that rose to his hazel eyes. "You bring a fresh perspective to a woman's life. Authenticity is the real key to my articles, which of course I hope to capture with your story." He made a few notes. Then, "How does your husband feel about you doing such dangerous work?"

Mary wondered if he knew he intruded on the personal; but then, it's what human interest articles were made of.

She swallowed. "I'm very fortunate. We're a team. This summer, he'll be here in Cannon Beach and rent out our horses to people who need a mount, to accompany the postal carrier, tourists wanting a ride on the beach."

"And you have no children?"

She blinked. "We have four. Two girls and two boys." Mary could hear the pride in her own voice even as the reporter looked up at her. "They give us lots of surprises. They and their child keeper."

"You hire someone so you can have a career?"

Mary stiffened her shoulders. "I believe Mrs. Duniway dealt with that in one of *her* articles in *her female* newspaper that she ran for almost twenty years. *The New Northwest*? She had six children if I recall. She hired help. Her husband understood too. We women are capable of being good wives and mothers and having careers."

"Oh, yes, I didn't mean to imply."

"Yes, you did." Mary smiled, calmed her voice. "You're forgiven." It would do no good to make an enemy of a man with the power of words at his fingertips. "A moment of enlightenment?" She grinned.

He touched his forehead to her, a "hats off" acknowledgment.

"Perhaps you can help another career woman," Mary continued. "We'll be looking for a new child keeper before long. The one we have now found a mate and will be off and married soon. Maybe your article will bring us a new hire."

Later, quite a number of people commented when she and John went to church the Sunday after Mr. Slauson's article appeared. It was one of the days when the pastor couldn't come, so they all took turns choosing a special verse and relating how it spoke to them. Mary picked Ecclesiastes with its ebb and flow about time, "A time to tear and a time to mend" being a favorite. Afterward, people who had read the article had slapped John on the back telling him he had chosen well to be married to such "an uncommon woman." Much to Mary's relief, John didn't seem to mind the attention nor the notoriety of his wife.

As they rode home, the children squabbled in the back of the wagon, then giggled merrily over something, their moods shifting in a moment. Mary decided she was uncommon. All women were, in their own way. She might not find happiness in the everyday of peeling potatoes or bathing children. Instead, she found her strength in oiling a horse's leather harness or in the sound of the wind at the ridge after making a safe crossing. These experiences refueled her, helped her be grateful for the blessing of the people she loved—her children included—being willing to set sail together on an unfamiliar sea. The sacred, she decided, was everywhere. One just needed to notice.

chapter
66

C oastal sunsets are the splendor of the sea. Mary wrote
the words in the small notebook she had started to carry.
It was long and narrow, like the reporter's. She'd sewn a
pocket into her split skirt (replacing John's worn pants) so she
could pull it out to write while she rode or while she rested as
Prince ripped at grass.

Today she'd made her delivery at the Austin House and once
again had gone on to see if Jewell had perhaps returned to build
a new rush-mat hut. No sign of her. Where was she? She missed
her friend.

As she came away, Haystack Rock rose up before her. Puffins
flashed red beaks she could just make out, and seagulls hovered,
screaming at their mates or maybe those puffins. She walked beneath
Herbert's Wedding Tree, Prince behind her. She sat on a driftwood
log and pulled out her pencil and pad, the rock speaking to her now.

-------------------- Haystack Rock --------------------

> *Mighty Monarch of the deep*
> *Where briny waters lave thy feet*
> *And while winged seagulls pause to rest*
> *Upon thy topmost pointed crest*

Long have you thus a sentinel stood
Who knows how long you thus may stand
To cast your shadows on the sand.

She made a few corrections, changing "on thy topmost pointed crest" to "upon." The words were formal, and she wanted them that way, to capture the majesty of the rock, its awesomeness. She'd share it with Belle, who had begun writing poetry herself, whimsical things about boots being mittens for her feet or a neighbor's new spotted dog having "black measles." She was an inventive child. They all were.

They continued on, finished the route, Mary making notes now and then she'd weave into a poem, each delivery a new adventure even when everything went as planned.

The air held autumn in its hands.

It was a new day as Prince and Mary headed north from home. "Once we're along the narrows we'll stop for lunch. How does that suit you, Prince?" Just thinking about what the new childminder had packed with the jam and biscuit made her mouth water.

Prince stopped to take a bite of clay. "Looking for a little salt?" She took the moment to step off him.

Then, in the swish of a tail, Prince lost the footing of his back feet. As though in a terrible dream Mary watched the path give way, loose gravel keeping Prince's hooves from gaining purchase as he clawed at the side, slipping, sliding backward and lunging to get back up, instead scraping soil down fifty feet or more with his hindquarters now upended; his head caught in the brambles and facing the cliff, this one with no hope of survival if he breached it. He lunged, wanting to pull himself up, but slid another 150 feet toward the edge, stopped with a grunt by a tree that swung him around. The stock saddle, heavy as it was, helped break his fall.

"Oh dear God, please, don't let him slide more, please." Mary was already on her way to him, on her bottom, legs outstretched on the steep descent, sliding as he had.

If Prince went over this edge, it was 300 feet to the sea.

Heart pounding, keeping her words as calm as she could, she reached him, saw the bulge at his side. *A broken rib. Maybe more than one.* The heavy mailbag lay like a gravestone on the trembling horse.

Prince flailed, snorted, his eyes white with fright.

"It's alright, alright." Mary's words soothed, then scolded to put herself in control, to calm her own pounding heart. "You be still. Be still now." Prince listened, lay breathing heavily, nickered, trusted. "Don't let me fail him," she breathed out her prayer. "Don't let me fall." She checked his legs. Scraped but not broken. "I'm going to pull these bushes, untangle you, get you faced uphill. You settle. It'll be alright."

She had gloves in her pocket and put them on to yank against the shrubs, the barbs. She both cursed them and praised them and the tree for stopping his glide. If she could get him angled uphill and then urge him upright, they might make a diagonal path to intersect the trail and slowly make their way forward. It would take hours. She had to be sure-footed herself, the pitch and grasses slippery like ice. Sweat beaded her brows. Her hat had been taken by the wind as she worked. "We can do this." Each time Prince struggled to get upright, she shushed him like a child, and he calmed, trusting.

She did what she had to do.

She didn't know how much time she'd spent, but by the sun it was well past noon. She had removed as many of the obstacles as she could. "It's time, Prince. Easy now." She tugged on the lead rope only slightly. He'd been on his belly and then his side for a long time. Now he pawed with his front feet, lurched, hesitated, stood.

"Yes, yes." Calm, reassuring.

Trembling, he hung his head, the mailbag lopsided on his rump. "We'll fix that in a minute, Prince." An offside bag would fret most horses. Mary touched his head, neck, flank, and rump. Drops of blood curdled against his gray side.

The bulge at his rib cage.

She didn't know if he could walk yet, but he could stand. That was half the battle.

"We're about twelve miles from Cannon Beach." She talked to herself. Or maybe the words were prayers. "We have to angle our way back up."

Prince limped even without the weight of the bags that Mary had removed and thrown over her shoulder. They began, each step a prayer, the hours of upward climb a weight of worry. Then, at a creek in a ravine, they stopped. Prince drank. They reached Cannon Beach at dusk.

Should they stay the night? No, better to go. John could treat him, that bulge especially.

Lydia sorted the mail quickly so they could take the Front Road along the beach before the tide shifted. Mary rubbed liniment on Prince's legs and side. As night settled in, Mary's lantern lit their way. She would have to tell John, no hiding this disaster. Would he ban her from mail delivery? She'd know soon enough.

"You're late. What happened?" John brought a lantern out to the barn, worry in his voice.

She told a version, one that didn't have as much danger as there was. "I think he has a cracked rib. But he's doing fine. I rubbed liniment on it. We rested some before starting back."

"Looks like maybe two ribs," John said.

He gentled Prince as Mary filled up the horse's trough, gave him water. She brushed his roached neck, put him up in the stall. He hung his head.

"You didn't do anything wrong, my friend. Things happen. You rest." To John she said, "I'll sleep out here. Take Jake for the Tillamook run in the morning."

"Nothing more you can do for him. I can finish the delivery tomorrow. You need rest too."

"No, please, John. It's my responsibility. Don't . . . don't."

He nodded. "We talk later, ja? But now, come inside. Your children miss you. And I, I want to hold you, safe."

A crescent moon sliced the sky as John put his arm around her shoulder and she leaned into him as they walked toward the house. One day she might write about Prince's close call, but for now she inhaled the moonlight with a sigh of gratitude.

chapter
67

"J ohn! You won't believe this!"

John looked up as Mary trotted on Jake into the yard. Several weeks had passed since the episode with Prince. That's what Mary called it, an episode. But it still rattled John, increased his worry every time she set out. The horses nickered to each other. Alice ran out of the house at Mary's voice. She dismounted beside John, as he bent over Prince's hoof, pounding a shoe nail in. Leonard held the halter.

"Hi, Mama."

"Hi, my boy." Mary hugged her son, then patted Prince. "He's looking good, healed up."

"What won't I believe?" John let the foot down, stood, and stretched his back. He'd keep shoeing his own horses but maybe he'd stop doing it for others, train someone younger, shorter, and stockier to do that hard work. Through the open door, the scent of hot iron came from his farrier's fire. Still, horseshoeing brought coins into the purse.

"The cannons. They've reappeared."

"Says who?" He'd heard rumors before.

"George Luce. Not far from Austin's. George saw them on his delivery route. They showed up where James Austin always hoped

272

they would, in that little creek nearby. So sad he didn't live long enough to see them."

"Must have been the king tide washed them up." John felt the excitement.

"Lydia's hoping you can bring a team and haul them inland before the sea takes them back."

"When was the last time they were sighted?"

"Years ago." She sighed. "But you'll have to haul rescued cannons out without me. I've got that delivery to make to Tillamook."

He was proud of his wife. He knew she would have loved the adventure of hauling the cannons from the beach, involving the children and the rest of the tourists still there. And the locals. But she understood her duties.

"Take the children, though. Herbie and Joe Walsh can help, if Herbie is still here. He was going to visit England. Goodness, what an adventure you'll all have!"

He heard the wistfulness in her voice.

"Maybe it'll be a false alarm," John said. "And there'll be another chance."

"Maybe." She pecked his cheek, then reached down to pat Max who didn't get up, just raised his head. He showed his age but still barked when a coyote came too close or an elk herd passed by. He just didn't chase them anymore. "You best get going. Me too. Sure glad you bought the team. You're going to need them to race the tide." She called to the new child tender and the children, told them to pack a bedroll. "You're headed to Cannon Beach."

"Won't you come, Mama?" Belle came out of the chicken coop, let unfurl the scarf around her head. Four-year-old Alice held a wicker basket of eggs in both hands, trailing her big sister.

"I have other obligations. People are counting on me. Take the kites. Johnny, Leonard, help your father. Have fun, girls."

Mary mounted up and was gone. Nellie trotted after her a ways, then turned back. John watched his wife leave. That woman, his wife, the adventure of his life.

"That's a cannon?" Johnny asked. He'd gotten out and fast-walked in front of the team as it pulled up onto the beach. The tides had been in their favor along the mountain's base to Arch Cape, so they made it to Austin's just as the tide strolled back in.

Ahead of them sitting in the creek like a rock squatted a pile of metal. That's how it looked to John. George Luce might have been mistaken, but as John approached on foot, he could see a shape that might have been a cannon before it became a deposit for barnacles.

"Glad you made it," Joe Walsh said. He appeared sober. "That's it. What we been waiting for, aye." He had chains with him and others gathered around while John wrapped the links over the metal. People brought their shovels, as much of the cannon sank into Mountain Creek's sand. Men suggested a hook of some sort. People speculated about the weight and whether there'd need to be more horses. The wind blew swirls in the sand as gulls gave their opinion of the activity. It was fall, though some of the summer cottage residents remained. Women came out in their shawls to watch. As the afternoon wore on, a few brought sandwiches to the men. Dogs—including Nellie—scampered about. John stopped paying attention to anything but the metal and the advance of the incoming tide.

Then a cheer went up as the horses dug in and the metal blob began to move, easing its way out of the creek, away from the sea that licked to take it back. John guided the team and they strained. But they pulled the cannon, dragging it across the sand to land in front of the Austin House. Men with shovels helped arrange it like a headstone, a monument to a man who had hoped he would retrieve it. Lydia wiped tears from her cheeks. The cannon from the 1846 ship *Shark* lay in the seagrass and sand in front of Lydia's Austin House.

"Ja," John said, wiping his brow. "The namesake of Cannon Beach has come home at last."

chapter
68

The children were still talking about the cannon recovery a week after the event. Mary had sauerkraut stewing on the stove.

"It was almost as much fun as the Fourth of July celebrations," Belle said. "Merritt led a song he said was from you, Mama, about staying no matter how."

"Did he?" Warmth flooded her face. It brought back the memory of their wedding party and their friends and neighbors singing to her words to "stay no matter how."

"It's a song of resipence. Re-silence. Re-sil-i-ence, he said. That's a big word."

"So it is. I wrote that song for your daddy. When we got married."

"Will you write one for me, Mama?"

"Maybe we'll write one together."

Her daughter loved words. Something they shared.

"We had fun, Mama." Mary put the round curling iron onto the stove to heat it before she'd put another crimp into Belle's peach-colored hair. "There were cookies and music. I wish you could have been there. I wish we lived at Cannon Beach all the time. We slept out on the sand and Papa built a fire."

"You didn't happen to see Jewell, did you?" Belle shook her head no. "I wonder what's happened to her. Maybe the next time we go to Astoria I'll go out to the Clatsop encampment and see if they know anything about where she might be."

"I'd like to go there, Mama. We can buy new shoes?"

"Sit still." She held the curling iron. "I can talk to you without you turning around."

"If we can't live at Cannon Beach," Belle continued, shopping forgotten as she held a mirror before her face, "maybe I could go live with Gramma and Grandpa. I really liked that school at Scholls Ferry."

Mary felt her stomach clench. Did her daughter want to leave because her mother wasn't doing such a good job? Or did she just like her grandparents?

"Gramma says they have a new Kodak. She'll teach me how to use it. Maybe take pictures of me."

"A camera. How nice." She wondered if Herbie got his photographs and the postcards made up.

Photographs. They should take some family shots.

A picture rose as a memory, the one her mother had grabbed from her that day, left her with an emptiness as cold as a Hug Point cave. The boy in the picture. The sad little girl who stood alone.

Belle crossed her arms. "I don't like nannies. I'd like you to stay home, Mama."

"Let's finish up your hair. We can talk more after church."

But Belle didn't raise the subject after church and Mary didn't want to tiptoe there either. They had a few more weeks before school started, so she could put off any unpleasantness that such a discussion might raise. She was good at that, putting some things off. But she was better than she'd been, her bravery reaching toward dealing with the trials of parenting and working things out with her husband. It was a good sign that her daughter could bravely ask for what she wanted. It had taken Mary a while, but she hoped Belle's asking happened in part because Mary was a good model.

Mary's life was full of adventures, and having a family—with

276

help—was one of the greatest. John walked beside her on that journey. Her life had room for all of it, that's what she'd discovered. She wanted her children to know that too. They could all walk together through the driftwood and shifting sands of the Crying Sands Beach.

It's what happened when you stepped out in faith and sailed the sea in a sieve.

The Jumblies

by Edward Lear, author of "The Owl and the Pussycat"

I

They went to sea in a Sieve, they did,
  In a Sieve they went to sea:
In spite of all their friends could say,
On a winter's morn, on a stormy day,
  In a Sieve they went to sea!
And when the Sieve turned round and round,
And every one cried, "You'll all be drowned!"
They called aloud, "Our Sieve ain't big,
But we don't care a button! we don't care a fig!
  In a Sieve we'll go to sea!"
    Far and few, far and few,
      Are the lands where the Jumblies live;
      Their heads are green, and their hands are blue,
      And they went to sea in a Sieve.

II

They sailed away in a Sieve, they did,
  In a Sieve they sailed so fast,
With only a beautiful pea-green veil
Tied with a riband by way of a sail,
  To a small tobacco-pipe mast;
And every one said, who saw them go,
"O won't they be soon upset, you know!
For the sky is dark, and the voyage is long,

279

And happen what may, it's extremely wrong
   In a Sieve to sail so fast!"
      Far and few, far and few,
         Are the lands where the Jumblies live;
       Their heads are green, and their hands are blue,
         And they went to sea in a Sieve.

III

The water it soon came in, it did,
   The water it soon came in;
So to keep them dry, they wrapped their feet
In a pinky paper all folded neat,
   And they fastened it down with a pin.
And they passed the night in a crockery-jar,
And each of them said, "How wise we are!
Though the sky be dark, and the voyage be long,
Yet we never can think we were rash or wrong,
   While round in our Sieve we spin!"
      Far and few, far and few,
         Are the lands where the Jumblies live;
       Their heads are green, and their hands are blue,
         And they went to sea in a Sieve.

IV

And all night long they sailed away;
   And when the sun went down,
They whistled and warbled a moony song
To the echoing sound of a coppery gong,
   In the shade of the mountains brown.
"O Timballo! How happy we are,
When we live in a sieve and a crockery-jar,
And all night long in the moonlight pale,
We sail away with a pea-green sail,
   In the shade of the mountains brown!"
      Far and few, far and few,
         Are the lands where the Jumblies live;
       Their heads are green, and their hands are blue,
         And they went to sea in a Sieve.

V

They sailed to the Western Sea, they did,
    To a land all covered with trees,
And they bought an Owl, and a useful Cart,
And a pound of Rice, and a Cranberry Tart,
    And a hive of silvery Bees.
And they bought a Pig, and some green Jack-daws,
And a lovely Monkey with lollipop paws,
And forty bottles of Ring-Bo-Ree,
    And no end of Stilton Cheese.
        Far and few, far and few,
            Are the lands where the Jumblies live;
        Their heads are green, and their hands are blue,
            And they went to sea in a Sieve.

VI

And in twenty years they all came back,
    In twenty years or more,
And every one said, "How tall they've grown!"
For they've been to the Lakes, and the Torrible Zone,
    And the hills of the Chankly Bore;
And they drank their health, and gave them a feast
Of dumplings made of beautiful yeast;
And everyone said, "If we only live,
We too will go to sea in a Sieve,—
    To the hills of the Chankly Bore!"
        Far and few, far and few,
            Are the lands where the Jumblies live;
        Their heads are green, and their hands are blue,
            And they went to sea in a Sieve.

Read on
for a *sneak peek* at
the next book in

The Women of Cannon Beach series.

Available April 2026.

prologue

Wave Woman tells the story. Three canoes with tall sails threw smoke at each other. Poof! Poof! Soon only one ship remained above the water. Broken, it limped onto the shore. Men with skin the color of sand—and one whose countenance was of black earth—carried a box onto the beach. They worked to fix the broken ship while guarding the box. Then four men carried the box up onto the mountain. They returned without it and without the man with skin of black earth.

While they worked to make the ship want to return to its purpose, objects began to appear on the beach. Chunks the size of the box. Bigger chunks, massive like horses. Small ones, white with a wick twisted around them—beeswax these were named. They came from one of the ships that had thrown smoke.

The day came to take the restored ship back onto the sea, but it was not to be. The waters were angry, and the breakers broke the ship into greater pieces than before. The ship gave itself to the sea. The men escaped and swam onto the beach. The people told them that some things cannot be restored. They must be transformed. Four men with faces the color of sand went north along the beach to the big river; the others stayed, built huts, made lives with some of our women. They vowed to stay no matter how.

chapter
1

Mary Gerritse reached across the bed linen to touch her husband's hand. She didn't know if he was awake, but even in his sleep John opened his palm and cupped her fingers into his. The sound of the waves washing ashore proved a lullaby. In their nearly twelve years of marriage, never once had he jerked his hand away, or turned over when she reached out. It was a luxury she hadn't always counted, his presence and his total acceptance of her no matter what disagreements they might have about her need for adventure. He was her best friend and she his. What more could one ever hope for?

She spoke her silent prayers, withdrew her fingers while he slept, and rose to face the day. She had a horse to saddle and a mail delivery to make to Tillamook on the north Oregon coast. It was a new century, this 1900, full of promise.

"I suppose I should have come from your Astoria and taken that marvelous toll road I read about that an Englishman built. Herbert Logan?" The woman sighed, a happy sound. "But the ship came into Tillamook Bay and the quartermaster told me I could go with the postal deliverer overland across Neahkahnie Mountain and avoid the tolls altogether. Have I said those names properly? He said the views were quite spectacular coming up from the south."

Mary loaded the mailbags onto Jake's rump at the hitching rail outside the lighthouse. The woman speaking wore a velvet green dress with a peplum jacket that reminded Mary of her own wedding dress minus the Minnesota buttons, as she thought of them. The woman surely wore a corset, while Mary no longer did. The woman's hat sported a pheasant feather that draped down over her eyes. It lifted with the morning breeze drifting across the spit that jutted into the Pacific.

"Yes," Lizzie, the Tillamook postmistress told her, "that's how you say it. Your English accent makes it sound quite exotic. *Teal-a-muck*," she repeated. "Mary will get you to Cannon Beach in no time."

"You'll have to ride Baldy, who will plod you along safe as a snail, which is exactly how fast he travels." Mary would ride Jake and trail Baldy and Prince, giving the latter a break from the heavy mailbags. Mary had ridden Jake from home to Cannon Beach, trailing Baldy. They'd returned to their Manzanita farm, spent the night, then picked up Prince as well. They'd all spent the last night in Tillamook.

Now the pack animals were loaded with crates full of items for the Austin House. Mary thought Prince could use more days of "light duty." She loved that horse and felt defensive when John commented that he wished she'd taken better care of his horse. He'd smiled as though teasing, but she knew he worried over his animals. Still, he should know that she worried over them too. Especially Prince.

The English woman appeared to be in her late thirties, with hair the color of coal and arched eyebrows that didn't look like they'd ever seen the pencil. She had a soft voice.

Mary led Baldy to the stepping block but had a second thought. An English lady might not feel comfortable riding astride. "We'll pick up a sidesaddle at our farm. Meanwhile you can ride pillion if you'd prefer."

"That would be delightful."

Mary placed Baldy into the string ahead of Prince, then settled the woman on Jake. Riding pillion, both of her booted feet hung off Jake's left side. The woman would steady herself using Mary's waist. Mary noticed she had tiny feet. Jake turned his head once to look at her, then back, unimpressed. "What's your name, if I may ask?"

"Olivia. Olivia Benton."

Mary caught her breath. *Olivia Benton. Herbert's letter recipient?* Could there be more than one English Olivia? "I'm Mary Gerritse. If you don't mind my asking, do you know Herbert Logan or have you just heard about his road?"

"I do know him. It's why I'm in America, actually. I'm looking forward to surprising him."

The party of two women and three horses stopped at the Gerritses' Manzanita farm on Oregon's North Coast. Olivia scanned the horizon, while Mary brought out the sidesaddle. She stopped to share the view of white sands and foam like gray lace bordering the waves. The ocean sported its calmest personality. Mary sighed. She loved this place.

Olivia smiled as she sat in her familiar way on the sidesaddle. Mary returned to the barn and told John who their passenger was. "I want to get her to Cannon Beach as soon as we can. I'm not sure that Herbert hasn't already left."

"Take the beach road around Hug Point, then. You should hit the tide right."

John kissed her goodbye, patted Jake as Mary mounted.

The morning was light chatter between the women, the creak of leather a rhythm Mary thought she might put to words one day. Up and over the mountains they rode, the spectacular views causing Olivia to gasp.

As they approached that Hug Point beach, it looked like the tide was going out. Mary remembered the week before they were married twelve years past when she and John and Herbert nearly died by John's miscalculation of the tide. The massive sleeper wave and the sinkhole that one couldn't see until they were in it, but for a miracle, would have taken their lives. Mary hesitated as she watched the waves. Maybe they should go inland but it would take longer and she wanted Olivia to get to Herbert just as soon as possible. If she was wrong, their lives were at risk, the horses' safety too.

Gulls called their way over the little party. Mary took a deep breath. She prayed they would be fine.

To Be Continued . . .

discussion questions

1. How did Mary's quest for adventure strengthen her marriage? How did it impact her family? Have you ever chosen an unusual route in your life where friends and family wondered, "What are you doing?"

2. Who was the biggest risk-taker in this story? Mary, Herbert, John, Amanda, Jewell? Have you ever taken a risk that you later regretted even though you discovered something important about yourself in the process?

3. Was Mary suffering from postpartum depression or was she struggling with the constriction of roles many women found themselves dealing with at the turn of the century—or even now? Could both things be true? Or was Mary simply too concerned about finding her own way?

4. In the research for this book, the author learned of Mary's long confinement in a Portland hospital and that, following her release, there were no more children born to her and John. She also began her postal career then. Did the

author's handling of that major life change ring true for you as the reader?

5. Mary has bits of information about her origins that are confusing—Minnie instead of Mary on her marriage certificate, her mother's alarm about the photograph—but doesn't want to confront her parents. We know some of what is happening through Amanda's eyes, but how might Mary face this unknown? Have you ever put off facing a family secret?

6. Which of the women in *Across the Crying Sands* interested you most: Mary, her mother Amanda, Jewell, or the elusive Olivia whom we'll learn more about in book 2? What about them intrigued you? Who do you want to know more about? And what do you think happened to Jewell?

author's notes
and acknowledgments

Nearly fifteen years ago, Suzy Johnson Wintjen arrived at the Hulda Klager Lilac Gardens in Woodland, Washington, where I signed books. She had what she believed was my next story of a remarkable historical woman, Mary Edwards Gerritse, one of the first to carry mail on the dangerous Oregon coast. I hope I was polite and took the information, making no promises. During the ensuing years, Suzy and her husband Collin became not only stellar Mary supporters but also research resources, tour guides, and friends. Along with Suzy's splendid research and computer skills, copyediting perusals, and her support of me as a writer, Mary's story remained in my creative satchel as a possibility. Now, in this Cannon Beach Series, it's a reality. I couldn't have done it without Suzy. Thanks are not enough.

I do have Mary walk through some pathless woods and make new trails. But as always, I hope to stay true to the spirit of these women whose lives I share with readers. As portrayed, Mary and John's premarriage near-disaster, their lives with burned-out occupier cabins, the births of their children, Mary's wondering about her family of origin, their interconnectedness with her parents, and of course her love of horses and the challenges she had on the trail are based on fact. Whether Mary struggled with her role as a mother is conjecture, but based on the facts that she did cook for a crew John was on, leaving young Belle with her parents, I wondered. They did hire a child keeper during Mary's years as a postal deliverer. Mary also spent three months in the hospital for an unknown operation and there were no more children born to them after that. I gave her a diagnosis and also introduced someone who might have helped her come to terms with being "different," to make the decision to become that mail carrier along the coast and be part of the development of Cannon Beach. She is a beloved historical figure, and I hope I have only endeared her story more by identifying some of the challenges she might have faced. Mary did write poetry that she signed as Mary Edwards. I gave her the love of Edward Lear's poem "The Jumblies," a favorite of mine. Mary read Charlotte Brontë and Dickens, so she might have known of Lear.

John's story is also supported by history: his running off to sea early in his life, sailing around the world, meeting Mary, and setting the wedding date in November on his birthday so he wouldn't forget their anniversary. He was a jack-of-all-trades, a hard worker, and did leave Mary alone on their forest claim while he ran the coastal mail route. He was employed at various hotels, worked on the *Columbia*, and was gone for three months at a time and during Mary's hospitalization. Like Mary, he also appears to have liked adventure. The cannon's disappearance and reappearance is noted in most books about the north coast history; its reappearance toward the end of this book is a part of the Gerritse history too. The other two cannons did not appear until 2008.

Herbert Logan was the impetus and primary funder of the Elk Creek Road Company. His English history as a remittance man (along with Joe Walsh) is part of the local lore, as is his building of the Elk Creek Hotel and his sawmill. He did have some sort of creeping paralysis, loved his silver candlesticks, and brought a Chinese man to cook for guests. He did dress for dinner. Someone rode with John and Mary to Astoria before their wedding and survived the near drowning at Hug Point; Mary talks about this event in an interview where she says she can't remember who the man was who was with them. I decided it was Herbert Logan. In that same interview, Mary says they stayed at the Elk Creek Hotel (1888), but other sources say the hotel wasn't built until 1893 or later. I let there be some semblance of that hotel—because Mary said it was there.

For the historical readers, a point of explanation. I did know that some towns were not officially known as the names used (Manzanita, Arch Cape, even Cannon Beach) in this book but for ease of reading, I've made them proper nouns before they were officially named. I hope historians will give me a pass.

Some of the characters have the names of real historical people—Merritt and William Batterson; James and Lydia Austin; Lizzie, the Tillamook postmistress; and William and Amanda Edwards, Mary's parents. Mr. Batterson's wife did take their daughter and leave for California. An older son did die, and Merritt stayed on with his father, who was the local teacher and justice of the peace. He was the officiant at Mary and John's wedding. The marriage certificate does say "Minnie Edwards." Mary's parents' story does begin in New York, then on to Minnesota to Scholls Ferry to Nehalem and back to Scholls Ferry. There will be more about the circumstances of Mary's birth and her parents' dealing with that. The incident on the trail that resulted in a newspaper article by Mr. Slauson is historical. James Austin did name the area as Cannon Beach and sadly died before the cannon reappeared. But he'd been correct about where it did.

Other characters were pure figments of my imagination—the hospital visitor, Rita, and Jewell, though she is a composite of the Clatsop-Tillamook-Nehalem people who kept the stories and who lived on that stretch of flat beach long before settlers discovered that shore. I ascribe to the wisdom of author William Kent Krueger who also writes of Indigenous people while he isn't one. In *Spirit Crossing*, he acknowledged if he errs in presenting a culture not his own, that it's not intentional, and I hope, not detrimental. "My wish in some small way is to open hearts and minds of readers to the enormous struggles our Native brothers and sisters face every day." In books 2 and 3, there will be more women of Cannon Beach. I hope you'll join me in their discovery.

I'd be remiss if I didn't express my gratitude to the Clatsop County Historical Society, the Cannon Beach Historical Society, the Nehalem Valley Historical Society that features a film *Homestead: The Life and Times of Mary Gerritse with Liz Cole*, the Seaside Museum and Historical Society, and the Oregon Historical Society for access to collections that included Mary's memoir, a separate interview with a librarian friend, postmasters at Cape Meares Lighthouse, discovering the poem Mary wrote about Haystack Rock, and other tidbits about cannons and beeswax that lend richness to a story. Several nonfiction books served me well. I include a list of them and their authors below.

I had the privilege of using one of Dana Huneke-Stone's poems to lead into this story. Her book *Amuse-Bouche: A Taste of Melancholy* found its way to me as a gift. I read one of her poems each morning as I wrote, a kind of meditation connecting me to my Muse, Mary's story, and the sea. I'm grateful to her for both writing these precious poems and allowing me to include one. Special gratitude goes also to my faithful friend Janet Meranda who, for ten years now, has perused my manuscripts seeking errors I have time to correct. However, any errors or omissions all still belong to me. My friend and draftswoman Susan Baily undertook the task of mapmaking with my odd instructions that dear Jerry would translate but isn't able to anymore. She did a splendid job and I'm so grateful. Thanks as well to Gary and Margie Waite for their enthusiastic support and their generosity in sharing their home at Cannon Beach. My new website maven, social media guru, and great-niece, Sarah Robinson of Robinson-Design.Co, came on board just when I needed her. I'm grateful. Her mother designed my first website back in the nineties.

"Thank you" is an insufficient expression to my editor Andrea Doering, who Zoomed with me monthly, helping me write a different kind of series. She kept the harpies at bay and led the team at Revell with whom I am so grateful to work, especially editor

Barb Barnes who "gets me." So do Robin Turici, Karen Steele, and Lindsay Schubert, who work their magic for me at Revell. I thank them. CarolAnne Tasai was an early researcher of Mary's story. I'm thankful for her presence in my days. Along with Kathy Gervasi of Tillamook and Madeline Olsen of Manzanita, Suzy and Collin Wintjen of Seaside, I had the gift of coastal boosters willing to share their joy about coastal living. My new agent, Linda Glaz of Linda S. Glaz Literary Agency, stepped in as my former agency closed with the passing of my long-term agent Joyce Hart. Linda and I are on a fine journey together and I'm grateful.

Thank you to family and friends, prayer partners and faith communities from across the country who continue to encourage my writing and my spirit. I'm especially grateful to readers, to those who receive my *Story Sparks* newsletters (jkbooks.com), follow me on my Facebook author page, and give me feedback about how the stories touch their lives. Thank you for making room in your lives for my stories. And to Jerry, as we navigate these new chapters in our lives together, thank you for always being there. There are others, too many to mention, but hopefully you know who you are and accept the depth of my gratitude.

Two books will follow in the Women of Cannon Beach Series. Mary's life is a testament to strong women who love family, friends, and faith. She loved Cannon Beach too. I hope to meet you (with her) on those Crying Sands next year.

Warmly,
Jane

resources

Jane Comerford, *At the Foot of the Mountain: An Early History* (Dragonfly Press, 2004).

S. J. Cotton, *Stories of Nehalem* (Forgotten Books, 2018).

Cumtux: Clatsop County Historical Society Quarterly 7, nos. 3–4; 9, no. 3.

Deborah Cuyle, *Cannon Beach*, Images of America (Arcadia Publishing, 2016).

Jill Grady, *Cannon Beach Cottages* (World Dancer Press, 2005).

John Delbert Griffin, *Reflections on Early Cannon Beach* (unpublished manuscript, c. 1969).

Peter Lindsey, *Comin' Over the Rock: A Storytellers History of Cannon Beach* (pub. by author, 2016).

Terence O'Donnell, *Cannon Beach: A Place by the Sea* (Oregon Historical Society, 1996).

"Oregon's Manila Galleon," Special issue, *Oregon Historical Quarterly* 119, no. 2 (Summer 2018).

George Wilder, *Mary Gerritse: Mary's Story* (unpublished manuscript).

Scott S. Williams et al., "The Beeswax Wreck of Nehalem: A Lost Manila Galleon," *Oregon Historical Quarterly* 119, no. 2: 192–209.

Jane Kirkpatrick is the *New York Times* and CBA bestselling and award-winning author of forty books, including *Something Worth Doing, One More River to Cross, Everything She Didn't Say, All Together in One Place, A Light in the Wilderness, The Memory Weaver, This Road We Traveled,* and *A Sweetness to the Soul,* which won the prestigious Wrangler Award from the Western Heritage Center. Her works have won the WILLA Literary Award, the Carol Award for Historical Fiction, and the 2016 Will Rogers Gold Medallion Award, and have been short-listed for the Christy, Spur, and Oregon Book Awards. Jane divides her time between Central Oregon and California with her husband, Jerry, and Cavalier King Charles Spaniel, Rupert. Learn more at JKBooks.com.

Dear Reader,

Thank you for selecting a Revell novel! We're so happy to be part of your reading life through this work. Our mission here at Revell is to publish stories that reach the heart. Through friendship, romance, suspense, or a travel back in time, we bring stories that will entertain, inspire, and encourage you. We believe in the power of stories to change our lives and are grateful for the privilege of sharing these stories with you.

We believe in building lasting relationships with readers, and we'd love to get to know you better. If you have any feedback, questions, or just want to chat about your experience reading this book, please email us directly at publisher@revellbooks.com. Your insights are incredibly important to us, and it would be our pleasure to hear how we can better serve you.

We look forward to hearing from you and having the chance to enhance your experience with Revell Books.

The Publishing Team at Revell Books
A Division of Baker Publishing Group
publisher@revellbooks.com

WEAVING THE STORIES OF OUR LIVES

Get to know Jane at

JKBooks.com

Sign up for the *Story Sparks* newsletter.
Read the blogs.
Learn about upcoming events.

@TheAuthorJaneKirkpatrick   @Jane.Kirkpatrick.3